BOOKS BY

Cecelia Holland

Rakóssy   *1967*
The Firedrake   *1966*

RAKÓSSY

RAKÓSSY

Cecelia Holland

Atheneum   New York

1967

FOR MY FATHER

sine qua non

Note

The Magyar nobility of the sixteenth century did not have titles, although their de facto power over their subjects was as absolute as that of the aristocracy in the Western monarchies. I have given János Rakóssy and Louis Malencz titles to make their ranks clear.

With the exception of the Archduke and Duchess, Suleyman the Magnificent, and the facts of the Turk invasion and the Battle of Mohács, the people and events of this tale are figments of my imagination.

Cecelia Holland

The world is too wicked, and does not deserve to have many wise and pious princes. Frogs need storks.

MARTIN LUTHER, 1523

RAKÓSSY

My dear Count," Kamal said. "Nothing would please me more. But Mustafa my master gave me this specific instruction. I am to sign nothing that is not also signed by Baron Rakóssy."

Count Malencz said, "János Rakóssy is a black traitor."

"Granted. But a man whom it is imprudent to ignore, and my master prefers to be prudent."

Malencz frowned and looked at the papers on the desk. His large white hands lay flat before him. The firelight played on the carved surface of his signet ring. Kamal permitted himself to covet that ring. He thought, He is wondering if he dare tell me to sign or leave, and Rakóssy be damned.

The spring ritual, Kamal thought. Five years of tradition can be as binding as five hundred, given the proper . . . It was comforting to know that Malencz would do the same things each spring. That reminded him of Harun. Kamal smiled gently on Malencz.

"Levolt has never signed one of our treaties," Malencz said.

"Levolt does not hold Hart Castle," Kamal said. "Nor does Levolt suffer from an acute temptation to break treaties. If Rakóssy signs the treaty in our presence, we know that he knows of it, and when he breaks the treaty he has no recourse to the excuse of ignorance." Kamal steepled his fingers. "Also, we can assign the blame properly, and you, my dear Count, are exonerated."

Malencz looked obliquely at Kamal, probably remembering the times that the Turks had broken the treaty, but he said only, "A man like Rakóssy, a breaker of faith with Turk and Magyar alike, should not be tolerated. It is a condition of war that we must tolerate him."

"Extremely well put," Kamal said. He had a reply framed already, but Malencz spoke no Turk, and in Magyar the phrases lost their amusing nuance. Kamal said, "Sometimes it is wisest to trap a breaker of oaths in the net of his own duplicity."

Malencz appeared to consider this. He said, "I suppose I must summon him."

Kamal bowed slightly. Malencz rapped his ring on the desk. A servant appeared at the door. Kamal relaxed, smiling.

"My compliments to Baron Rakóssy," Malencz said to the servant. "And will he join us here immediately."

So Rakóssy had already been summoned to Vrath. Kamal felt it the moment for a raised eyebrow. Malencz refused to look at him and the gesture was spoiled.

Kamal was mildly irked. "A good winter," he said, arranging the folds of his sleeve.

"Yes. We had hoped for more snow."

Kamal's head jerked up; he had not thought Malencz capable of irony. He saw that Malencz had meant no irony at all. Malencz was staring at the treaty as if he were reading it. His left hand was poised over the desk top, wrist on the wood, the fingers ready to drum.

Malencz was getting soft, Kamal thought. Always before he had waited until Kamal demanded it to summon Rakóssy from Hart Castle to the treaty conference. Kamal was briefly concerned: it was to the Turks' advantage to treat with Rakóssy only through Malencz, whom the Turks never fought.

The door opened, and the servant entered, stepping aside. "Baron János Rakóssy. Sir Denis Rakóssy."

Kamal straightened. A tall, slender young man came gracefully through the door, paused, and bowed to Malencz. Malencz rose, smiling. The young man was blond and elegant. Malencz greeted him elaborately. Kamal looked away from them, straight into the black eyes of János Rakóssy, shorter and stockier than his brother, swarthy as a Turk. Rakóssy looked positively sleepy. He nodded to Kamal and went on, past his brother and the enthusing Malencz, to stand behind one of the chairs by the fire. Malencz turned, saying, "Sir Denis, be seated, if you will. My lord." He glanced at Rakóssy.

Rakóssy sat. His brother sat to his left and a little behind him.

"The terms of the treaty are as usual," Kamal said. "With one or two unimportant exceptions, dealing with the procedure for exchanging prisoners."

"The point of exchange will be before Hart Castle," Malencz said. "And I might add that the shift is well warranted, considering what happened last year."

Rakóssy mimed innocence and indignation. His face slipped immediately back to dark boredom.

"The other details are petty," Malencz said. "If we sign the treaty now, we will be sooner at supper."

"Let me see the treaty," Rakóssy said.

Malencz leaned back. "As I said, the changes are unimportant and indeed wise. Why quibble?"

"I like to know what I'm signing."

Kamal rose, picked up one of the copies of the treaty, and handed it to Rakóssy. "For your perusal," he said, and bowed with a flourish.

Rakóssy could not read. He took the paper by the edge and held it over his shoulder to his brother. He looked at Kamal. His face was amused. Kamal returned to his chair and the arrangement of the folds of his sleeve.

Denis read the treaty in a voice without inflection. It was a long treaty. Rakóssy slid down in his chair, put his head back, and stretched out his legs before him. He listened with his eyes half shut. Kamal thought that he was not listening at all. He was doing this to perturb Malencz. A glance at Malencz told Kamal that Rakóssy was succeeding admirably. Kamal watched him. The left corner of Rakóssy's mouth drew down. Kamal knew this for a sign of unmitigated hilarity. Denis read the significant passage and went on, and Kamal saw no change in Rakóssy's expression. He thought, Harun, you are all but home.

"Signed this and so forth and so forth," Denis said.

"About the exchange of prisoners," Rakóssy said. "You credit me with five. I have six. I will dispose of the sixth as I see fit."

Kamal sat up straighter.

"Only last Christmas you told me you had five," Malencz said. "Where could you have gotten another since then?"

"In a raid."

"You raided, in the middle of winter?"

Rakóssy shrugged. He looked at Kamal. "It gets boring in Hart around January."

Kamal swore to himself, smiling. Rakóssy had found out about Harun and taken another prisoner so that he could keep Harun for his own uses. Kamal schooled his face to courtesy and disinterest.

"You lie," Malencz said, without schooling his face.

Rakóssy blinked.

"At any rate," Kamal said, "the prisoner will have to be exchanged."

"But Mustafa has only eighteen Magyars in Cliff's Eye," Rakóssy said. "My lord Count has eight here in Vrath, Levolt has five in Kutess, and I have five."

"Six," Kamal said. "He must be exchanged. That is the sole reason for these treaties."

"Oh? I thought they were to keep the peace."

Kamal unclenched his fist and smiled.

"Who is this prisoner?" Malencz said.

Rakóssy did not look at Kamal. "Mustafa ibn Ismail's young brother."

"Harun was captured in the late summer and he was warded in Kutess," Kamal said. "How can you have him?"

"This is an outrage," Malencz said. "You make a mockery of me, Rakóssy. You mock me and the King's honor and the honor of all Magyars. This man is an important political prisoner."

"And mine," Rakóssy said.

Malencz opened his mouth, shut it, and leaned back in his chair. Rakóssy was angelic. Denis looked bewildered and frightened. Of course, Kamal thought. He's only just come home. Now he knows.

"Damn you," Malencz said. "All right. Do as you please. Be careful that you don't provoke me into informing the King of your . . . misconduct. Kindly remember that I am your military superior. Would you care to sign the treaty now?"

"Of course, my lord."

He rose. Malencz signed the three copies of the treaty and sealed them with his ring. Kamal signed Mustafa's name and his own directly below it. Rakóssy could write his own name; his untutored handwriting looked narrow and awkward beneath Malencz's and Kamal's. Rakóssy used the last of the wax to put his seal on the pages. He straightened, took one of the copies, rolled it up, and handed it to Denis. He stood, sliding the signet ring on and off his forefinger.

"And so, my lords," Kamal said. "My dear Count, you mentioned supper. If I may have a moment to refresh myself in my chambers . . ."

"Of course. Perhaps you would care for some wine now?"

"Ah, thank you," Kamal said, "but the dictates of the Prophet . . ."

"Milk, then." Malencz jerked his head toward Rakóssy. "Baron?"

"Thank you."

Malencz summoned the servant and ordered him to fetch wine and milk. He turned heavily toward Kamal. "If you will excuse me a moment, my lords."

"Of course."

"Please make yourselves comfortable. I shall return in a few moments." Malencz shot a vicious glare at Rakóssy and marched out.

Kamal sat down, sighing. "What a tedious man."

Rakóssy laughed. "He's a fool."

Kamal made a gesture. "You are to be congratulated on your coup, Rakóssy. My master will be most upset."

"Upsetting Mustafa is my life's goal. When are you going back to Cliff's Eye?"

"As soon as possible. After last year's . . . ah . . . lesson, I have no desire to remain long this deep in Magyar territory."

"I never repeat myself," Rakóssy said.

"What happened last year?" Denis said.

Rakóssy glanced at him.

"The exchange of prisoners was held before Vrath," Kamal said. "On the way back, your most astute brother attacked us and . . ."

The servant came in with the milk and wine, poured them into Malencz's finest crystal goblets, and departed, all in silence.

Kamal looked back at Rakóssy. "And beat us rather badly," he said. "Boy, your brother is a veritable devil."

Rakóssy looked at Denis. Denis glanced away. Kamal said, "I wonder what's keeping our illustrious host."

"I can guess," Rakóssy said. He got up and went to the window. He looked out a moment and sat down again. "He's down in the courtyard by the Countess Gate."

"Mustafa will be happy to know what happened to the envoy from Belgrade," Kamal said.

Rakóssy was staring straight ahead. He was as motionless as stone.

"Not very talkative today, are you?" Kamal said.

"Malencz makes me sick."

"He must. You haven't touched your wine, and it's probably his best."

The door opened and Malencz came back into the room. He sat down. "I trust you will excuse my absence."

"By all means," Rakóssy said.

"Sir Denis," Malencz said. "How wonderful to have you back again. Tell me, did you enjoy Italy?"

"Very much, my lord."

"I hope you and your lord brother will stay awhile here. I would enjoy talking to you. I traveled in Italy as a boy."

"We'll be leaving when Kamal leaves," Rakóssy said.

"Oh? Is your escort waiting for you outside?"

"You have no escort?" Kamal said.

Rakóssy hesitated. He turned his head and looked at Kamal. "I left them outside," he said.

Kamal blinked. He rose. The tone of this meeting had changed suddenly. "My lord, if it please you, I believe I shall return immediately to Cliff's Eye. I have no desire to wear out my . . . ah . . . white flag." He smiled and bowed to Malencz, to Rakóssy, to Denis.

"If you're going," Rakóssy said, "we will leave too. My lord, if you will excuse us. Come on, Denis."

Denis stood up. Malencz said, "Good day, then."

Rakóssy, Denis and Kamal went together out into the corridor. Kamal walked down toward the stair to the stable courtyard. He said, "What do you intend to gain by this?"

Rakóssy spoke Turk. "Malencz was talking to his constable in the courtyard. I think he plans to hold me here. I don't think he will if I am in your company, Kamal."

"And what makes you think that I shall not detain you with me, when we are without these mighty walls?"

"Don't be too smart for your own good, Kamal."

"Perhaps I am. Enlighten me."

They went down the stair to the court, and Rakóssy sent a boy for his and Denis' horses. Kamal raised his hand and one of his Turks appeared. Kamal told the Turk to assemble his escort and prepare to leave.

"As I said," Kamal said, wheeling. "Enlighten me."

Rakóssy was staring up at the great outer wall of Vrath. He turned back.

"To reach Cliff's Eye, you must ride straight across my land. You don't know where my escort is, or how large it is. And you have only twenty-five men, Kamal."

"And because of such an uncertainty I am to give you what amounts to an escort out of Vrath?"

"Yes." Rakóssy looked back at the wall.

Kamal said, "Whatever the pit that spawned you, Rakóssy, it should take you back." He turned on his heel and walked away.

Denis said, "I don't understand this at all."

"I didn't think you would."

"Kamal doesn't look very happy."

Rakóssy put one hand on his hip. "No, little brother. He isn't. Amazing, isn't it?"

Denis bit his lip.

The stableboy led their horses out into the courtyard. Rakóssy went to his black mare and mounted. She half reared and he moved with her, talking to her. He looked over at Kamal and saw that Kamal recognized the horse.

Kamal mounted his own horse and rode over. "That's Harun's mare," he said.

"Do you want more proof that I have him?"

"No." Kamal rode away. He rode up beside his captain and said, "Rakóssy and his brother ride with us."

"How far?"

"Not far at all."

"My lord—"

"He has his men out there somewhere."

Kamal thought, Here, I am at Malencz's mercy; outside, at Rakóssy's. He saw Rakóssy riding toward the gate. Kamal felt the dangers around him like a fence of spears. He sucked in his breath. The portcullis was going up, slowly, and Rakóssy had pushed his way to the front of Kamal's men to watch it. Kamal went up to him.

"Don't dream that I will forget," Kamal said.

Rakóssy looked at him and back at the gate.

"My first concern," Kamal said, "is to see that my men are safe. My second will be to repay this."

He turned and signaled to his men. They started out through the double gate. The outer gate was standing open. Rakóssy turned in his saddle to look up at the castle tower. Kamal followed his eyes. Malencz stood on the balcony above them. He stood unnaturally straight. Rakóssy wheeled the black mare and rammed her between two Turks toward the open outside gate. Kamal was immediately separated from him by two or three men. He saw Rakóssy lean out and catch his brother's rein.

Rakóssy swung the mare away from the Turks as soon as he was through the gate. He and his brother galloped off to the south. Kamal rode to the head of his troop. He saw Rakóssy rein in a little distance away and look back. Kamal waved his arm and started almost due east, along the riverbank.

Rakóssy let go of Denis' rein. He glanced at his brother and swept his gaze over Vrath Castle, Kamal and the country to the north beyond the river.

"Where is Kamal going?" Denis said.

"Taking the long way home." The left corner of Ra- kóssy's mouth drew down. "I hope he gives Mustafa my especial regards."

"Now will you tell me what's going on?"

"I brought you here to learn. The only way you can learn is to keep your eyes open and your mouth shut."

"I don't speak Turk, and you—"

"Now, that's one thing you learned, isn't it?"

Denis flushed.

"Let's go home," Rakóssy said. "It's going to rain."

Mustafa said, "Sometimes, Kamal, 1 think that your use to me is extremely limited."

He looked at Kamal across the stretch of empty room, snorted, and looked out the window at the mountains, brilliant against the clear, rain-washed sky.

"I don't see what I could have done," Kamal said.

"Kamal," Mustafa said. "Kamal, you are very dear to me, as dear to me as my brother. I could not love you more if you were braver, or stronger. But wiser, Kamal. Just a little wiser?"

"Enlighten me, my lord."

Mustafa gathered up his robes and hurled himself into a chair. "You should, very simply, have let Malencz ar- rest him."

Kamal thought this over. He shut his eyes. "I see."

"Yes. You were in a position to destroy Rakóssy in a single stroke. You could have taken him prisoner, handed him over to Malencz, and asked of Malencz one simple favor in return. My brother. And why did you not pursue this wonderfully bold, dramatic, Turkish design?"

"I didn't think of it."

"Why?"

"My lord, I beg your pardon for my failure."

"Do you know why, Kamal? Because Rakóssy started to give you orders, and you, Kamal, you would rather take orders than do anything else in the world."

Mustafa shot out of his chair. He went to the window and poured a cupful of clean mountain water from the ewer on the table there.

"And Rakóssy knows it," he said. "He knows you, Kamal, as well as your own father knows you. Kamal, aren't you ashamed?"

Kamal's eyes were clamped shut. "My lord."

Mustafa drank the last drop of the sweet water. He turned and without a word flung the cup through the window. He waited, serene, until he heard the cup smash on the gravel of the courtyard below.

"Someday," Kamal said without opening his eyes, "you are going to hit someone doing that."

"Ah, Kamal, permit me to apologize. I have taxed you beyond your strength, demanded more of you than it is in your power to give. Go. You pollute my brain."

Kamal slunk out.

Mustafa slouched into his chair. He propped his feet on the stool.

"Rakós'," he said, "Rakós', what are you trying to do with us?"

There was something here that he thought he should try to understand. Rakóssy had deliberately provoked Malencz. Possibly he had underestimated his ability to do so. Possibly he had not thought that Malencz would try to arrest him. It was a very serious thing to do. If Malencz and Rakóssy were near open war, Mustafa could extend his operations against Malencz. There was little chance of a change in Rakóssy's style.

"Rakós'," Mustafa said, "damn your soul. If you have one."

He had to get Harun back. He lifted one hand to the little silver bell on the table beside him. A slave answered the ring.

"Send Abdul Mohammed here," Mustafa said. "Immediately."

"János, wake up."

Rakóssy opened his eyes. He turned his head and looked out the window. It was bright and windy outside.

"János?"

"Come in. Ivo?" Rakóssy got out of bed. The floor was cold. He sat on the bed and pulled his feet up under him. He roared for Ivo, his servant, and raked his fingers through his hair.

Denis came to the foot of the bed. "There's a messenger here from Cliff's Eye."

"So you wake me up."

"It's important, he says. Besides, you've had enough sleep."

Ivo brought Rakóssy's clothes. He put water on to heat and got out a razor. Rakóssy dressed, swearing at the chill of the floor. "What happened to my rug? Bring me my boots. And my belt." He cuffed Ivo. "Hurry up before I take a whip to you." He stamped his feet into his boots and sat down while Ivo strapped on his spurs. Denis stood uncertainly by the door.

"I'll tell you when I've had enough sleep." Rakóssy shoved him out of the way. Ivo held out his doublet. Rakóssy thrust his arms into it.

"Do you want me to shave you, my lord?"

"No. You're a born butcher. Get out of here. Get my rug back. Tell Anna I want breakfast in the great hall, and it had better be hot when it gets there. Denis, come with me." He took his swordbelt from the peg by the door, buckled it around his middle, and pounded out.

"Don't worry, Ivo," Denis said. "He's just—"

"It's all Mari's fault," Ivo said.

"Who's Mari?"

"Denis!" Rakóssy shouted.

Denis went out after him.

Rakóssy went straight to the great hall and flung himself into a chair. The hall was long, narrow and not very well lit. He looked up at the crossed halberds over the hearth and the painted coat of arms. Ivo jogged in with a covered dish. He pulled over a little table and set down the dish. Rakóssy took away the napkin and looked down at the meat and eggs. "Where's my milk?"

Ivo left at a run. Denis came through a side door with the Turk messenger. Rakóssy was prodding the meat with his dagger. He looked up.

"Abdul Mohammed." Rakóssy pointed at a chair with his elbow. "Mustafa loses no time."

Abdul Mohammed grinned. "On this matter, no." He spoke Turk.

"Speak Magyar," Rakóssy said. "My brother has no Turk."

"As you will." Abdul Mohammed glanced at Denis. "My master thinks perhaps you had a reason for making poor Kamal to be a fool."

"For that, no."

"But you have Harun."

"Down in the dungeons."

Ivo came in with the milk. Rakóssy drank it and sent him for more.

"Ransom," Rakóssy said. "Nothing more."

"Oh? And what can Cliff's Eye offer the Lion of Hungary?"

"Don't call me that." Rakóssy wiped his chin and the two days' growth of his beard. "I want three thousand bezants."

Abdul Mohammed blinked.

"Three thousand," Rakóssy said.

"Dinars."

"Bezants."

"That's a lot of money."

"He has it." Rakóssy took the second cup of milk and drank half of it. "He got that much at least from the sack of Belgrade, and where would he spend it?"

"Yes. I am to see Harun and know that he is well."

"As you wish."

"My master will accept the terms, then. He will bring the ransom here, to the point of exchange, on that day."

Rakóssy pushed away the dish. "Tell him that I shall personally count every bezant. Denis, take Abdul Mohammed down to the dungeons. Take Arpád or Alexander with you."

"Yes, János."

They left him. He sat with his head resting against the back of the chair. He shut his eyes. Within a few moments he was fast asleep.

Malencz's eldest son supervised the exchange. Some fifty of Malencz's men lounged on the slope below Hart Castle, and a hundred Turks sat their horses in orderly rows opposite them. In the space between, the exchange was conducted with bored formality.

A hundred yards west of the point of exchange, Mustafa himself on his white-footed chestnut mare watched Rakóssy count gold bezants into leather sacks. Arpád, Rakóssy's second-in-command, stood nearby, looking now and then at Harun. Both Kamal and Denis were with Peter Malencz overseeing the exchange of prisoners.

"As sticky-fingered as any Jew," Mustafa said.

Rakóssy dropped the last bezant into the last leather sack. "With reason," he said. He straightened and held out his hand. "Ten short. Give me them."

"Alas." Mustafa searched his clothes. "I don't seem to have that kind of money anywhere with me. Perhaps we can leave it on account."

Rakóssy snapped his fingers.

"Rakós'," Mustafa said, "your major failing—aside from a lack of breeding, education and religion—is that you want—and completely, I'm afraid—a sense of humor." He shook his head. "Of all the gifts that Allah has given men, surely the finest and the most consoling in this vale of pain . . ."

He paused and eyed Rakóssy. "No. A pity." He took a handful of bezants from his sash and dropped them, one by one, into the trampled grass. "Ten," he said. "My fool of a brother, if you please."

"Arpád."

Arpád cut Harun loose. Rakóssy was staring at the gold, shining in the beaten grass.

"The horse," Mustafa said.

"She wasn't part of the bargain," Rakóssy said. "I like her."

Harun put two fingers in his mouth and whistled. The black mare lifted her head and came slowly forward, her reins trailing. She passed Arpád and Harun and thrust her head under Rakóssy's arm.

"One would expect better taste of a beast of her breeding," Mustafa said. He called to Kamal to bring another horse. Kamal jogged over almost at once. The exchange was finished, and Malencz's men were riding off. Levolt of Kutess stood watching them.

Rakóssy mounted the black mare. Mustafa said, suddenly, "What will you do with your new treasure, Rakós'?"

"I'll shoe my horses with it for the ride into Cliff's Eye."

Kamal was staring at Rakóssy. Harun mounted. Mustafa wheeled his horse. The chestnut mare moved with short, neat steps, like a dancer. Her scarlet trappings swayed. The little bells on her harness rang like silver. Rakóssy glanced once at Kamal and nodded absently. He listened to the bells and watched the flutterings of the tassels on the mare's saddle cloth. The Turks galloped away. The sound of the bells died softly.

"What are you thinking about, János?"

"None of your business."

Zoltan," Denis called. He rode over to the side of the road and dismounted.

The priest stood up. "Good morning, Denis. Are you riding alone? Your brother will be very angry."

"To hell with him," Denis said. "Where have you been?"

"Down there." Zoltan nodded to the village. "The headman was sick. He wanted the last rites, which I administered." He put his hand on the sack beside him. "Well. How do you like Hungary again?"

"I've been back almost a month."

"Ah, but you've been on the move. It's a beautiful spring, isn't it?"

"Yes. Are you in a hurry?"

"No. I have to say Mass tomorrow morning."

Denis laughed. "I won't keep you that long. I just wanted to talk to you."

"About your brother."

"Well, yes."

"Denis, I gave up trying to save your brother a long time ago. I rarely see him. I never talk to him."

"Save him?"

"His soul, Denis. His famous soul."

"Why famous?"

"Well." Zoltan sat down again. He leaned over and picked a flower and put it behind his ear. His cassock was tucked up between his legs, and his calves were ridged with muscle and old scars. "The people in the village think that he sold his soul to the Devil for a charmed life and fortune in battle. The Turks, I'm told, believe so too. I think it's possibly the only point of agreement between them."

"Peasant superstition."

"Perhaps. But superstitions have their roots in truth, sometimes. You've been away, Denis. You came back just in time for the fighting season."

Zoltan twined grass between his fingers. He looked off at the valley and the tangle of huts and gardens.

"He is much like your mother," Zoltan said at last. "Restless, impious, arrogant, and cold. He has some virtues which your mother, if you'll pardon my saying so, did not have."

"Mother was very strange."

"So she was."

"But János is stranger."

Zoltan braided the grass. "Not really."

"He almost got us into terrible trouble at Vrath. Count Malencz was furious."

"My lord doesn't think that Malencz does enough against the Turks. He hates Malencz."

"I don't think he knows what he's doing."

"Oh, yes. Yes, he knows what he's doing. Sometimes I think that everybody in the world is traveling through a dark cloud, and they do things expecting something quite different than they should. Your brother knows exactly what he's doing and what will happen. Perhaps it's another thing the Devil gave him. I have great confidence in your brother."

"Confidence? In János?"

Zoltan got up and started toward the castle. Denis led his horse along beside Zoltan.

"He's very capable," Zoltan said. "Look up there. He keeps one hundred ten knights in Hart, and almost thirty servants. The knights do nothing but fight. They don't herd. They don't garden. They must all be outfitted and mounted and the horses must be tended, too. Your brother probably doesn't know exactly how many peasants live on his land, but it can't be more than five or six hundred. He protects them from the Turks so that they can support themselves, he sees that the Gypsies and the Jew traders come through here, and he supports his knights and his castle servants and the horses, without taxing his people a single head of cattle, a single lamb, or an old carrot. He's very capable."

The gate of Hart Castle opened. A dozen knights rode out and jogged down the hill. Several women followed them, walking, carrying baskets on their arms. They were going down to the gardens by the stream, Denis knew, to tend them and to gather vegetables. He watched the knights turn west, riding at a trot.

"They're going to raid," Zoltan said. "They'll bring back a herd of Malencz's sheep and cattle. If they were hunting they'd have bows. The hunting isn't very good anymore. Some say the Turks drove off the game."

Denis said nothing. He wondered how Zoltan knew and how Zoltan, a priest, could condone it.

"We eat better and more often, in the hard season, then most of Malencz's people," Zoltan said. "It's hard to be a zealot on a full belly."

"I've heard it just the opposite."

"Zealots love to starve."

They went through the gate. Rakóssy was standing next to the pump, supervising while three sweating men fixed the pulley. He looked over, saw Denis, and waved. He looked back to the pump. Denis called a stableboy to take his horse. He went over to Rakóssy. His heels clicked on the paving stones of the courtyard.

"Up early, little brother."

"I wanted to ride."

"Oh? New sport in Italy? I told you once that you have to take somebody with you when you ride."

"I wasn't going far. Just down to the village."

Rakóssy started toward the stable. Denis said, "Where are you going?"

"Check the stable for winter damage." Rakóssy nodded back at the pump. The men there were drawing up the old rope. It was wet and filthy and covered with slime. Things grew on it.

"Everything inside the walls needs to be mended, patched or replaced," Rakóssy said. "The whole place is falling to pieces."

"It looks better than before I left," Denis said. "I always remembered it as colder and wetter."

"That's because it was down by the stream."

"There are more people to take care of it now."

Rakóssy grinned. "Where were you going?"

"Nowhere special."

"Don't ride alone. It's dangerous."

"I didn't remember."

"Naturally."

They went into the stable. Denis looked around. Rakóssy swung the door on its hinges.

"What happened to the dogs?" Denis said. "Lightning, and Red—we used to have a whole pack."

Rakóssy tapped the wooden stable door. He took a piece of chalk from his doublet and marked an X on a rotten panel.

"They died off," he said. "I don't hunt. I sent the falcons to the King."

"That's a shame."

Rakóssy went farther into the stable. He looked up at the wooden ceiling, at the wide crossbeams. "Does that beam look sagging to you?"

Denis squinted at it. "A little," he said.

"We'll have to put a prop under it."

The walls of the stable were of stone; the horses were hitched to iron rings set into the walls. Only Rakóssy's black mare had her own stall. Denis said, "That's a lovely horse."

"Pure Kohl Arab. Mustafa had her brought up from Constantinople under a full guard."

Rakóssy poked and shoved at the props, studied the beams, and made chalk marks on those to be replaced.

Denis said, "How did you get her?"

"Levolt offered to sell her to me."

"That's how you knew Harun was in Kutess."

"Yes."

Denis looked down toward the end of the stable and laughed.

"You still have the cats."

"They catch mice."

"Look at that."

Rakóssy turned. A big orange cat was lying on the rump of the last horse, fast asleep. The horse was dozing. The cat was sprawled comfortably over the horse's slacked hip.

Denis said, "That's beautiful."

Rakóssy went down to the rack at the end of the stable and took down a long whip. He shook it out, worked it over near the horse, and cracked it. The horse leapt awake. The cat, startled, dug in her claws to keep from slipping. The horse neighed shrilly and bucked. The cat clung with all four paws. The horse kicked out violently. The cat leapt down and streaked for the hayrick.

Rakóssy laughed and coiled up the whip. Denis said, "That was cruel."

"I wanted to see what she would do," Rakóssy said. He went to the frightened horse and calmed it down. "Bring me that pitch pot."

Denis brought the pot. Rakóssy swabbed pitch over the long furrows on the horse's rump. The horse stood, quivering.

"You've broken up a beautiful friendship," Denis said.

"He'll forget all about it when he heals."

Rakóssy went through the rest of the stable. Denis trailed along behind him.

"What are you going to do with that money?" Denis said.

"That's my business. Why is everybody so interested in that money?"

"It's a fortune."

"I'm taking it all to Buda in a couple of days."

"Can I go with you?"

"No. You stay here and make sure nobody burns the place down."

Denis followed him out of the stable. Alexander, Arpád's brother, was standing near the gate. He came over and said, "Have you gone through the kitchens yet?"

"No."

"One of the scullions got himself bitten by a rat."

"A rat? Did they kill it?"

"Yes. It was this big."

"Someday I'm going to have the hide off that woman's back."

Denis said, "Is the scullion all right?"

Alexander pulled his mustache. "I guess so."

Rakóssy started for the kitchens. Denis took a step after him. Alexander caught his arm. "Stay out here," he said. "It's a better show when you're not in the middle." Alexander whistled, and everybody in the courtyard came lazily to attention. Rakóssy went through the kitchen door. There was a moment of taut silence.

Fat Anna, the cook, hurtled through the door and fell into the courtyard. She swore and got to her feet. Rakóssy appeared in the doorway. He held the corpse of a gigantic rat in one hand. He leaned against the doorjamb and tossed the rat into the yard.

Anna began to scream curses at him. Rakóssy waited until she was out of breath. He came down the steps from the door slowly and headed for Anna. She stood her ground a little while. When he was within two paces of her she began to back up.

"You get rid of those rats," he said, "and clean up every inch of that kitchen, or I'll peel your skin back and open your fat gut."

"Stay away from me, you dog-eating—"

Rakóssy hit her in the stomach. She doubled over and he tripped her. She lay, gagging, on the stones of the courtyard. He said something Denis could not hear and walked away. Anna rose after a while and shook herself, so that all her fat body rippled. She looked around her and went back into the kitchen.

Rakóssy came over to Alexander. "If she wants help for the rat hunt, give it to her."

Denis looked at his boots. Alexander went away.

"How long will you be in Buda?" Denis said.

"Not long enough for you to turn Hart Castle into an enlightened bit of paradise or a commune. I won't expect you to keep my discipline, but don't attempt to win everyone over by loving kindness."

"Why not?" Denis said, looking him in the face.

"Because it won't work." Rakóssy stamped off.

Denis went up to the library. He settled himself with a book. He could hear the noises from the courtyard through the window; he closed his ears to them and read.

Rakóssy was away almost two weeks. The Jews came and went. For a while, everybody in Hart and the village below it had bright new clothes and jewelry. Denis spent most of his time in the library. The castle required little attention. The brothers Arpád and Alexander organized the knights and the keep, where the knights lived, and the servants had their own routines. One day Arpád came to Denis and told him that Anna wanted the kitchen inspected. Denis went down and found the kitchens clean and ratless.

"We killed twenty-two big rats," Arpád said. "Big. Like this."

"I'm going to roast them for your brother's table," Anna said.

"Just don't feed them to me," Denis said.

Anna laughed, showing all her teeth. "For you, little one, grapes and lamb." She went back into the pantries.

"You should have hit her," Arpád said.

"No," Denis said, and went back to the library. He heard Arpád shouting in the courtyard below. Denis could remember when his father had spent hours in deep discussion with priests and learned laymen from all over Hungary, Bohemia and even Austria, often right in this room. It was different now. Only this room was the same. It was here that he had learned to read. He settled himself with the *Vita Nuova*, taking notes and pretending he was organizing a lecture. When he was done, he emendated his notes and rearranged them.

He had the choice now of beginning the *Commedia* immediately, with about two hours before dinner, or of reading something else and waiting for a fresh day. He remembered something one of the doctors at Louvain had said—that the great masters should be approached only after a good night's sleep and a full meal. He stood up to put the *Vita* on the shelf and stood reading the titles of the other books. The door opened and Rakóssy walked in behind him.

"János," Denis said. "You startled me."

"Everything's all right?"

"Yes, just fine."

Rakóssy took off his cloak and hung it beside the door. "I want you to write a letter for me."

Denis went to the desk. "Of course."

Rakóssy shut the door. He stretched. His eyes moved uneasily over the shelves of books.

"I don't think I've ever seen you in here before," Denis said.

The corner of Rakóssy's mouth drew down. "It doesn't particularly appeal to me."

Denis sat down at the desk, took a piece of paper and a pen, dipped the pen in ink, and said, "I'm ready."

Rakóssy prowled once around the room, his eyes wandering, leaned on the desk, and stared at the books.

"Don't sit on the desk like that. You'll break it."

"You sound just like Father."

"You really don't want me to write this letter, do you?"

"It has to get written."

"I mean, you don't want me to know what's in it."

Rakóssy looked down at him. He looked amused. "Don't say the obvious. I don't think it can be helped."

"Do you dislike me because I can write?"

"My God, no. Why should I?"

"I don't know. It just seems an unfair advantage."

Rakóssy shrugged. "Father's predilections. It was his money."

"He tried to teach you."

"So he did."

"It's odd, you look like Father, and I look like Mother, but I'm much more—"

Rakóssy waited for him to finish. Denis put the pen back into the inkwell.

"Your father's son?" Rakóssy said.

"I'm sorry, János."

"Little brother, you credit me with feelings I have not got. As for your unfair advantage, it isn't much of an advantage at all."

"What do you mean?"

"You've been to Italy and France and you speak Italian and French and Latin and Greek, but if I wanted you to write Turk, you couldn't do it, and you can't write German, although I wish you could. You're precious little use to me, for all you've been across Europe and back. As for being like Father, I would only wish that on my enemies."

"That's unfair. That's a terrible thing to say. Father was—"

"A scholar. Write the letter in Latin."

"All right. But go slowly so I can translate."

"To his Magnificence the Archduke Ferdinand . . ."

Rakóssy looked down. Denis was not writing. Rakóssy said, "Is anything troubling you, little brother?"

"To his Magnificence the Archduke Ferdinand," Denis said, and wrote.

"Greetings. I have just now come back from repaying the agent of the Fuggers in Buda."

"You borrowed money from the Fuggers? Father would turn in his grave."

"Probably. I—this is the rest of the letter. I shall come to Vienna in the late summer. I will bring with me thirty knights and my brother, Sir Denis Rakóssy, who will act as my secretary. This must be completely secret in Hungary. For this reason I send this letter through my own means instead of the Fuggers'. I ask you to present my compliments to the Lady Catharine."

Rakóssy stared. Denis said, "Is that all?"

"Yes. Put some fancy end to it."

Denis corrected two or three mistakes and copied the letter over.

"Have you been dealing with them long?"

"The Fuggers or the Hapsburgs?"

"Both, I guess."

"Almost two years."

"What for?"

"Because I enjoy being three thousand bezants in debt. And . . ."

Denis wrote carefully. His handwriting was beautiful. "And what?"

"You sound like a priest."

"Why did you borrow it?"

"Because I needed it."

"Why?"

"Denis, don't be stupid. I don't want to tell you. I don't intend to tell you. You'll find out in good time. Stop asking me questions."

"I'm sorry."

Rakóssy said nothing. Denis wrote a courtly closing to the letter. He said, "Shall I sign it?"

"I'll sign it." Rakóssy took the pen, inked it, and leaned down to write his name. He straightened away from the desk. Denis sprinkled sand over the page and shook it gently. Rakóssy melted wax over the candle and put his seal below his name. He put his signet ring down on the desk. Denis watched the ink dry and the seal cool. He sat still, trying to decipher the design on Rakóssy's sword hilt.

"I'm getting married," Rakóssy said.

Denis's gaze flew to his brother's face. "What?"

"I am. In the late summer, in Vienna."

"Who is she?"

"One of the ladies-in-waiting to the Archduchess. Catharine de Buñez. She's supposed to be the bastard daughter of the King of Aragon."

"Good Lord, isn't that high?"

"We're the same rank." Rakóssy shrugged. "The blood relation to the Hapsburgs is nil, and they want to be rid of her."

"But, János, you're nothing but an obscure border baron."

Rakóssy's black eyes flashed. "That depends on who you are, little brother."

"This is all because you hate Malencz."

"Of course I hate Malencz. Everybody hates Malencz, except the Turks, and they love him."

"Have you met her?"

"Yes."

"When?"

"I went to Vienna last winter."

"Do you like her? Is she pretty? Is she nice?"

"I prefer her sister, to tell you the truth. But the sister's married."

"The wax is cold."

"Heat it up again."

"Ivo told me you were—I mean, that you were courting some girl in the kitchens."

"Courting her? I'm sleeping with her. She's a Slav. Do you think I'd marry some Slav girl from the kitchens?"

He took the wax and sealed the folded letter. "Get Stepan Hálasz."

Denis called for a page and sent him for Stepan. He came back, settling into his chair again.

"I'm fascinated," Denis said. "I didn't think you'd ever get married."

"I have to get an heir. You don't think I'd leave this to you, do you?"

"I hadn't thought of it."

"You couldn't handle one half of it."

"I don't suppose I could."

"Then why don't you do something about it?" Rakóssy turned. The door opened. It was Stepan. Rakóssy
said, "Take two fast horses and ride to Vienna. Give this
to the Archduke's secretary, Mansfeld, in the Hapsburg
palace. If you have any trouble seeing him, tell them
you're from Hart Castle in Hungary. Nothing more,
you understand?"

"Yes, sir."

"And don't tell anybody where you're going."

"Yes, sir."

Rakóssy dismissed him. He swung back toward Denis.

"Why don't you learn how to fight? Or speak Turk?
Or even German? Learn to be of some use?" He turned
and snatched his cloak from the rack. He slammed the
door behind him.

In the late spring the Turks broke the treaty. They attacked a cattle camp, ran off the herders, and took the cattle back into the hills. A Slav brought the news to Hart a few days later. Rakóssy took fifty men and headed into the mountains.

Once they had left the foothills, they were in the heart of Mustafa's territory. Rakóssy knew the mountains along the border of his land almost as well as he knew his own hills. He cut straight across to the road that led south to Belgrade and waited by it for a few days. There was no sign of a supply train coming. Rakóssy got bored. He divided his men into two bands and sent Arpád with one south along the road to destroy any bridges they could find within four days' ride. The other twenty-five men Rakóssy led toward Cliff's Eye.

The mountains along this stretch crawled with Turks. The Magyars stayed on the move, eating what they could find along the way. On the second day after they had left the road, their scouts sighted a small band of Turks headed slowly east. Rakóssy circled around in front of the Turks, set an ambush and sprang it that evening. They killed two Turks and ran off their horses. The remaining Turks stood off their second charge, and Rakóssy quit. He headed northwest.

That following morning they camped in a gorge running east to west just below the timberline. A little boiling stream raced along one side of the floor of the gorge. Rakóssy posted sentries on the banks and rode along the gorge, alone, toward the east. The gorge ended in a waterfall that spilled over a cliff to a narrow valley.

Rakóssy went back to his camp. Most of his men were asleep. He found Alexander, rolled in a cloak, and woke him up.

"What's down there?" Alexander said.

"No way out. It's a very neat trap. Wake everybody

up. We're moving out."

Alexander got up, yawning, and started waking up the men. He called two men to carry the one who had been wounded in the ambush. Rakóssy rode down the gorge to a place where horses could climb the walls and went up. The sentries had seen nothing.

"If you see a large band of Turks—anything over fifteen—we scatter and go home," Rakóssy said. He told this to all his men. He took the bridle off the mare and loosened her girth. He found a thicket, wrapped himself in his cloak, and slept.

Alexander woke him up at twilight. "There are six Turks riding on the other side of the gorge," he said.

"Scouts?"

"They're riding pretty fast."

Rakóssy stood up slowly. He went to the edge of the trees. All around him his men lay in the brush, tense and silent. The Turks were galloping through the scattered pines on the other side.

Alexander said, "I don't understand this."

Rakóssy tugged his mail shirt straight. "We're being herded. Like that time we got caught on the mountaintop."

"Herding us north? Then let's go south."

Rakóssy shook his head. "He's probably got us ringed, except for the east. And east's that cliff. We'll break up and go home."

He put his hands around his mouth and made a sound like a woodcock's call. The brush around him rustled. Slowly his men gathered around him.

"How is Martón Nagy?" Rakóssy said.

"Healing fast."

"Good." Rakóssy sat on his heels. His men drew closer. "We're going to scatter. Pál, you and Michael Szabo take Martón back. Be careful. Take your time."

"What about the horses we captured?" somebody said.

"Leave them. You couldn't get them through the

Turks anyway. Take your time and be careful, all of you."

They left, padding softly away through the trees toward their horses.

Rakóssy got Alexander by the sleeve. "Meet me at the Old Man by tomorrow moonrise," he said.

"What for?"

"Never mind. Just meet me."

Rakóssy turned and went after the black mare. He stood by her, talking to her, until he was sure everybody had gone. He led her up the slope toward the timberline. The moon was coming up. He climbed a tree and looked out. He could see nothing but the trees and the silver of the moonlight. The roar of the stream in the gorge reached him faintly. He climbed back down the tree and mounted the mare and turned north.

He rode at a walk, keeping just below the timberline. Toward midnight he heard horses coming up from below. He pulled the mare into the shadow of a twisted old pine and dismounted. He put his hand on her nostrils.

Eight Turks in single file rode out of the trees and onto the naked slope, into the full glare of the moonlight. Their helmets and the tips of their lances flashed. There was no wind. They came slowly toward Rakóssy. He held his breath. They turned uphill again and rode toward the heights, where they could see more of the slope.

He started to breathe again. The Turks stopped and looked back the way they had come. Rakóssy led the mare away from them, his hand still clamped over her nostrils. When the trees were thick around him he mounted and rode on.

Twice before dawn he stopped and dismounted while bands of Turks rode by him, moving slowly and headed east. After dawn he was almost afraid to ride on. He saw no Turks and thought he was out of the circle that they had been building around him and his men. He relaxed enough to doze in the saddle. At noon, without warning, he was jumped by a good fifteen Turks.

The mare bolted at the first shout and headed for the thick of the forest. Rakóssy steered her around an impenetrable thicket and across the slope of the land. The Turks yelled and whooped and charged after him. He heard them calling wildly back and forth behind him, but he could not hear the words. He thought that they were as surprised as he was.

The mare broke out into a meadow and sprinted. She leapt a little stream, skidding on the soggy, slippery grass, and he spun her around and headed for the nearest trees. A lance wobbled past him. The mare thundered through belly-high grass into the trees and he bent in the saddle, his head by her neck, to avoid the swinging branches. A branch raked across his back. He turned slightly and saw that the Turks were still in the meadow. He spun the mare straight down the slope. Almost at once they reached another meadow. He raced her to the eastern edge, where the grass grew thinnest, and dismounted. He listened. The Turks had lost him in the trees. They were spreading out to find him again. He led the mare into the forest and made her lie down in the lee of the rock where the dead leaves were drifted high. He lay down beside her, one hand on her head, and waited.

The Turks called to each other. Three of them rode into the meadow he had just left. They spread out, looking for signs. The ground was too hard to hold tracks.

Now he could understand what they were saying. They knew that it was Rakóssy they had flushed. One of them suggested that they head north, because he had been going north when they jumped him. The others thought this was a rotten idea.

There was a shout from the trees. Somebody had found a trail. The three in the meadow galloped back. Rakóssy strained his ears. He caught the Turk word for deer and a shout of laughter.

He lay still. The mare twitched once, trying to get up, and he pressed her head down. The smell of decaying leaves was all over him. He yawned. The sound of the Turks moving in the forest died away. He got up and let the mare rise, mounted, and turned north. He rode cautiously, staying under the highest trees.

The Old Man was a rock formation just northwest of Mustafa's fortress at Cliff's Eye. When Rakóssy got there Alexander was cooking a dove over a low fire. Rakóssy circled the rock entirely and came in, unsaddled the mare, and let her go. Alexander took the dove off the fire and split it. He handed the bigger half to Rakóssy.

"Have any trouble?" Rakóssy said.

"I went all the way up to the heights and came that way. I saw some Turks but none of them near me."

"They're thick as fleas on this slope." Rakóssy cracked one of the bird's small bones between his teeth and sucked out the marrow. He spat out the crushed bone and gristle. "Did you see anything of that valley where Mustafa keeps his herds?"

"No. I didn't go that far west."

If I were Mustafa, Rakóssy thought, I would go toward Hart and try to pick off anybody trying to sneak back that way. "I'd guess he's pulled off most of his herders."

"Aha. You're going to steal his cattle."

Rakóssy laughed. "Not quite. Wake me up at dawn." He lay back and went to sleep.

He woke up by himself at dawn. Alexander was fast asleep. Rakóssy climbed up to the top of the Old Man and lay on the cool stone, looking west down the slope. He could see the crag that overhung Cliff's Eye. He could see nothing moving. Turks moved like ghosts in these mountains.

He went back down and woke Alexander. They rode together down to the edge of the valley where Mustafa kept his herds. The valley was almost circular, flat and wide. The slopes were thick with aspen and larch. All the herds were crowded along the southern edge where the spring was.

"Do you see any guards?" Rakóssy said.

"No."

"There they are. Over there."

The guards were up on the western slope, nearly under the trees. They had a fire going. Rakóssy had seen the smoke of it first.

"I'm hungry," Alexander said.

"So am I. Let's start a fire."

"Are you crazy?"

"No." Rakóssy dismounted. He heaped up brush against a tree. "That grass is dry as tinder. It hasn't rained in three weeks."

"Oh. I follow you."

"That's good."

Rakóssy made a pile of brush against the tree as high as his shoulder. Alexander said, "I think they've seen us."

"The fire will cover us."

"They have. Here they come."

Rakóssy bent down. He struck a spark with his tinder-box. The spark leapt into the brush and died. He swore steadily. He knelt and tried again. This time he let the spark flare up in the box's tinder. He knocked the fire into the brush. It caught with a roar.

"Let's go," Alexander said.

Rakóssy stirred the fire with a long stick. When the stick was burning, he mounted the black mare, still holding the stick.

"This way," he said, and headed around the valley, striking for the herds. Alexander followed him. Rakóssy signaled him to come abreast of him and leaned down, trailing the burning stick through the grass. The stick began to burn up toward his hand. The mare snorted and tried to break his strong hold on the rein. The grass burst into flame like a trail behind him. The fire on the stick singed his hand, and his sleeve began to smoulder. He hauled himself back into the saddle and flung the stick away. The grass was burning in a wide swath behind him.

The Turks wavered between attacking Rakóssy and Alexander and fighting the fire. Half of them raced for the burning grass. The rest swung around to head the Magyars off. Rakóssy charged the mare straight at the herds. The cattle were already nervous from the smell of fire. The black mare was tired and stumbled once, almost throwing Rakóssy. He steadied her and galloped around the farthest edge of the herds and began to shout and whistle and wave his arms. Alexander followed him. The great-horned cattle flung up their heads and bellowed. The horses began to bunch up a little way away. The herd stallion bugled and drove them together. Rakóssy yelled and crowded the mare into the cattle.

The cattle broke into a shambling trot, their horns clashing and ringing like swords. The horses followed them. They headed straight across the valley. As soon as they were in a full run, Rakóssy turned west. He waved to Alexander and raced for the cover of the trees.

They rode straight for Hart Castle. The Turks were too occupied to chase them. From a ridge well west of Cliff's Eye Rakóssy could see a tower of smoke rising toward the sun.

"Good enough," he said. "Come on. I'm hungry."

Arpád and his men returned to Hart two days after Rakóssy. He had burned two bridges and started a landslide to cover the road in a little pass. He had not lost a single man. Rakóssy nodded.

"Everybody's back except one—what's his name from Mohács," Rakóssy said. "He may just be cornered, or he may be captured."

"Maybe he went back to Mohács."

"Maybe. Could you make a map of that part of the road you traveled on?"

"I don't think so."

"But you remember it."

"Yes."

"Go find my brother and tell him everything you can remember about it. Everything. South of Robbers' Pass."

"Yes, sir."

"Leave me alone."

Arpád left the room. Rakóssy went to the great hall and sat down. He put his feet up on the table. His boots were filthy. He thought of—what was his name? The men all called him Mohács. If he was cornered, he would probably surrender.

He wondered if Malencz would attack him this year. He doubted it. Malencz would try to go through the Diet of Hungary first. He was glad that Malencz was the King's commander in the south—if anybody but János Rakóssy had to be. Malencz was a fool and worse, but Rakóssy never lost his temper with Malencz. Levolt, now, Rakóssy lost his temper with Levolt as often as he saw him. Because Levolt was stupider than Malencz and small-thinking. Malencz had big thoughts, at least.

If Malencz attacked him this year it would be difficult. He got up and took off his mail shirt and sat down again. Next year for Malencz. Unless the time ran out on him. By next year he would have handled Levolt, too.

The door behind him opened. Soft footsteps came toward him. Two hands laid themselves on his shoulders, and Mari's voice said, "Weary, my lord?"

Rakóssy looked at her right hand. She was fingering the cloth of his shirt. She wore a new ring.

"The Gypsies came while I was away."

She laughed. "The villagers ran them off. They stole a baby."

"Gypsies don't steal babies. The villagers need a lesson."

She laughed again. She sat down on the arm of his chair and carefully settled herself back until she lay in his lap, with her arms around his neck. "I missed you," she said.

"All of me?"

"Don't be coarse, Jansci."

"No."

"Smile a little. There, you look best when you smile."
She put her hand against his cheek. "You look like that
big painting of your father."

"The devil I do. It doesn't look much like him, either."

"You do."

She ran her fingers lightly over his face. The light
cloth of her bodice clung to her breasts. He touched the
cloth. It was damp.

"Sweating rather more than usual, aren't you?"

"Damn you." She sat up. Her weight slid off the arms
of the chair and came full on his legs. He jerked away.
She started to fall and he caught her. She stood up and
pulled the damp cloth away from her skin.

"You damned bastard."

"At least I know that you go to the trouble of making
yourself enticing." He stood up. She smiled and leaned
against him.

"Let's go upstairs," he said.

"You still haven't kissed me." She fooled with the laces
of his shirt. "I can't be very enticing."

"Let's go upstairs. I'll kiss you then."

They went upstairs. They made love and Rakóssy sent
Ivo for something to eat. It was still daylight. He lay beside her, thinking of Malencz.

"Jansci," she said. She turned over. She crossed her
arms behind her head. "What are you thinking about?"

He reached down and pulled the cover up over her
breasts. "Not about you." He stretched.

"Do I bother you?"

"If I said yes, you'd be all over me, and if I said no,
you'd be angry."

"I mustn't, then."

"Oh, you do. You do."

"Good." She rolled over again and breathed into his
ear. "You bother me, you know."

"Women. You're all mad. Shut up for once, will you?"

She breathed into his ear without saying anything. He thought about Malencz. After a while he stopped thinking about Malencz and reached for her.

They ate in bed. Ivo served them, keeping his eyes on the floor, on the ceiling, on Rakóssy, while Mari sat eating, smiling, not caring that her back was naked. Rakóssy lay back again and thought about Denis. Ivo left. Mari climbed out of bed and put her clothes on. Rakóssy watched her. She had a big, beautiful body. Her face showed the Slav blood in her.

"Jansci," she said, "if I told you I was going to have a baby—"

"You'd be lying. The Gypsies were just here."

"Well, I could have wanted it."

"Too bad for you."

She laughed. She flung herself across the bed and kissed him. "You're wonderful."

"I'm also going to be married."

"Married? You?" She raised herself on her elbows. "Who is the unfortunate lady?"

"Spanish noblewoman. Go tell everybody. They'll laugh their fool heads off."

"Pity." She sat up and combed out her hair with her fingers. "I'll miss you."

"Oh, I'll be around."

"Not you. You're the faithful type."

"Why do you think that?"

"Oh, reasons."

"She's a stick, this one. She lacks your—" he patted her left breast— "equipment." He got out of bed and dressed.

"If you imported one all the way from Spain, you could have gotten a good one."

"Vienna. And I tried. Very hard."

"And failed? You?"

"She got herself married."

"So somebody closer to the tree caught the fruit that you shook down?"

"Quite." He buckled his belt. "You aren't really pregnant, are you?"

"No."

"Good. It might not appeal to my bride."

"I thought she was a stick."

"Even sticks have feelings. She's very . . . intelligent, and I like her. We were good friends in Vienna."

"Can I wait on her?"

"I think the comparison might be too much for my blood."

"Oh, Jansci, please? Anna hates me. She gives me all the dirty work. I had to clean out the soap pot yesterday and it ruined my knees, kneeling on the stones all day long. Look."

"All right. But as soon as anything happens, out."

"Good." She went to the door. "Shall I come back to-night?"

"Yes."

"Good." She laughed. She shut the door softly.

He grinned. Catharine's reaction to Mari might be interesting. He went to the window and looked down toward the mountains. He wondered what Mustafa was thinking about.

Mari started paying attention to Denis in the next few days. She came up to Rakóssy's room once and he said, "What are you trying to do to my brother?"

"Seduce him. Maybe he'll teach me to read and write."

"You'll have to teach him something. He's probably still a virgin."

"Actually, he's quite charming. If you pay some attention to him."

"He's not your breed."

"No, he's a real Greek. But he's fun. He's told me a lot about Italy. It must be very interesting. Jansci, stop."

"Um? Saving yourself for Denis?"

"He's very nice."

"Yes. He's very nice. He's very useless, too, and he has the spine of a . . . of a . . ." He searched for some spineless thing.

"Jansci, you're being cruel."

"If you were in my position and stuck with a brother like a soggy sweetmeat—"

"Jansci, don't get so excited."

"I'm not excited. And be quiet." He shut his eyes. "Be quiet for once, will you?"

Denis, Rakóssy realized, liked to talk to Mari, but he either did not intend to or did not know how to let her seduce him. It was a hot summer, and getting hotter, enough to sap anybody's strength. Mari dropped Rakóssy entirely, gave Denis another try, and finally settled on Arpád. Since Arpád and Alexander split the post of second-in-command between them, a rumor started that Mari was Arpád's when Alexander was out raiding with Rakóssy, and Alexander's when Arpád was away. It was pushing into midsummer, and they fought almost every day. Rakóssy thought that Fat Anna, who hated Mari, Arpád and Alexander almost equally, had started the rumor to get Arpád and Alexander fighting. The rumor didn't bother Arpád at all. He was openly Mari's lover, and even if the rumor were true he was willing to share anything with his brother. Almost all the young women in the castle had plots to get Rakóssy, and Ivo was in great demand, since he alone could know for sure who went up to Rakóssy's room at night. Ivo said that the whole castle was amazed that Rakóssy had not yet gotten himself another mistress.

"The conniving around this castle is enough to drive me out of my mind," he said to Denis.

"The morals are what irritate me."

"Who—Mari? Mari looks out for herself."

"She's terribly sweet. But she's so . . . I suppose it's the Slav in her."

Rakóssy grinned. "It's the Slav in her, the Greek in me, the Czech in Arpád, and even the Magyar in some people."

"I'm as Greek as you are."

"Yes. Aren't you glad you have me around? All this vicarious sin and you can stay as angelic as ever."

"I don't know. Mari isn't my idea of a good—you know."

Rakóssy blinked. "You mean you—"

"I'm not as innocent as I look." Denis blushed. "I'm not exactly a virgin, you know."

"I didn't. Why not Mari? She's a handful."

"I'm not going to take your leavings."

"Pride. A deadly sin. She's not my leavings. I'm her leavings. She doesn't want me anymore." He broke off a chunk of bread.

"Why?"

"I told her about Catharine. Mari's honorable. She's quite a woman. You could do worse."

"Well, Arpád's got her now."

"So he does. You could get her back. Pass me the milk."

"Let's not talk about it."

"Shy?" Rakóssy said. "All you have to do is—"

"For the love of God, János."

Rakóssy grinned.

The summer wore on. The Turks burned a lot of the hay and Rakóssy had the horses put out to graze rather than use the feed in the castle. He led one raid deep into Mustafa's territory, laid an ambush along the road to Belgrade, and captured a whole convoy of supplies. He lost half of them on the way back, and when he reached Hart the castle was in an uproar. Mustafa had attacked in force. Denis described the attack, excited even now.

He had been talking to Father Zoltan when he heard the horns blowing. He got to the courtyard just as the last of the horses was galloping in through the gate. The courtyard was filled with loose and frantic horses. Alex-

ander led the defense, arming everybody with crossbows. Mustafa had brought a small bombard and bashed
in the roof of the stable with a big stone before they
finally drove him off.

"You were with Zoltan?"

"Yes."

Rakóssy walked away without saying anything more.
He went down into the basement of the castle and found
Zoltan's cubicle. Zoltan was writing a letter.

"I hope," Rakóssy said, "that's to the Bishop, asking
him to relieve you here."

Zoltan turned. He stood up. "It isn't, my lord."

"Stay away from my brother."

Zoltan looked down. "He seeks me out. I don't—"

"You carrion crow, I said stay away from him. Give
me back talk, and I'll kick your tailbone through your
front teeth."

Rakóssy slammed the door shut and went upstairs.

He wanted Denis to come raiding with him. Denis
would not go. He said calmly that he was a coward and
that he preferred talking to Father Zoltan.

"Not even Father was a coward," Rakóssy said.
"You'll go. Not this time, but the next."

Denis looked down at the courtyard. "Where are you
going?"

Arpád came behind Rakóssy and said, "We're ready."

Arpád was a head taller than Rakóssy, broad-
shouldered and thick-boned. Denis had always been a little afraid of him. Seeing him now, in the doorway of the
library, he began to tremble. Above his huge, droop-
ing mustaches Arpád's eyes were carefully blank. Denis
thought he saw contempt in Arpád's eyes.

Rakóssy turned and said, "Go down and wait for me in
the courtyard, Arpád."

He looked back at Denis, waiting until Arpád had
gone. He said, "You'll come raiding. If I'm ever killed,
somebody has to be here to give orders. These sheep will
follow but they won't lead. You're the only one who can

tell them what to do, if I die."

"If you're ever killed. If you die. You're human, János. You could die today. Where are you going?"

"None of your business."

"Nothing is ever my business until you want me to do something for you. If I'm supposed to take over when—when you die, maybe it should be my business."

"All right. Malencz has sent a hundred knights to garrison the old wooden fort by Etzel's Well. I'm going to drive them off and burn the fort."

"Etzel's Well? Isn't that on Malencz's land?"

"Yes. But it's too close to mine. I don't want him there."

"You don't want him there. That's no reason to attack him."

"Too bad."

"Zoltan's right, then. You are plotting against Malencz."

"You stay away from that damned priest. You wanted to know, and I told you. Now you don't like it. I take it back. I never told you. Sin in ignorance, brother."

"I'm not going to let you."

"Just how are you going to stop me?"

Denis sucked in his breath and started toward Rakóssy. He put his hand on the dagger in his belt. Rakóssy side-stepped calmly and slapped Denis across the face. Denis reeled back. Rakóssy went slowly after him. Denis tried to rush by him, and Rakóssy hit him in the pit of the stomach. Denis fell, retching.

"Would you rather I dragged you out into the court-yard and beat you up in front of everybody?"

"I hate you, János."

"That's Christian of you. Don't get up or I'll hit you again." Rakóssy backed away. "I've got plenty of time."

Denis gathered himself and lunged for Rakóssy's legs. Rakóssy dodged easily and kicked him in the head. Denis cried out. He lay still.

Rakóssy watched him. He was surprised that Denis

had gone for him the second time and he had not meant to kick him. He saw a tear on Denis' face, just above the scrape on his cheek.

"I don't think I can stand it," Denis said. "I wish I were dead."

Rakóssy bent and picked him up. "Don't cry, for the love of God. If you were a girl, everything would be different and better. Denis, don't cry, damn it."

Denis lifted his eyes slowly to Rakóssy's. Rakóssy said, "I want nothing from you but obedience. I don't care if you hate me or if you burn with brotherly love. All I want is obedience. If I say you are going to raid, little brother, you will raid. And stay away from that priest."

"I hate you."

"You've already said that." Rakóssy gave him a little shake. "Stop crying. Sit down. Read something." He turned and went out. Denis put his head down and wept.

Rakóssy stood outside the library door, listening. He looked down at his fist. He wished it were all over, everybody safe and the Turks beaten and Malencz finished, and he older and Denis back in Italy, going to school. He unclenched his fist and went out into the courtyard.

They reached Etzel's Well at sundown and found Malencz's men already in the wooden fort. Rakóssy had brought only seventy-five men with him, but they all had bows. He set up a camp at the gate of the fort and ordered bonfires lit. There was no moon that night. Rakóssy kept half his men on sentry duty while the other half slept, changing the guard at midnight. Rakóssy did not sleep at all.

At dawn a man under a white flag came from the fort. Rakóssy rode alone to meet him.

"I am Sir Martón Vidor," the man said. "What is the meaning of this?"

"I want you and your men out of this fort by noon.

Go back to your master and tell him not to try it again."

"You must be mad. This is my lord's land."

"Possibly."

Sir Martón spat. "The King will hear of this."

The left corner of Rakóssy's mouth drew down.

Sir Martón turned and galloped back to the fort. Rakóssy jogged to his own lines and dismounted. Arpád came over. "I've got ten men with longbows making fire arrows."

Rakóssy nodded. He looked at the sun. The sky was slowly clouding over.

"Are you worried about your brother?" Arpád said.

"When I want to tell you my problems, you'll know about it."

Arpád said nothing. Rakóssy stamped by him, watching the fires.

"That damned brother of his has him worried," Arpád said to Alexander.

"Not him. No sheep like that can bother him."

"What would happen to us, say, if he died?"

"Why—"

"The brother would be baron, and we'd be right back where Papa was when old Alexander was baron. Yes, my lord, No, my lord, Malencz coming to visit, and half of us out hunting some other way to keep fed."

Alexander looked for Rakóssy and saw him standing slouched by one of the fires, watching the wooden fort. Rakóssy glanced up at the sun and back at the fort.

"Remember when he became baron?" Alexander began to laugh. "Rode right over to Vrath and demanded his knights back."

"And had us rebuilding Hart before we were even out of mourning." Arpád turned too and looked at Rakóssy. "He was a silly-looking little brat, wasn't he?"

Rakóssy came toward them. He looked toward the fort every other step.

"Do you think they'll leave?" Arpád said.

"They'll leave," Rakóssy said. "One way or another.

Get the crossbowmen up closer to the gate. It's almost noon."

Arpád went to move the crossbowmen. Rakóssy stared at the fort. He turned to Alexander.

"If they attack us, nobody gets mounted. The bowmen can cut them down to size."

Alexander nodded. Half the crossbowmen jogged up past them and knelt, their bows unwound, talking. Rakóssy called the other men up and ordered them to a place three or four hundred feet from the first group and about the same distance from the gate. He paced nervously back and forth between the two groups. He told them all not to shoot until he gave the order.

He hoped that Vidor would surrender without fighting, but he knew that he would not. He watched the gate for a while, looked at the sun, and sat down on his heels.

The gate opened and he jumped up again. Horsemen galloped through the gate. He lifted his arm, waiting. When most of the horsemen were out the gate and charging, he dropped his arm.

In the first volley of bolts, the front rank of horsemen hurtled down. Horses kicked and screamed and ran wildly back toward the fort, plunging through the ranks behind. Some of the fallen men got to their feet and ran toward Rakóssy's men with their swords raised, awkward in their armor. Rakóssy said, "Keep shooting."

His men shot as fast as they could crank up their bows. They knelt to steady their aim and shot into the spreading mass of the knights. The bolts riddled the oncoming horsemen. Rakóssy, standing, saw them pitch to the ground and lie still, crawl, or get up and try to run. From the fort came the shrill blast of a horn. The knights wheeled and rode or ran on foot back to the gate. Rakóssy looked at his own men. Not one of them had been touched.

A white flag appeared at the gate. Vidor rode out toward them, alone. Rakóssy walked slowly out from between his lines, watching Vidor. Vidor sat stiffly in his saddle the prescribed distance from the gate, scowling. Rakóssy passed a body and glanced at it. The man was not dead. A bolt's wooden fletching thrust up from his belly.

Vidor said, "We will leave. This is against all honor."

"Take your dead and wounded with you."

"There is no dishonor in being beaten by a trick," Vidor said loudly.

"Well, you could have saved twenty or thirty men by giving up without a fight," Rakóssy said. "They probably all feel better knowing that they're still honorable. Get going. Don't try anything dishonorable. We'll be watching you."

Vidor spat. "Scum." He wheeled his horse and rode back. Rakóssy smiled.

Vidor and his men spent until late afternoon patching up their wounded and collecting their dead. They left just before sundown. Rakóssy took six men to burn the fort. They built bonfires against the walls and lit them. The wood was old and hard. It caught fire in sluggish ripples. Rakóssy felt the heat growing. Suddenly the whole wall was burning. His men backed away, weeping from the heat. Rakóssy stared at the flames. They leapt up roaring, high above the top of the wall. The black mare quivered and he put his hand on her neck. She jumped sideways, moving away from the fire. Rakóssy wheeled her and rode off.

As soon as Rakóssy had left for Etzel's Well, Denis went to find Zoltan. The priest noticed the scrape on Denis' cheek, but he did not mention it. They talked for a while, both of them nervous. Denis wanted to ask Zoltan about the new heresies, but Zoltan was not interested and Denis did not press him. Finally Zoltan said that he was tired and wanted to sleep, and Denis left him.

He went down the corridor toward his room, passed his brother's door, and after a moment turned back and went in. When Rakóssy had rebuilt Hart, he had left it exactly as before, on the inside. This had been their father's room. It was the same as it had been the day the old man died, but for the new clothes and the litter of János' personal things on the top of the chest. And the absence of books. It had been a shock to come home and find Hart on the top of the hill. But here, it was almost the same. He sat down on the foot of the bed and looked at the huge portrait of his mother. He remembered the picture much better than he remembered her.

I do look like her, he thought. And I have the Greek name. I was hers, when I was born, and János was Father's. Strange. János was . . . what—three?—when I was born. Not old enough for Father to know that he wasn't the son he wanted.

When I was a little boy, I would come here every afternoon. His father would read to him, one finger following the words so that Denis learned to recognize them. One night he remembered especially. Father was reading in Latin, explaining and tracing the words, and I was on his lap. Mother came in, dressed the way she did when she rode. It was dark out, I remember that. He remembered that his father had been worried about his mother.

"When did you get home?" his father said.

"Just now."

She came farther into the room to hang up her cloak, and Denis, safe on his father's lap, saw that János was at the door. He had been hidden before by his mother in her heavy cloak.

"You took him with you," Denis' father said.

"Yes."

"I've told you a hundred times, he's too young to go riding all day long and doing God knows what out there, growing up like some Slav peasant's brat. János, come here."

János looked at his mother.

"Don't look at her. Come here."

His mother stood there, watching his father, tall and blond, beautiful. The boy János, like some troll or changeling, came softly across the floor, his hands behind his back.

"What did you do today, János?"

"I rode in the mountains."

Denis sat on his father's lap and watched János. His brother's black eyes stared at him, not seeing.

"What else?"

"Nothing."

"Come, come, you must have done something." Denis' father looked up at the woman. "What did you do, Theo? Whom did you see?"

She smiled. "Nothing, as he says."

"Well, János, would you like to read?"

"No."

"You've forgotten everything I taught you, haven't you?"

The stony black eyes, lifting, stared at Denis' father. "Everything."

"Go to bed."

János turned and went out of the room.

"What have you done to him?" Denis' father said.

She smiled. "I? Nothing."

"You've ruined him. He's a stupid lout of a boy. A dull brat without obedience or kindness or gentleness."

"Perhaps if you spent more time with him?"

"I can never find him to spend time with him. When I do find him and try to teach him something, you take him off and teach him to forget it."

"He rides wonderfully, Alexander. He jumped his horse over a windfall today that must have been as tall as he is."

"I thought you said that you did nothing."

"If he didn't want to tell you, why should I?"

"It's dangerous. Why do you let him jump something that high? He's only nine years old. He might have been killed."

"Not Jansci."

No, the older Denis thought. Not Jansci. But it was wonderful, then, when Father was alive. A home full of books and laughing people, when János and Mother were the ones who were wrong. And after Mother died, there was only one left to bother us. He did not remember that János had been lonely. When their mother died, János hardly marked it. He certainly did not act as if anything were different; he was fourteen, and he simply stayed out of their father's way. The old man was increasingly sick in those days and rarely left his room—this room. János took care of things. Even old Alexander had to admit that he did well. Denis rarely saw János in those days.

He stood up and walked around the room. The litter of little things on the top of the chest was what a child might collect. There was a small wooden thing, like a toy cart with two wheels, on one side of the chest, and he picked it up to look at it. János never changed. He was the same when I came back as when I left. After six years. No change at all. I'm certain there was a change in me.

An arrow on the chest, and a little blackened coin, and the buckle from a spur strap.

Of course, János had never been the intractable boor their father had thought. The old man had been terribly disappointed in the way he had turned out and had exaggerated everything. Why did a boy turn into something exactly wrong? Especially an older son. It wasn't only Mother. She was only his accomplice. Denis thought, It must have been deliberate. Yet—once their mother had said, "Jansci is all Magyar, without an inch of Greek in him." But János, just the other day . . . A sort of atavism, maybe, throwback instincts dormant through generations, lighting finally on one unsuspecting child in his cradle to curdle up the gentle, cultured blood in his veins.

János still carried certain marks of his father, of course. And really his ambitions and his cold-blooded-ness were more modern than atavistic, like one of the Italian princes who delighted so in mazes. Giangaleazzo and Cesare. Denis had heard great tales of such men in Italy.

When he thought about it the wicked János of his daydream bore very little resemblance to the real János, and he gave up trying to decipher him. He knew he was trying to punish János for kicking him. He left the room and went to his own and slept.

Rakóssy stayed near the burned-out fort for several days, waiting to see if Malencz would come. He did not. Rakóssy thought, when I get back there will be a formal protest and a threat to have me summoned to Buda. He rode slowly home. Perhaps the Turks were raiding. They had been quiet for a while—Mustafa was probably working out a gigantic scheme. He would use that as an excuse not to go to Buda.

Alexander rode up to him, when they were almost to Hart, and said, "Arpád thinks you're worried about your brother."

Rakóssy rolled sideways in his saddle and brought his eyes slowly up to Alexander's. "I'm touched at your concern. You tend to your brother, and I'll tend to mine. The Devil take you. You're turning into meddling women."

Alexander shrugged. He rode beside Rakóssy, saying nothing.

Rakóssy turned again. "Get the hell back with the rest of them."

Alexander fell back obediently.

Rakóssy looked straight ahead. He had almost forgotten about Denis. He would have to do something about him. He remembered the child Denis sitting on their father's lap, reading. Denis, blond, grave, reading along. His mother had disliked Denis, but Rakóssy remembered being fascinated by him and wanting to take care of him and play with him. Once he had even asked Denis to come with him and their mother off to the mountains, but Denis had said no.

Probably they were all like Denis in Italy and France. The young men were like that in Vienna. Denis would love Vienna. Catharine would love Denis. They were about the same age. Catharine always seemed much older.

She learned fast too. He had taught her Magyar. Until he met her he had never believed that a man and a woman could be friends.

That was before I found out I'd be marrying her. Instead of Carlotta. He thought of Carlotta and laughed.

They reached Hart, and Rakóssy took the black mare to the grazing land and let her go. Walking back to Hart, he thought of finding Denis to apologize for kicking him. He decided against it. It made him angry to think about it. He went up to the great hall, got out a map, and studied it, planning his next raid.

What's Mustafa like?" Denis said.

Rakóssy looked up. "You've met him."

"I mean, what's he like to know?"

"Oh." Rakóssy leaned back. He called in a servant to clear away the dishes, put one foot against the table, and rocked the heavy chair gently back onto its hind legs. "He's . . . very interesting. You might get to talk to him someday. He never talks Magyar, so you'll have to learn Turk. He has this . . . odd way of talking. He always says things in three times as many words as he needs."

He grinned. He was not looking at Denis, and Denis thought he had almost forgotten his presence.

"Does he speak Magyar?"

"I don't know. I suppose he does. Naturally it's very useful to him to work through agents instead of in person."

"Why?"

"Oh, well, it's an advantage when he's trying to handle me, especially if he works through an agent and through Malencz, it keeps me from . . . My position isn't as strong if it isn't openly recognized. Officially, he treats with Malencz, so he's above me, he keeps me unofficial."

Suddenly he threw back his head and laughed. "Christ, he has the most incredible style."

"Do you like him?"

"I suppose so."

"Does he like you?"

Rakóssy snorted. "All is not sweet honorable competition between us, little brother. It doesn't make any difference. We're going to Vienna very shortly, and you can study the effects of policy better there than here. I've got one more raid to work out, but you don't have to come with me this time."

He got up and left the hall. Denis sat a moment, thinking. He thought perhaps he should ask to be allowed to go along on the raid, but he was unsure, and finally he went to the library to read and forgot all about it.

Rakóssy carried out his raid a few days later. In the first days of autumn they left for Vienna. The ride was swift and uneventful. They reached Vienna at noon of a bright, windy day and rode buffeted through the crowded city up to the west gate of the Hapsburg palace. The knights muttered and pointed and laughed. Denis rode close to his brother, embarrassed.

"You'd think they'd never seen civilization," he said.

"They haven't." Rakóssy turned to watch a coach pass, drawn by six big bays. The curtains were drawn, but a woman's hand lay on the sill of the window, glittering with rings.

At the gate a sentry ordered them to halt. Rakóssy rode forward a little.

"János Rakóssy," he said. Denis did not hear what the sentry answered. Rakóssy gestured. The sentry stepped back and saluted him. The gates opened. They rode through them and into a road leading through a park.

"This is magnificent," Denis said.

The park was brilliant with flowers and fountains. Two young men cantered by them on white horses.

"The Hapsburgs are rich," Rakóssy said.

"Is the Emperor here?"

"The Emperor is fighting in Italy. He'd rather not be here, probably."

"Why? This is lovely."

"The heresy, for one thing. Or haven't you heard about the heresy?"

"Which one?"

"Some monk's trying to reform the Church all by himself."

"Oh, I've heard of him. Everyone at the universities is very excited about it. They seem to think he will."

"The Emperor's having more trouble with him than with the French king, apparently. I wish they'd catch him and hang him."

"Why?"

Rakóssy did not answer. They drew up before a court-yard and Rakóssy dismounted. He called to a group of pages and they ran up to hold his and Denis' horses. The pages all wore beautiful livery and behaved very courte-ously. Denis dismounted. He heard his brother's voice in the midst of the pages and realized that he was speaking German.

"Arpád."

Arpád jogged up.

"This boy will show you where to go. All of you. Denis, stay."

The Magyar knights rode off. Rakóssy crooked a fin-ger at a page in blue and rose. He spoke to him for a moment and started off into the palace. He looked as if he knew where he was going. Denis followed him closely. He had to trot to catch up. Rakóssy went through a door, turned left, and without any hesitation started up a flight of stairs. They passed a gaggle of girls in glowing pale satin and lace, girls with their hair heaped up on their heads in sleek coils. Rakóssy strode through a curtained archway and into a great corridor. Denis trailed him, his head stuffed with the smell of perfume and the sight of young enchanting faces.

Harquebusiers stood at intervals along the corridor, and pennants fluttered in the breeze that swept in through the tall windows. The corridor was full of sun-light. The ceiling was ornately carved. He thought he heard the murmur of a thousand voices from the closed rooms, behind the hangings, as if the whole palace sang with light and beauty. He wanted ten eyes to look and a dozen ears to hear.

Rakóssy marched down the corridor as if he owned it. He spoke a single word to a harquebusier and led Denis through a closed door.

This was an office or an antechamber. Courtiers stood along the walls, talking. Their clothes were stiff with gold braid, and jewels flashed at their ears and wrists.

Denis sniffed their heavy perfume. He saw the courtiers watching him and his brother out of the corners of their languid painted eyes. He felt uncomfortably dressed. Rakóssy, in his black cloak and high Hungarian boots, looked calmly out of place. He stood by the desk, one hand resting on the quillon of his sword.

The man seated behind the desk looked up and said something in German. Rakóssy said, "Baron János Rakóssy von Ungarn."

"*Ein Moment.*"

Rakóssy glanced at the courtiers. Some of them knew him and bowed, their lace fluttering. He saw that Denis was red with embarrassment. The man behind the desk was talking to a pensioner. The pensioner argued and Mansfeld, the secretary, only talked, but the pensioner lost and stalked away with a curse.

"Now, my lord." Mansfeld turned back, smiling. "His Excellency is not free today. However, if you would care to wait, I will see that he knows of your arrival and perhaps tomorrow he will see you. Your chambers have, naturally, been arranged, and I will assign several pages to you and your escort. I assume that you will prefer your own men as sentries. That has been anticipated."

"My lady de Buñez—is she at court?"

"I believe so, but, as you know, my good lord, I am not officially in charge of her affairs. If you will wait a moment . . ." The secretary rang a little bell. A page came forward. The secretary sent him to the chambers of Lady de Buñez.

A second page came in and put a note on the desk. He bowed and backed off a few steps to stand with his hands behind his back. The secretary said, "If you would care to see the Duke of Brunswick, my lord, he has requested that you . . ." Mansfeld read the note while he talked. He stood up. "His Excellency requests your presence at dinner. The page will escort you to your chambers and thence to his Excellency's. If I may be of further service, please do not hesitate to inform me. Good day."

The page turned smartly and led them out. Denis said, "Where are we going?"

"To change clothes and then to dine with the Archduke. The ways of courts, little brother, are sometimes devious."

They passed through corridors filled with sunshine. The page opened a huge door, stepped aside, and said, "Your baggage has been brought up, my lord. I will await you outside."

Rakóssy nodded. He went through a smaller door. Denis followed. Rakóssy said, "Anything we wear is going to make us look like poor relations." He snapped his fingers and another page appeared. Rakóssy said something in German and the page bowed smartly and trotted out. Rakóssy sat down on the bed and looked over at Denis, who was staring around the room.

"They live well," Rakóssy said. The page returned with a pile of clothes, laid them tenderly on the bed, and knelt to take off Rakóssy's boots. Rakóssy stripped off his doublet and shirt and rummaged through the pile of clothes. Denis dressed by himself, while the page danced around Rakóssy, shining spurs and buttoning buttons and lacing laces. Denis almost laughed, but sat down instead. Rakóssy ended up looking exactly as before, only a bit cleaner. They went back to the corridor and started after the Archduke's page. Two Magyars with halberds passed them and took up stations by the doors.

The page led them through the glowing palace, opened a big oak door, entered, and said, "His lordship the Baron Rakóssy. Sir Denis Rakóssy."

"How does he know my name?"

"The ways of courts."

They advanced into a wide room with a tiled floor. Six people sat at a massive table under the windows. These people stood. A tall, handsome young man came around the table, smiling.

"Baron Rakóssy. A pleasure."

Rakóssy bowed over the Archduke's hand. "My

brother speaks no German, your Excellency. If you will permit me."

"By all means."

"Denis. The Archduke Ferdinand." He bowed toward the Archduke. "He speaks French, I believe."

"Your Excellency," Denis said.

"Ah. Sir Denis. It is a pleasure. May I present the Archduchess, your countrywoman. Sir Erich Markwald and his lady, Carlotta. Father Peter Munch. Your lord brother's betrothed, the lady Catharine de Buñez."

Denis spoke compliments and greetings. He glanced at his brother. The Archduchess was speaking to Rakóssy, and Rakóssy nodded, smiling. They were all seated, Rakóssy next to the woman he would marry and to whom, as yet, he had not spoken. The conversation slipped back into German. Denis was thankful to be quiet.

These people disturbed him. They all seemed too young, except for the priest. Catharine de Buñez looked older than he had expected. She had beautiful hair, the rich gold of Spanish blondes. Her eyes were gray, large and wide-spaced. All her features were large. She saw Denis staring at her and smiled. She turned to Rakóssy, who was listening to the Archduke tell a funny story.

"János," she said in Magyar, "your brother seems fascinated. Hadn't you told him?"

"I don't think he actually believed me." Rakóssy crooked a finger at a page and told him to pour wine for him and for the lady Catharine. "You remember it. The language."

"If I'm to live there, I may as well be able to complain so that the people can understand me. Did you have a good journey?"

"Excellent." Rakóssy lifted his wine. He looked at the lady Carlotta. "A good, quick trip. I don't think it will be as easy going back."

"Probably not, considering the baggage you will be packing. Don't stare at Carlotta, my dear. Erich suspects you already."

Carlotta was in conversation with the priest, a very old man who nodded all the time. She darted glances at Rakóssy, lowered her eyes, smiled, and moved her small hand in a light gesture.

"Your sister's beautiful," Rakóssy said. "Any man would stare."

"János, this is unkind," Denis said.

Rakóssy drank wine. "Be quiet, little brother."

"Sir Denis," Catharine said, "haven't you gotten used to your brother yet? János, stop staring at her."

"Giving orders already? You aren't in possession of me yet."

Catharine looked at Denis, smiled, and tipped over the wine goblet before her. The wine splashed over the table and drenched Rakóssy. He stood up, throwing the chair over backward.

"My dear, how could I have been so careless," Catharine said idly. "Now you will have to retire and change. A pity. Michael."

A page came over, the same page in blue and rose that Rakóssy had spoken to in the courtyard. The Archduke was on his feet. "My aunt must be beside herself with joy," he said. "My lord, please accept my apologies. By all means, change your dress and return as soon as possible."

Rakóssy turned toward Catharine, bowed, and said, "You infernal bitch."

Catharine raised her eyebrows. "Come back soon, belovèd."

Rakóssy wheeled and bowed to Carlotta. "It is a pleasure to return to the realm of the magnificent Carlotta."

Erich lurched to his feet. Rakóssy strode out, followed by the page. Erich flung his crumpled linen to the table. "If it please your Excellency, my wife is ill. May we have permission to retire?"

"As you will, Sir Erich."

Erich and Carlotta left. Catharine leaned back. She began to laugh. Denis sat bolt upright. He heard the Archduke and duchess laughing.

"Do you think me unworthy, Denis?" Catharine said. "We may speak French, if you wish."

"Well, Catharine," the Archduchess said. "What do you think of your wild stallion of a Magyar now?"

"I think he's marvelous."

"My aunt," the Archduke said to Denis, "thinks that she can tame anything."

"I don't want to tame him, my lord. He is magnificent."

Denis said, "He's vicious and heartless. He did that just to hurt you."

"Yes," the Archduchess said, "and he never seems to recall that I speak Magyar as well. I heard what he called you. I think you should repudiate him."

"I will never give him up, my lady. I love him."

"Love. That's no reason to marry any man. You marry to be made happy. This man will make your life a hell, Catharine. My lord, is there no way to—"

"Make a man love a woman?" The Archduke drew his perfumed napkin through his fingers. "No. Catharine, you may call off this marriage, if you wish, without any fear of my breaking our agreement. That is settled, and between him and me."

Her face was perfectly calm. "I want him, my lord, and I mean to have him. I think I'm a match for him. Will you excuse me?"

"Of course."

She rose and swept a deep curtsy. She was very tall, Denis saw. He stood.

"May I escort you, my lady?"

"Thank you, Sir Denis, but this, I believe, is a piece of work best attended to alone. Thank you."

In the corridor, she paused. A page hurried by, swearing under his breath. She turned and went down the hall. It took her almost fifteen minutes to reach the apartments where Rakóssy was staying.

A Magyar knight with a halberd stood by the door.

She faced him and said, "Open that door."

"Am I supposed to?"

"Open it, knave."

He opened it. She took a deep breath and went in, shutting the door behind her. Another Magyar stood by Rakóssy's bedroom door.

That one ignored her and she opened the door herself. Rakóssy was standing by the window, staring out, naked to the waist. His dirty shirt was flung over a chair.

"You are angry with me, János."

"Angry? I'm in a killing rage."

She sat down. "You don't seem to realize that I have some pride too."

"You haven't got me yet. You shouldn't be here without a duenna."

"My dear, I trust you."

He snorted. "You love to make me look ridiculous."

She stood up. "It is fun. The Black Baron Rakóssy, flawed. A satirical play."

He said nothing. He leaned against the window frame.

"Erich was furious. He left right after you did—with Carlotta. I think he will go straight back to Schloss Markwald. Do you want to fight another duel over her?"

"God knows I'll never fight a duel over you."

"Erich is a famous duelist. Much better than poor Sebastian."

"He's a fool."

"Come back to dinner."

"No."

"You act like a spoiled boy who has been denied something he should never have wanted." She looked around. "Where is Michael?"

"I sent him away."

She went to the windows. The gardens lay below, drawn straight and neat with roses and hedges of thorn. Two gardeners were working almost directly below this window.

He put his hand on her waist. "Catharine," he said.

"Don't tell me you're sorry, my dear."

"I'm not."

"We should go back."

"Are you angry?"

"No. Are you?"

"Not any more. I've always liked you, Catharine. I just can't get used to the idea of marrying you."

"Do you think you would enjoy being married to my sister?"

"I hadn't really thought about it."

"She told me that she would never go to Hungary. She said you made it sound frightful."

"When did she tell you that?"

"After she married Erich. She told me that I was lucky to be getting you, but that she could never live too far away from a court, without a lot of servants, and in the middle of a war."

"But you're looking forward to it."

"Frankly, yes. I'm awfully tired of this court, János. Hungary sounds much nicer."

"You may not like it. Or being married to me."

"We're being married the day after tomorrow. And it will be, 'fore God, the quietest, most secret wedding ever performed in the Hapsburg palace."

"Nothing could please me more."

"Now will you come down to dinner? Put a shirt on. You look like a wild barbarian out of the hills."

"I am." He looked down at her. "If only you looked like your sister."

"That," she said, "is a compliment."

"You have a mole on your cheek. You didn't have it last winter."

"Last winter, moles were not in fashion. I covered it with cream. Of course, last winter, you were not aware that you would be marrying me and you didn't look very hard. Come along."

He followed her out.

In the corridor, she said, "My nephew says that I may decline to marry you and your alliance will still stand."

He looked at her. "Why tell me that?"

"I've been trying not to."

They walked the length of that corridor and turned into another. Rakóssy said, "Thank you."

"What?"

"Thank you for telling me."

"You're welcome."

He opened the door for her. She swept past him, and he heard her murmur to the Archduke. He went into the room, drawing the heavy door closed behind him.

"Cannon," Rakóssy said. "Thirty-five cannon." He hauled the canvas back over the dismantled guns and walked on.

"They're ugly," Denis said. "What do we need cannon for?"

"The Turks."

"We've been able to fight them off before without cannon."

"You don't like them?" Rakóssy threw back the canvas on a fourth wagon and looked in.

"They're obscene."

Rakóssy climbed into the wagon. "And effective. I hope." He sat down on a cannon barrel and rolled a keg over to him. He anchored the keg between his knees and pried up the bung with his dagger. He shook out a handful of black powder.

"What's that?"

"Gunpowder. The Turks used it against Belgrade." He crushed the powder between his fingers.

"Is this why you borrowed money from the Fuggers?"

"The money was only part of it. I am marrying these. Plus a promise to support the Archduke for the Hungarian Crown and support the Emperor against the heretics."

"How do you propose to get them to a battlefield?"

"Battlefield, hell. These are going on the walls of Hart and—"

"And?"

"Hart."

"And Vrath?"

"Little brother, whatever gave you the idea that I would lend these to Malencz?"

"I wasn't thinking that you would lend them," Denis said. "Mustafa will be surprised. Are you getting troops, too?"

"The Emperor needs the troops to fight the Pope with, now that he's taken care of the French." Rakóssy stared at nothing. "He will . . ."

A coach clattered up and jerked to a stop. Rakóssy straightened. Denis turned to look where he was looking, and saw the shade fall back across the window. Rakóssy watched the coach roll off.

"Who was that?"

"Who?"

"In the coach."

"I don't know. Probably a spy." He rolled the keg back to the corner of the wagon and counted the kegs. "He's given me enough powder to take Constantinople."

"Is Catharine coming with us?"

"Is Catharine coming with us where?"

"You're terribly thick today, János. To Hungary."

"Do I look like a man who would desert his wife?"

Denis smiled up at him. "Yes."

"She's coming." He jumped down from the wagon and drew the canvas over the kegs of powder. "I do like her, you know."

"I do too."

"She's very entertaining. I don't particularly like my women so civilized." He nodded to the Magyar guard by the wagons, and they fell in closely around them. "We can eat in our rooms," he said to Denis. "I'm seeing Brunswick this afternoon."

"What about?" Denis said, walking.

Rakóssy shrugged. "Brunswick is something of a fighting man. I may need his influence."

Rakóssy walked through the gardens, keeping by habit to the shadows of the hedges. The moonlight was dull and hardly lit the most open lawns. He found his way without hesitation, even after almost eight months. He crossed the narrow path that led to the fountains, slipped through the hedge, and stopped dead, still in the deep black shadow of the hedge. He studied the pavilion. It was dark, a tiny house of painted wood, drowned in climbing roses. He sat down on his heels, his back almost against the hedge, and waited.

The sickle moon rose higher. A Turkish moon. That was probably a bad omen. The light played tricks with his eyes. He heard footsteps in the grass and tensed. The hedge rustled. Carlotta, wrapped in a dark cloak, pushed through the hedge and almost ran across the lawn to the door of the pavilion. She knocked. After a moment, she opened the door.

Rakóssy walked softly across the lawn and came up behind her. She did not hear him. She tried to see into the dark pavilion, whispered a curse, and took a candle from her cloak. Rakóssy put out his hand and took it from her.

She gasped and whirled, her hands rising.

"János. You frightened me."

"Did I?"

He laid his fingers along the edge of her jaw. She smiled. Her lips were trembling. Her eyes shone. He bent toward her and she closed her eyes and held up her mouth to be kissed.

* * *

Denis, in borrowed finery, saw Catharine at the court and went to her. She sat in the light of a huge chandelier, talking to an elderly dowager. As Denis came over, she smiled and made room for him beside her.

"Have you seen my brother?" Denis said.

"I dread the thought." She smiled again. "Lady Margaret, may I present Sir Denis Rakóssy. The Countess of Zweibrucken, Denis."

"You must be his brother," the Countess said. "My, you two are as different as could be, aren't you? You must pardon me, my French is a trifle rusty. Your rogue of a brother has caused quite a stir here."

"A crow among peacocks," Catharine said.

"A barbarian. But you are educated, Sir Denis." The Countess called a page and sent him for sweet wine and cakes. "Surely you've studied in Italy."

"At Padua. And at Louvain."

"Oh, didn't you love Italy? Did you go to Rome? You must have. The Count and I saw the most lovely collection of Roman and Greek statuary there. At the palace of one of the Cardinals. What is his name? Anyway, it was marvelous."

"At the Medici Palace?" Catharine said.

"The very name."

"He isn't Cardinal anymore," Denis said. "He's the Pope."

"Not for long," the Countess said.

"Let's not talk politics," Catharine said.

"Oh, definitely not." The Countess took a bite of a cake. "Ugh. Nuts. I hate them. Those Italians are so charming, Catharine. Marry an Italian, if you ever get the chance."

"Oh, no. I've heard the most naughty stories about Italians." Catharine disposed of the Countess' rejected cake. "Besides, I intend to make the first the last."

"We all start out thinking that. Where is your brother, Sir Denis?"

"I don't know."

"Catharine, your sister isn't here either. I'm not so old that I don't know what that means."

"Erich has been announcing loudly that he locked her in their suite."

"She's in the east wing, isn't she?" the Countess said. "My dear child, anyone could sneak out of there. Nobody but a blind man could have trouble getting out. I know, because I've sneaked out of there myself, in my youth. Several times." She nodded to Denis. "Several. My first husband and I met in the gardens below. He was trying to get in and I was trying to get out. I dare say I could do it now. As for you, Catharine, you're a fool. A talented, educated lady marrying a man who can't keep his hands off another man's wife."

"I rather think it's the other way around," Catharine said. "Carlotta finds him irresistible."

"Who wouldn't?" The Countess swallowed a cake. "If I were twenty years younger—"

"I'm rather glad you aren't."

The Countess laughed. She took another cake. "These are fruit. They're very good."

The court was putting on its nocturnal display. The sight of courtiers was beginning to bore Denis, and the conversations made him nervous. He fussed with his rings. He noticed several people watching him.

Catharine said, "Sir Denis, would you escort me to His Excellency?"

"Of course."

"Lady Margaret, will you excuse me?" Catharine rose. "I do so adore talking to you, but I've just recalled that the Archduke asked me to join him to hear his new lutenist, and I see they're gathering up there now."

"Catharine, I know I bore you silly, but you're such a pleasure to have around and you're so sweet about it, I can't help it. Here, young man, you may kiss my hand."

Catharine smiled. Denis bowed over the Countess' fingers and gave Catharine his arm.

"Am I really so unlike my brother?" he said.

"Night and day."

After a while, maneuvering her through a dancing figure, he said, "He isn't worth you, Catharine."

"I'm beginning to find this song everyone sings a bit wearisome," she said. "Oh, Denis, don't look so abashed. You dance beautifully."

"Thank you."

The music stopped, and they went to find wine and cakes. Several young courtiers came over and they talked. Catharine listened to Denis discuss Italian philosophy. One of the young men made a joke, and the little gathering burst into laughter. A courtier named de Guzman plucked a scented handkerchief from his sleeve and made an elaborate display with it, pretending to wipe his eyes.

"Miguel," Catharine said, "I do believe that you've been at my lady Cordobés' scent pots again. Here." She captured the kerchief and sniffed. "I believe I may faint. One of you must surely catch me and wave your hands."

"Oh, Catharine," de Guzman said. "You must. We could have the whole court on its ear. Swoon here, my dear lady." He knelt with a flourish and indicated his knee. "I shall sweep you away, with all your skirts arustle."

"I shall scream and deliver a long speech," a young Italian said.

"La. And tush. And sweet my lords. You would have my betrothed at your throats." She parodied a swordsman's flourish with a long cake. "And he would slash you, thus, and rip you, thus, and give you the coup, thus —and what would my lady Cordobés do?"

"Catharine, protect me from your vicious lover." De Guzman snatched back the kerchief and pressed it to his brow. "Now I may faint."

"Yes, do." Catharine sat down. She smiled up at them. "Just think, my boys, in a few days I shall be free of all this."

They gasped and fluttered. "Say nay, dear Catharine,"

a young Fleming said. "Stay with us, who love you."

"But I'm going with Denis, who loves me. Don't you, Denis?"

"With all my heart," he said, smiling.

"And with my toad-prince, who when I love him will turn miraculously into a handsome young man. Will you miss me, my lords?"

"We shall all die without you. We shall languish. We shall all ride out with the Emperor to die on the point of some dastard Frenchman's rapier, all for love of you."

"Nonsense. You will go back to your Ficino and your pretty ladies with their scent pots to pilfer, and never think of me more."

"Ficino?" De Guzman postured. "I? I assure you, dear Catharine, I am of no sort of Ficino breed. Besides, I am too busy reading these lovely heresies."

"This monk," Denis said. "Tell me more about him."

"He's a fanatic from Wittenberg," the Fleming said. "A few years ago he tacked up a list of grievances against the Pope on the chapel door there. We haven't been rid of him since. I think he's mad. The German princes, the dogs, have all gone over to his side and are backing him because he gives them whatever they want."

"What kind of philosophy does he follow? My brother wishes they'd hang him. We had a fellow at Louvain when I was there who did a lot of talking about . . ."

Catharine sat among them, listening with only part of her mind. Her mouth felt tight from smiling so much. She thought of Rakóssy and Carlotta together somewhere, and of Erich, hunting for them. Erich had killed eight men in duels.

He did not love her. Perhaps he never would. Probably. She was a fool to think that he would ever love her, simply because they were such good friends. He was a man of powerful lusts, a vicious, black-hearted man.

And I am plain, and sensible, and fond of talking to old ladies and boys, and I do like it here, and Hungary sounds so cold and dark.

"Catharine," de Guzman said. He took her hand and bowed over it. "Beautiful lady, are you happy?"

She smiled brilliantly at him.

"Are you tired, Catharine?" Denis said.

"No. I'm quite all right." She rose. "Don't you know that nobody goes to bed before dawn here? Only pensioners and people wanting favors go to bed early, so that they can be up early and go stand in lines." She turned. "Miguelito, please do bring me a glass . . ."

Rakóssy was coming toward her. The young courtiers saw him and parted, quieting, to let him through. They greeted him uneasily and said nothing after they had greeted him.

"Good evening," he said, looking generally around at them.

"We didn't expect you tonight," Catharine said.

"You look sleepy," he said. "Let me take you to your apartments."

"Thank you. Yes." She smiled at the young men, put her hand on Rakóssy's arm, and let him lead her out, across the hall, and through the doors.

"What do you want to say, János?"

"We were caught."

"You and Carlotta."

"Yes."

"Has he challenged you?"

"He challenged me."

She shut her eyes. "When do you fight?"

"We fought. I killed him."

She sighed. Her legs were weak. "Thank God."

He opened a door, looked to see if the room was empty, and drew her inside. She sat down in the only chair.

"Were you worried about me?" he said.

"He might have killed you."

He sat down on the floor in front of her and folded his arms on his knees. "I apologize. It was not what you would call the best moment."

"You apologize for the moment, but not for the act?"

The left corner of his mouth drew down. His eyes were unblinking on hers. "For the act, never."

"I'm glad you didn't have to pay for it more dearly. How is Carlotta?"

"Inept."

"I didn't mean that. You are horrible."

"She is. Do you still want to marry me?"

"I don't know."

He looked down.

"Do you want me to?" she said.

"Do I want you to want to marry me?"

"János."

"Catharine, my mother was Greek. Our children will be only one-quarter Magyar. I would prefer to marry back into the blood. But I will need the influence of the Emperor behind me, given one or two things. If I do not marry you, he can shrug off our alliance at any future moment, and he might, when his brother has the Hungarian Crown. But if I marry you, the chances are better that he won't."

"You are frank."

He shrugged. "I like you. I don't often explain things."

"Yes. Thank you."

"Will you marry me?"

She felt only dull irritation. She was grimly tired. She felt her eyes burn with tears. She put her hands to her face.

"Don't cry." He put his arms around her. "Don't cry. The fairy tales, remember?"

"I should never have told you those damned fairy tales."

She sobbed. He held her tight.

"Once my mother and I were out in the mountains," he said. "We cooked a rabbit and ate it. We didn't talk much. We sat there by the fire and all of a sudden she burst into tears."

"What is that supposed to mean?"

"That women cry at the strangest times."

"Strangest times?" She wrenched herself away from him. "Good God."

He sighed. His hand rested on the nape of her neck, his fingers against her hair.

"You can marry Carlotta now," she said.

"I don't want to marry Carlotta. She bores me."

"And you want to marry me."

He looked at her. "Yes."

"All right," she said. "I will."

He took her by the hand and led her to her rooms. At the door, he kissed her on the forehead. "Go to sleep," he said. "Good night."

"Good night."

She watched him go down the corridor, his sword swinging lightly at his spurred heels.

Rakóssy headed for his rooms. He rounded a corner and saw de Guzman standing there. Behind him were half the young men of Catharine's circle.

"My lord," de Guzman said. He and the others came briskly to attention.

Rakóssy stopped raggedly. He was very tired. "Yes."

"You have insulted the lady Catharine de Buñez. I challenge you in the presence of witnesses."

Rakóssy stared at him. "By the seven little Devils." He went on past de Guzman. De Guzman caught his arm. Rakóssy wheeled. "Take your hand off me."

De Guzman's fingers slipped from his sleeve. "Do you accept?"

"God, no. I have better things to do than chase around killing greensick boys."

He went on down the corridor. At his door, he turned and bowed. "Gentlemen." His Magyar opened the door for him and he went in. Once in the room, he stopped and stood still, thinking, and finally threw back his head and laughed.

They were married in the morning chapel. The bishop married them, very quickly and quietly. The Archduke had heard about the duel and ordered Rakóssy to leave for Hungary as soon as he could pack up and go. Rakóssy's knights and Catharine's relatives and suite attended the ceremony. When the ring was on Catharine's finger and all the vows said, she was taken to her apartments and Rakóssy went to supervise the loading of the wagons. He sent a coach for her, and she came to the west gate in it, and looked out and saw the wagons with the cannon, and the Magyar knights riding up and down. Rakóssy saw her and rode over. The black mare danced under him.

"Are you ready, Catharine?"

"Yes."

"We'll leave the coach outside the city. It would never last to Hungary. You can ride in a wagon if you want. I have a horse for you if you want to ride."

"All right."

He swung the mare and cantered up the line. The wagons began to move. She watched through the coach window. He was everywhere, cursing the drivers and the great stubborn oxen, shouting orders. She felt her heart leap. She was going to Hungary. I am going to Hungary.

Denis jogged up. "Good morning."

"Good morning, Denis."

"You looked beautiful in the chapel."

They were moving through the city. The sharp voices of the people reached her ears. "Isn't it marvelous? We're really going."

"Yes."

"Hungary," she said.

Denis grinned. "It will take us some time, with these wagons."

"Is it a rough trail?"

"It's plain almost all the way. But we have to ford two

or three good-sized streams, including the Danube. It may be difficult."

The city boiled around them. "I feel as if I were in a ship, except that the waves are people," she said.

"You're excited, aren't you?"

"I have been this excited only once before. When I was ten. I sailed from Cadiz to Genoa. I'm glad we aren't doing that again. The sea air was very bracing but a ship does not like my stomach. I can't lean out like this anymore, Denis. It's very tiring. Good day, sir." She plumped back into the seat.

"Then I'll ride with you," Denis said. He opened the door and got inside, looping his reins through the window. "You know, Hart is a little castle and not very comfortable. We have rushes on the floor and that sort of thing."

"He's told me."

"I used to think it was the grandest thing in the world, until I left."

"When did you leave?"

"Right after my father died, in '18. I was fifteen and I had my own valet. I felt very important, until I got to Italy."

"Then you're twenty-two now."

"Yes. There was one between János and me, but she died, poor thing."

"Why haven't you ever married?"

"I will, someday. Women of good birth are rare around Hart, and I never thought of it while I was away."

"Never?"

"Well, once or twice. But you'd be surprised how few well-born Italian and French girls want to marry the younger brothers of Hungarian barons."

She laughed.

"Father originally meant me to marry the daughter of a northern Count, but it fell through when he died."

"You'll marry someday."

"I'm sure I will."

They rode through the gate in the Ringwall and turned to the east. There they left the coach. Catharine rode on the lead wagon, between Denis and a sweating, cursing driver. She talked to Denis for a while, but soon it was too hot and dusty to talk. She was fast asleep before sundown, her head resting on Denis' shoulder and his cloak flung over her knees. She woke up a little when they made camp and watched the men swing the wagons into a square and build fires. She began to doze again.

Rakóssy's voice jarred her awake. He was swearing horribly. She sat up, trembling. He was beating one of the men around the head and shoulders with his riding whip. Catharine sat rigidly, staring at him, shaking with her heartbeats. The knight merely huddled at Rakóssy's feet, his arms over his head. Rakóssy flung down the whip, caught the man by the hair, and whirled him to face the wagon and the dry bed of an unlit fire.

The rest of the men were standing, watching, motionless; in the dim light of the other fires their faces shone with sweat.

"There is powder in that wagon," Rakóssy said, and shook the man he had beaten. "Black powder, you God-damned fornicator with dead bodies." He hurled the man away and kicked the firebed to pieces. He swung around to face the rest of his men.

"Don't be smug," he said. "It could have been any one of you. You're all just as stupid as he is." He glared at them. "Get to work. All of you."

They cringed away. Rakóssy saw Catharine. He hesitated a while and came over to her.

"Are you comfortable?" he said.

"What happened?"

"Pál was building a fire up against the powder wagon." He took a saddle pouch from the wagon behind her and fished around in it. He went back to the powder wagon and marked a big X on it with white chalk.

He came back, threw the chalk into the wagon, and sat

down. "This is going to take us almost a month, at this rate."

"They're frightened of you."

"When they do something wrong, yes."

"Don't they ever fight back?"

"They know they'd be beaten twice as hard if they did."

"Somehow," she said, "the logic of this isn't clear to me. Thank you, Denis."

Denis held out another bowl to Rakóssy and sat down on Catharine's left to eat. "Pál said to tell you that he's sorry."

"I'm sure he is," Catharine said.

"You see what you married?" Denis said.

"Shut up," Rakóssy said.

"I'm just—"

"I said shut up."

Denis looked at Catharine and shrugged. Catharine said, "Are you worried about something, János?"

"Not really. I'm going to sleep. Denis, rig up some kind of a tent for her." He got up and went away. Catharine saw him stop to talk to Arpád.

"Who is Arpád?" she said.

"Second in command. He and Alexander, his brother. Alexander's back in Hart."

"He's very big, isn't he?" She watched Arpád stooping slightly to talk to Rakóssy.

"He's supposed to be part Czech or even German."

"Is it so important to be a Magyar?"

"If you aren't a Magyar, you aren't a lord. Haven't you ever heard of the Tripartite Code?"

"No."

"Well, back about ten or eleven years ago, the peasants revolted. It was really awful. I remember once I was sent north with some knights, because Father was afraid they might attack Hart. After we put it down, they set up the Code. No peasant or descendant of peasants can own land or animals or anything. All the Magyars are equal—so I'm the equal of even Zápolya, the Prince of Transylvania. And the Magyars own the peasants and no peasant can protest any action of his Magyar overlord. Nobody really pays too much attention to your ancestry, as long as your name was on the records when the Code was made. Actually, though, the House of Rakóssy is very ancient and noble; we're descended from the House of Arpád."

"Well. I'm pleased I've married into a good family."

"On Mother's side we go back to the Macedonian dynasty in Constantinople."

"My."

"You're sleepy. Here, let me make you a tent."

He fixed up a tent on the wagon and spread a cloak out for her to lie on. She smiled. "Thank you, Denis."

"Good night, Catharine."

She climbed up into the wagon and lay down. She heard Denis talking to someone. She slept.

The next day they traveled through more hills. The days after she had trouble keeping straight from one another; they seemed always to travel at the same pace and through unvarying countryside. She talked to Denis and to Rakóssy. Rakóssy was not talkative and she decided that he was worried about something. He would not admit it when she asked him, and she knew enough not to press him. One night she told him another fairy tale, in German. For some reason he loved them. Denis told her that he had never liked to read with their father or listen to the old baron's lectures. He loved fairy tales. It was funny to see him sitting there with his arms on his knees, listening to a story full of trolls and giants.

She changed into riding clothes, borrowing trousers from Denis, and rode the horse he had brought for her. She had not ridden for a long time and after the first hour or so she got off and rode in the wagon, so sore that she could hardly keep her balance on the rocking seat. She kept riding, and finally she could stay in the saddle the whole day long. She could not put up her hair by herself and wore it down, gathered at the nape of her neck. At night she sat in her tent, combing her hair, and listened to the noises the men made in their camp.

Often they would sing. She had trouble understanding many of the words, although they sang in Magyar, but one long song she could understand much of. It seemed to have an endless number of verses.

"János," she said, "what is that song they were singing last night?"

"They sang at least four. What was it about?"

"Oh," she said, "it was full of mournful things. One of the lines was something about rocks and going barefoot."

" 'I am the wanderer, I am the barefoot wanderer in the rocks.' "

"Yes."

"It's a lament for János Hunyadi, the Champion of Hungary. He fought the Turks and beat them, right and left. That's a game, making up new verses."

"Why do you like fairy tales?"

He looked at her sharply. "Because they're true."

"True!"

"They're not like the things in books. I . . . They may not be true. They may be made up. You can't trust them."

"You mean that fairy tales must be true because they aren't written down?"

"Don't laugh at me." He smiled.

"I'm—I don't feel the faintest temptation to laugh. That's the oddest thing anybody ever said to me. You can't even read."

"The things that are written down . . . When you hear something you can know the man who says it and you can judge if it's true or not, but when you read something you don't know who wrote it and you can't judge it. It may not be true."

"They're just stories, the fairy tales. They're completely made up."

He shook his head. "You don't understand them, then.

You see? If you had written them down you would change them because you didn't understand them. But you just tell me and you don't say, 'Look, this isn't so,' or 'In the story this happened, but I know that can't be so, so I'll say that this happened.' "

"What do you mean, I don't understand them?"

He reached out and tucked a long wisp of her hair behind her ear. "You don't."

She began to get angry, and he saw it and laughed. "So," he said, "you see that I'm cleverer than you are."

Before she could force an answer through her throat, he had spurred the black mare and was galloping off. She sat in her saddle, staring after him, and planned scathing answers and proofs of her cleverness for the next time. But there was no next time.

The days moved on. Whatever he was afraid of did not appear, and he grew more easy the closer they came to his own country. The broad Hungarian plain fascinated Catharine. She loved to watch the herds of horses galloping over it. Denis told her that Hart was not like this.

"It's on the edge of the plain," he said. "Where the mountains start. Hart's in the foothills."

On the thirteenth day they reached the Danube again and forded it. The river was strong and rough with a thousand hands. Rakóssy drove the wagons into it like a dam, each team of oxen linked to the wagon ahead, so that the horsemen could cross above it. The great wagons, weighted with the cannon, struggled over the ford, lurching when the wheels ran into holes in the riverbed. Sometimes the oxen, losing their footing, plunged to their knees, their heads thrust back, fighting to keep their noses above the water, while the drivers lashed at them with their whips. Rakóssy ordered two teams of oxen yoked together to cross the heavier wagons.

"Is there no bridge?"

"North and south of here. Too dangerous."

Why? She did not ask him. He spurred the black mare

into the river and leaned down. He caught hold of the ring in the nose of the lead ox on the powder wagon and jerked. The ox stumbled after him, bellowing.

Two days later they saw a camp of Gypsies. Catharine had always heard that Gypsies stole children and cheated, but Rakóssy seemed glad to see them. He led the wagons to the camp and shouted for the chief.

A big, ugly man with scars all over his face strode up to them. He thrust his thumbs into his belt and said, "Rakóssy, is it. What are you doing here?"

"Going home. Have you seen any Turks? Or Magyars where they shouldn't be?"

"Not a one. Lonely down here. It's going to be a bad winter, so they say. Get down and drink with me."

Rakóssy turned and shouted, "Arpád, make a camp. We'll stay here until tomorrow."

Catharine rode up to Rakóssy. "What are we going to do?"

"I'm going to milk him, sweet." He looked at the Gypsy king. "This is my woman. Mine. Understand?"

"Hum." The Gypsy walked all around Catharine's horse, staring at her. "Want to sell?" He roared with laughter. Catharine flamed. Rakóssy was laughing with him. He swung off the black mare and tossed the reins to one of his men.

"János," Denis said, "you shouldn't—"

"Don't tell me what I shouldn't do. Come on, get down. We're with friends." He turned back to the Gypsy. "Eh, Trig?"

"Friends," the Gypsy said. "I am Trig Columbo, young master. The king of this humble little tribe. You are welcome to my camp." He turned and clapped Rakóssy on the shoulder. "Come along, friend. We have some liquor here."

Rakóssy went off with him. They sat down in front of a fire and Columbo took a jug of liquor from one of his women. He uncorked it and took a long swallow. "Now. What can I tell you?"

"Have you been north?"

"North, south, east, west. Gypsies go everywhere. Is it Buda you're after? I was in Buda only last spring. Or was it summer? Sometime. I was going north to see the Poles, but I changed my mind. Here."

Rakóssy took the jug and upended it. The liquor burned in his throat and punched around in his stomach. "Jesus," he said. "You make it stronger every year."

"Your mother used to say that. Now, there was a woman. If she would have gone with me, I would have made her the queen of all the Gypsies in Hungary."

"Malencz. Vrath Castle."

"Malencz? His son died. Hunting. He was gored by a wild boar. Terrible thing. Now he has only the ones in Buda who are—what do you call them?"

"Pages. A pity."

"His people don't particularly like him. The King says, 'I want money,' and most of the Magyars say, 'That's good, I want money too, everybody wants money.' But this Malencz, he gets the money and gives it to the King. And—here's something—he wants knights. He wants to fight sometime next spring. Who, he won't say. Where, he won't say. But he wants to fight, somebody not the Turks."

Rakóssy's mouth twitched. "A pity."

"There's some that say he was tricked into it."

"No man tricks another man into fighting."

A girl sidled up to them with food. She smiled at Rakóssy. Her white teeth were as sharp as a cat's.

"My daughter," Columbo said. "She's a piece, isn't she? I have to keep a watch over my doors, I'll tell you. She's smart, though. She's after Venn. Best horseman I have. He won't look at her."

Rakóssy looked at Venn, a tall, slender man in a vest sewn with gold pieces. Venn saw him looking, stared back boldly, and came over.

"Rakós'," he said.

Rakóssy said, "And how is Mustafa?"

Venn muttered something. Columbo laughed. Venn looked down at his hands. The girl came back with more food. She ignored Venn and Venn ignored her. She went away and Venn shot her a quick, cautious glance. He got up and went off.

"Venn's smart," Rakóssy said. "All he has to do is snap his fingers and that girl will fall into his lap."

"This woman you have. Is she your wife?"

"Unfortunately."

"Hah? What is this?"

"You've seen her."

"Yes. She's not beautiful. When did you look at her last? There's strength in that woman. And you—hunh. You snort after these flimsy things with their pretty faces and hips that show off everything they've got. Let me tell you, Magyar. A woman is a woman, and a face is a face, and after a while the face isn't pretty or plain anymore, it is this woman's face, and you love her."

"The Devil. I don't love her. I don't love anybody." He tilted the jug again.

"Your mother, now. There was a face, and a body, and the eyes, like . . . like . . ." He made a gesture like cupping water. "Eyes a man could drown in. I keep thinking they were black, but I know they were blue eyes. They were big and soft and they lied like black eyes. Blue eyes are honest and can't tell you stories."

"What about gray eyes?"

"Never trust gray eyes. They are honest like blue eyes, but cruel, too. I've never known a gray-eyed woman who wasn't cruel. Especially the ones with long nails. If they aren't scratching your face, they're carving holes in your shoulders."

"Malencz."

"Five hundred knights, they say he can call. Between him and Levolt."

"Levolt's out."

"Oh? Levolt was at Vrath only a little while ago. Give me some of that." He drank. "A stupid man, Levolt."

Rakóssy nodded and finished off the jug. Columbo threw it against a wagon and it broke. Columbo's huge laughter boomed out after it. Someone began to play a violin and the Gypsies sang. The Magyars were divided up among the Gypsy fires. Denis and Catharine came over.

"Eaten?" Columbo said.

"Yes," Denis said.

"Good. Here, boy. A little of this." Columbo uncorked another jug. Catharine sat down next to Rakóssy.

Rakóssy took her by the chin and turned her face toward him. He looked at Columbo. Columbo said, "Gray eyes. You tricked me, Magyar." They laughed. Rakóssy let go of Catharine's chin. Columbo burst into song.

"What was that about gray eyes?" Catharine said.

Rakóssy looked at her hands. "And long fingernails, too." He drank more of the liquor.

"János, you're getting drunk."

"No. Not yet." He listened to Columbo for a while and began to sing with him.

"Will they dance?"

"I doubt it."

"I thought Gypsies always danced."

"Only on special occasions," Columbo said. "Do you dance, lady?"

"Not like a Gypsy."

Rakóssy kept the jug he held for himself and told Columbo to find his own. He put his arm around Catharine's shoulders.

"You are drunk," she said.

He laughed. "Want some?"

"No."

Venn came over and sat down next to Denis. He yawned and turned to Columbo, on Denis' other side. He said something in Romany.

Columbo's daughter walked by, looking at the ground. Her face was solemn. Her bare feet moved slowly over the dust. Venn looked at her with his eyes half closed. Rakóssy looked down and saw Catharine watching the girl. Venn coughed and said something loudly to Columbo.

Catharine said, "She's pretty, isn't she?"

Rakóssy nodded.

Columbo's daughter stood a moment in the firelight, her head turned slightly away from Venn. She looked at him swiftly from the corners of her long-lidded eyes. Venn, caught watching her, jerked his head away. Columbo's daughter sauntered off, out of the firelight, headed for the low ground by the water.

Rakóssy said, "I hope you don't think me . . . lax."

Catharine started. "I hadn't thought of it. Somehow it seems to be something you do to my sister but not to me."

Venn rose and went off up the slope.

"Wait until we get to Hart," Rakóssy said.

"I'm tired. Can I go to bed now?"

"That would be a serious breach of etiquette." He drew his hand through her hair.

"János, you're stinking drunk."

"What I am I won't confide into your shell-pink virginal ears."

"You'll be very embarrassed in the morning."

"The hell. I'll be angry."

"I'm embarrassed now."

He laughed and drew away from her. He drank from his jug and talked to Columbo. She heard them speaking of Malencz and the Turks.

Columbo's daughter came back, smiling. She sat down behind her father and said something in Rom. Columbo laughed.

"She says that Venn is down by the water dreaming." He thumped his knee. "She'll have him yet."

Rakóssy looked over his shoulder at the girl. "He's lucky."

The girl smiled. "Thanks, Magyar." She lowered her eyes and looked quickly up at him again. "You have a wonderful horse."

"Yes."

"I wonder if she would let me ride her."

Venn came up the hill. Rakóssy saw him and saw that the girl had seen him. He winked at her. He lay back on one elbow and said, "Oh, there's a chance, little one."

Columbo looked around at them. He glanced at Catharine, at Denis, and at Venn. Venn came quickly toward them. Rakóssy, with his head almost in the girl's lap, stared lazily up at Venn.

Venn said something in Rom to the girl. She answered archly and shook her head. Rakóssy looked at Columbo. The corner of his mouth drew down. Venn stamped his foot and spat something at the girl. The girl sighed. She put her hand on Rakóssy's shoulder. Rakóssy kissed it. The girl laughed and got up, shaking out her skirts. She went off and Venn followed her.

Denis crawled around to sit next to Catharine. "Are you all right?"

"I'm tired."

"Let me—"

Rakóssy said, "Denis, take her to her tent. She's half asleep."

Denis got up, helped Catharine stand, and took her off. He said, "Don't mind him, Catharine. He's just trying to hurt you."

"I know."

Denis lingered by the wagon. "If you want anything, call me."

"Thank you, Denis." She smiled and went inside. She lay down and thought, I should have been gay and witty and flirted with him. I can just see me being gay and witty and flirting. He scares me to death.

Denis went back to the fire and sat down. "You bastard," he said.

Rakóssy looked at him. He laughed. "The Devil," he said. "I think my little brother has fallen in love with my wife."

"I have not. I'm just her only friend."

Rakóssy looked at Columbo and they both laughed. Rakóssy stood up, steadied himself, and walked between the fires toward the wagons. Denis started to rise. The Gypsy caught him by the arm.

"Stay here," he said. "Do you want to ruin her life? Stay here."

"Ruin her life?"

The Gypsy's eyes narrowed. "Stay here and learn something. Go after him, and you'll probably have all your teeth knocked down your throat."

Rakóssy vaulted into the wagon and slipped and fell. Catharine said, "Who's there?"

"Me." He fought the nausea in his stomach.

"Go away."

He stuck his head inside the tent. Her face, white and frightened, was only a hand's span from his. He grinned.

"I won't come any farther than this," he said. "Promise."

She moved a little and produced a long knife. "Don't."

The eyes over the knife were steady. Her face was still very white.

Rakóssy stared at the knife, rolled over onto his back, and howled with laughter. Tears streamed from his eyes.

"Catharine," he said. "Catharine."

"Stop laughing at me."

"Yes." He rolled over again. "I won't come in. That knife won't do you any good. It's dull. Take this." He gave her his dagger. "Don't cut yourself." He folded his arms and and put his chin on them. "I'm drunk."

"I can smell it. What is that?"

"It's something they make out of grain. It's poisonous."

"What do you want?"

"State my business and go?"

"János, you're so many different people I can't keep you straight."

"I'm very drunk."

"So."

"I wasn't really flirting with that girl. She wanted somebody she could throw up to Venn. I just co-operated."

She said nothing.

"Denis is madly in love with you."

"That's nice."

"Isn't it." He hiked himself up on his elbows. "That mole. It drives me crazy."

"Why?"

"There's a Turk poem about a mole."

"A poem?"

"Don't look so surprised."

"Tell it to me."

He recited it. She listened patiently. "Now translate it."

"I keep forgetting you don't speak Turk." He scratched his head. " 'O Belle of Shiraz, grant me but love's demand, and for your mole—that clinging grain of sand upon a cheek of pearl—Hafiz will give all of Bokhara, all of Samarkand.' "

"That's pretty."

"It's prettier in Turk." He touched her cheek with his fingertips. "Columbo said that gray-eyed women are cruel."

His fingertips were gently urgent, drawing her nearer to him. She shut her eyes. He kissed her. The smell and taste of the liquor repulsed her. His mouth was gentle. She felt herself relaxing. He kissed her eyes and her nose and her mouth again. His hands were buried in her hair.

"Will you let me in?" he said against her mouth.

"Un-unh."

"Why?"

"You stink of that liquor."

He laughed. "Then you get no more kisses, free. Anyhow, I'm not prepared, according to Columbo."

He drew away. He was leaving. She put her head down. "Why?"

"He says that I'll have to wear full armor in bed with you." He wiggled his way out. She heard him stand, curse, and jump to the ground. She smiled and shut her eyes.

Five days later Catharine and Rakóssy rode up to a ridge and looked east and saw the mountains.

Catharine cried out. Since they had left the Gypsies there had been nothing but the plain, a few salt marshes, and little hills. Now suddenly there were mountains, mounting shoulder on shoulder, their rock arching above the timberline, harsh under the late sun.

Rakóssy moved the black mare over a little. "You're sunburned," he said.

"I feel like a Gypsy." She lifted her hair in her hands and let it fall. The wind cooled her face, smelling of pine trees. "How do you find your way out here? Those mountains are wonderful."

"I grew up here."

"Are we that close?"

"Come on."

He galloped off. She lashed at her horse. She wished she could ride the way he did, all loose and supple, not thinking. He reined up on the crest of the next hill and waited for her. She could feel the steepness of the slope through her horse's muscles. The mountains reappeared the higher she climbed on the slope. She drew in beside him and he said, "Look."

She looked east. The mountains were stark under the brassy sky. She could hear the wind in the pines and smell the odor of the hills, like Austrian hills.

"Those are the Transylvanian Alps," he said. "We are two days' ride from the Turks."

"The Turks," she said.

"Are you afraid?"

"I'm homesick."

"Homesick."

"They look like the Austrian mountains. Except that there are Turks behind them."

"Not behind them. In them. These hills are mine. The mountains are the Turks'. You didn't see Hart."

He pointed again. She had missed seeing the castle. The mountains made it look smaller. She could only see part of it, half hidden behind a hill—a round of stone and a tower.

"It's different from Vienna," he said.

"Cliff's Eye. That's the name of the Turks' fortress, isn't it?"

He reached over and pulled her hair. "Don't be afraid." He shifted his weight and the black mare burst into a gallop. They rode down the slope, turned south, and swung around a promontory of trees. The wind was rising and the murmur of the trees engulfed them. They rode around the foot of the hill. The flash of Rakóssy's spur caught her eye and she glanced down at his heel. When she looked up, she saw Hart Castle directly above her.

It was smaller than she had expected, more like a hunting lodge, except that it did have a tower. It perched up on the top of the hill, ugly and squat, without any decorations or statues or even any pennants except the banner of the Rakóssys flying from the tower.

"This isn't like Austria," he said.

"No."

"The original castle was down where the village is now. Poor planning, but closer to the water. I tore it down when I became baron and rebuilt it up there. It took four years. We dug a well, too. The Turks kept attacking us. I finished it the year the Turks took Belgrade."

She stared up at it and looked down at the village, a straggling line of low wooden huts surrounded by fences and gardens. A stream traced through the middle of the village.

"Tonight," he said, "we'll sleep in a bed."

"I'm too tired for that."

"For sleeping in a bed?" He turned, looking back after the wagons. "Let's go."

They rode up the dirt path to the gate. Rakóssy

shouted. The gate opened. They rode into a little courtyard. In the middle of it a fat shaggy pony, hitched to a turnstile, walked a circle around the pump. The courtyard was full of people. She felt them all staring at her. She smelled bread baking. There was a crowd of women by an open door, all of them watching her with wide, curious eyes.

"Imre," Rakóssy said. "Come hold your lady's horse."

He dismounted and dropped the black mare's reins. "This place is a mess. As soon as I leave everything falls to pieces."

The people vanished. Catharine dismounted. The door where the women had sat watching slammed shut. Imre led her horse away. She looked up at the wall near the gate and saw a tall man standing there, stiffly at attention.

Rakóssy glared around at the stone walls. "Ignorant, lazy, filthy pigs," he said very loudly. "You all need a whip on your fat backsides. The Turks deserve you."

"János," Catharine said, "there's nobody here but him." She pointed to the man on the walls.

"They're all within earshot. That's Alexander, Arpád's brother." He took two steps toward the kitchen door. "Anna, you swine."

A towering fat woman opened the door. She had an iron spoon in one hand and a scullion in the other. "What do you want?"

Three wishes, Catharine thought, and giggled. Rakóssy shot her a strange look and she clapped her hand over her mouth. He looked back at the huge woman.

"I'm hungry. I want meat, wine, bread and apples, in my room, by the time I get there. Hop, you cross-eyed witch."

"Hop," she said. "When your father was alive, God rest his soul—"

"Get the hell back into that kitchen."

The door slammed. Rakóssy whirled and stamped off. He stopped a moment to inspect a drainage ditch, crossed the courtyard, and opened a small wooden door with iron braces on it. Catharine trotted after him. They came into a long, narrow hall. The sudden gloom blinded her. She stopped, waiting for her eyes to clear.

"Anna was cook for my father during his declining years," Rakóssy said. "She'd feed him milk pudding and broth so thick you could have walked on it. Finally she got to calling him Alexander. My father either didn't notice or didn't care."

"What did your mother say?"

"She was dead. This is the great hall. Not what you're accustomed to."

"What are those?"

"Old-fashioned halberds."

"That's your badge, isn't it?"

"Yes. My great-great-grandfather a couple of times over made it up. The silver deer are from a Hun legend, and I think the red's for blood, but I'm not sure." He sat down. "You know, you're looking very presentable."

"Oh. Thank you. What's your motto?"

He shrugged. "The original was in Latin or maybe Greek. It's carved on the badge. It means 'Forever,' whatever it is."

"It's Latin," she said, squinting up at the badge.

"Well, anyhow, my grandfather changed it to Magyar. 'Forever Thus.' So you can take your pick."

"What's yours?"

"I don't use one. Come on, she's had time to get our dinner up there by now."

He led her up to his room and opened the door. It smelled musty. He shouted for Ivo. Catharine sat down by the window. The food was laid out on the table there. The door opened and a young man and a girl came in. Rakóssy sat down and told the young man to open the windows and air out the room. The girl came over to Catharine and curtsied.

"My name is Mari," she said. "Jansci, does she speak Magyar?"

Rakóssy drank wine. "Catharine, she'll be your maid.

If you don't want her, I can get you another."

"Oh?" Catharine looked at Mari. "Do you usually call your master by his nickname?"

Mari curtsied again. "A slip, madam. My lord, are the wagons far?"

"No. They should be almost here."

"Mari," Catharine said, "please find me a comb and some slippers. Thank you." Mari left. "My father used to do that to the Queen, assign his mistresses as her ladies-in-waiting."

"She's Arpád's."

"But she was yours."

"If you want to be jealous of every woman I've ever had, you can be jealous of all the girls in Hart except Anna."

"What a braggart you are."

"Why don't you take orders and become a reformer, like that monk?"

"The prevailing opinion is that that monk believes in plural wives and concubinage. I'm sorry if I sound like the Grand Inquisitor."

"You do. Eat."

"What is this meat?"

"Goat."

"It doesn't taste like goat."

"Hungarian goats taste different from Viennese goats."

"I've never had goat before."

"Then how do you know it doesn't taste like goat?"

"It doesn't taste the way goat should taste."

"It's good meat. Eat it."

They ate in silence. Mari came back with combs, ribbons, slippers, and a fur robe. Rakóssy did not look at her until she rolled in a big wooden tub and put water on the fire to heat.

"What the hell do you think you're doing?"

"I'm drawing my lady a bath," Mari said and curtsied. She called to Ivo to bring more water.

Catharine said, "What a wonderful idea. I feel so dirty I should be peeling off in chunks. I'm finished eating."

"The wagons are here," Rakóssy said.

Mari came over and began to comb Catharine's hair. Their eyes turned steadily on him. He said, "I'll be down in the courtyard."

Mari curtsied.

"Quit that," Rakóssy said. He went out.

Mari laughed. Catharine said, "That was very kind of you, Mari."

"Thank you. Will you keep me?"

"Yes."

"I'm glad. I was afraid maybe I had done myself out of it."

Rakóssy supervised the unloading of the wagons and had eight of the cannon ranged on the walls of Hart, hoisting them up in pieces by pulley and putting them together on the ramparts. All afternoon they worked, and when it got dark they lit torches and worked by that light. The rest of the cannon he had stored in the stable. He sent several men to take the powder and shot to a dry place. He thought of firing one of the cannon, and sent Denis three times for powder and shot, only to call him back each time.

Finally he sent everybody off to bed. He saw Arpád walking with Mari, telling her wild stories. Denis had gone quietly away. Rakóssy went alone to his room.

Catharine was sitting by the window, bundled to the ears in the fur robe. The room was clean and her trunks were piled up against the wall by the window.

"Have your bath?" he said.

"Yes. It was marvelous. I like Mari."

"So do I."

She looked at him. He sat down and called to Ivo to take off his boots. He sent Ivo to bed and peeled off his doublet and shirt.

"Did you see the cannon?" he said.

"Yes."

She poured herself a cup of wine and took an apple from the dish. She stretched out, curling her bare toes. "I feel like a bandit chieftainess. Can I have my own Turkish slave and a sword?"

He went to the window and looked out. The corner of his mouth drew down. "I'll fetch you silk to make a turban with and a dagger to carry in your teeth, if you want."

"Can I ride among the peasants with a whip, overseeing their labors in the fields?"

"The peasants here are mostly herders, and you are not to leave Hart without an escort of at least five knights. Even if all you want to do is go down and swim in the lake."

"Where's the lake?"

"You can't see it from here."

"That would be a scandal. The Baroness Rakóssy swimming with her escort of wild-eyed bearded Magyar knights."

"If you see any of my men with a beard, you can order him to shave it off. They can have mustaches."

"All barbarians have beards. Why can't they have beards?"

"They're very . . . disadvantageous when you're fighting. The Turks all have beards. Mustafa ibn Ismail has a beard. A lovely beard, too. I grew one like it once."

"I thought—"

"I wanted to impersonate him. We looked like twins, with the beards."

"János, will you beat them?"

"The Turks?"

She looked up at him. His face lost the twist his smile gave it. He looked at the cannon on the walls.

"Why," he said, "that's why I married you, sweet. I sort of hope your nephews will beat the Turks and I won't have to do it all by myself."

"Humph. You'd think you were the King of Hungary."

"I'm not. The King's a fool. Anyone who goes near Buda is a fool, for that matter. They're all mad up there. That's why my commander's Louis Malencz."

"And it should be you."

"Yes."

"You're certainly modest."

"He's more help to the Turks than he is to me. When —if he weren't involved I might be able to beat the Turks in three or four years."

"I really don't understand this war."

"Nobody expects you to. I don't understand it either. You really don't want to go to bed with me, do you?"

"I didn't mean—"

"Of course you did. You've been acting like a nun about to be raped since we left Vienna."

"I have not. I'm just tired, that's all. And I do want to know what this damned little war is all about."

"You can't do this forever. However much both of us might regret it, we are married."

"Please, János."

He got up. "Well, I suppose I could sleep next door. Tonight." He went to his chest and opened it.

She looked out the window. The villagers were lighting fires down by the stream. She wondered if they were celebrating the marriage of their lord. "János," she said, "what do those fires mean?"

He leapt across the room to the window. "God damn them to hell," he said. He leaned out the window and shouted, "Everybody out! Arpád!"

"What's wrong?"

He turned. "Stay in here. The Turks are burning the village."

Rakóssy left Denis inside Hart and led all his men down toward the village. There was a strange, numb silence above the pounding of the horses' hoofs. The flames from the village were leaping and waving in the wind.

The Turks fled at the first sight of the Magyars. Rakóssy on the black mare veered away from his band and raced to head them off before they could stampede the herds by the stream. Half the Magyar band galloped after him. The Turks raced in a ragged line, shouting insults. Rakóssy drove his men straight at them. For a moment there was close, muddled fighting.

Rakóssy pulled out of the fighting and drew back, watching. He waved the other group of Magyars on. The Turks forced this band backward, trying to outflank them. There were only about seventy-five Turks. Rakóssy shouted and half of the men in the band that was fighting made a concerted charge against the Turkish left flank. The Turks saw that the other fifty Magyars were almost on them. They raced away. Rakóssy swore at his men. They chased the Turks along the stream.

The Turks led them through the marshy ground by the lake. The black mare stretched out. Rakóssy was six or seven lengths ahead of his own men by the time they were back on solid ground. He drew the mare down slightly. The Turks whirled and charged back, trying to cut off the left quarter of the Magyars. Rakóssy hauled the mare around and was surrounded by Turks.

"Rakós', Rakós'," a Turk shouted. "Get him for me, my children!" He laughed.

Rakóssy flung off one Turk and ducked under a scimitar. His men were all around him, hammering at the Turks. Rakóssy pulled the mare back into his own lines.

"Mustafa!" he shouted.

That laugh rang out again. Rakóssy drove the hilt of his sword into a Turk's ribs. Both sides were screaming insults. The darkness kept them from fighting well. The smell of sweat and close quarters made them choke.

A Turk on a tall horse charged Rakóssy. They fought clumsily for a moment. Rakóssy grabbed the man by the beard and dragged him off his horse. The Turk howled, jerked free, and dodged under the mare's belly. She reared. Rakóssy felt her lose her balance. He jumped free. His outstretched arms slid over a horse's sticky rump. He landed on his back and looked up at a horse's lathered belly. A hoof smashed into his side. He lurched up, caught a Magyar stirrup, and clung to it.

"Get out of here, my children."

Mustafa laughed again. The Turks retreated. Arpád shouted, "Hold, you dogs' dirt. Hold!"

Rakóssy knelt, his fingers wrapped around the stirrup. His side ached. Arpád bent over him.

"Ribs," Rakóssy said. "God damn it."

Arpád hoisted him up. Rakóssy said, "Where's my mare?"

"There."

The mare was trotting beside another horse, shaking her head. She was not limping.

"Get the villagers up into the castle," Rakóssy said. "We'll never get that fire out."

He slid into his own saddle. The pain drove through his side. He clamped his arm over his ribs. "I'm going back. Stay here until you're sure everything is taken care of."

"Yes, sir."

He rode alone up to the castle. He could barely breathe. Denis held the mare while he dismounted.

"I broke every rib in my side," Rakóssy said.

Denis and Catharine helped him up to his room. Denis took off his shirt and Catharine sent him away. She washed Rakóssy's side. "You're going to have a lovely bruise there, my dear," she said.

"That was Mustafa. I heard him."

"We couldn't hear anything."

"How much of the village was burned?"

"Practically everything."

"Ouch."

"This will hurt even more. Sit up."

He sat up, groaned, and started to lie down again. She

forced him upright and wound a bandage around his chest. "I was frightened," she said.

"Not for me, I hope."

"I have a weak heart."

"Thank you."

"Do you want some wine?"

"The ministering angel. You always seem to prefer me when I'm helpless."

She went around the room pinching out the candles.

He shut his eyes. "You call me 'my dear.' I find it very touching."

"Touching." She went to the head of the bed and put out the candle. "Good night. My dear. Where am I to sleep, by the way?"

"Right here."

"The Devil and the ministering angel in one bed?"

"You've got me so cinched up every move I make kills me, so you're perfectly safe."

"All right. I'm tired."

She went away from the bed. Rakóssy watched her in the dim light. He thought she would make a fuss about getting undressed, but she did not. She took off her clothes, piled them on the chair, and climbed into bed. She lay down, rolled over once, and sighed. From her breathing, he knew that she was asleep right away.

"Probably it was a trap," Kamal said.

"No." Mustafa shook his head. "No. He was gone, and for a long time. But no one in Hungary knew of it. Your informant, this Gypsy. Did he say how he knew that Rakóssy was not in Hart?"

"He saw him just this side of the Danube." Kamal shrugged. "At any rate, Rakóssy is back, and the Gypsy will serve us no more; his king found out about it and was angry. He brought us that news to defy his king."

"It's just as well," Mustafa said. "The Gypsies are Ra-kóssy's good and faithful servants and it is rarely useful to . . . patronize turncoats. The raid was rather successful anyway."

Kamal opened his eyes wider. "My lord, I doubt my ears."

Mustafa smiled, a quick flash of teeth in his impeccable beard. "He can be hurt. He was nearly killed. His life is not enchanted. Ah, Kamal, the war is safe again, the Devil is fled home to Hell, and we alone inhabit the earth. Do you understand?"

"I usually don't when you're in this mood."

Mustafa stroked his beard. "Of course not. He was nearly killed. That balances the disappearance into thin air of last summer."

Kamal smiled. He watched Mustafa preen himself. Kamal thought, This past season has been the biggest failure since we came into these mountains. But look at him. It was time to spring the last tidbit of information, the delicious news the Gypsy had mentioned in passing, useless but titillating.

"Rakóssy is founding a dynasty," he said.

Mustafa turned a fond eye on Kamal. "Rakóssy is a scion, my child. A son of dynasties. He could no more be a founder than I, the son of Ismail the son of Mehmet the son of . . . and so forth. A comparison of our genealogies might prove interesting, similar, like our fates. Except that I, unhappily, am unwed, denied such comforts, and he has taken to board and bed and bosom a daughter of the King of Aragon."

Kamal stared at him. Mustafa was combing his beard, finding an acute interest in each particular hair. Kamal said, "You amaze me, my lord."

Mustafa gestured neatly. "I pay attention to such things as dynasties more than is the wont of such as I. You recall that Harun my brother returned from Constantinople yesterday."

"Yes."

"He brought general news to us, of the well-being of the Sultan, may Allah bless his life, and of the power of the realm. And he brought me a special summons. I go to Constantinople in a month. Harun will go with me."

"Am I to be left in command of Cliff's Eye?"

Mustafa paused. Kamal watched the bright black eyes leap back and forth.

"Yes," Mustafa said. "As for Rakóssy's marriage to the Emperor's aunt, find another informant and discover what you can about her." He turned a blissful smile on Kamal. "I know that you will, in your infinite resources, learn all. Temper your might with caution and your mind with humility, and who can stand before you?"

"My lord," Kamal said. He kept his voice neutral.

Mustafa turned away again, adjusted himself in the chair, and appeared to ponder.

Kamal said, "Another raid, perhaps?"

Mustafa shook his head. "No." He blew out his cheeks and smiled again, not looking at Kamal. "No, I think that the next few weeks, plus the winter, should be a time for rest, for quiet, for meditation on the lessons of the past. Besides, we don't have the men or the supplies. The bombard isn't fixed yet."

"And Rakóssy's cannon?"

"Are no concern of ours, at the moment. Nor Rakóssy's bride, save that I would know more of her. Nor Rakóssy's ambitions. Leave me." He glanced out the window. "It's very nearly time for prayer."

"My lord." Kamal bowed himself out.

Mustafa thought briefly of the Gypsy, whom he had questioned privately after Kamal had finished with him. He remembered the look on Kamal's face when Mustafa revealed that he knew of Rakóssy's marriage. The memory wiped away any temptation he might have had to inform Kamal of his own conversation with the Gypsy.

He steepled his fingers and blew lightly on his fingertips. Rakóssy's ambitions. He had thought for a long time that Rakóssy was involved in some great plot to . . . But he had expected nothing quite so magnificent, so complex and delicate, so perfectly delightful. It proved once again Mustafa's fondest belief, that a clever plot, well conceived and strictly executed, was more advantageous than simple direct action. Rakóssy could not know how beautiful his timing was.

The woman, the woman . . . She was the master stroke. An Imperial bride, a new voice, a stranger seen but not met, refreshing after five years of the same people. He wondered how he could turn all this to his own uses. He was a hot-blooded man, Rakóssy. Hot-blooded, black-hearted, and cold in his mind, a nice balance of humors. How to tip the balance? He was a fragile thing, Rakóssy. So much of his success depended upon his . . . The cloud of superstitions and rumors and half-beliefs and terrors that surrounded him . . .

"*La ilaha il-Allah; Mohammed-un rasulu-llah.*"

Mustafa rose and washed his hands and feet and face. He went to the southern corner of the room and knelt to pray.

Alexander said, "This came while you were gone. I meant to give it to you yesterday, but I forgot. Special messenger it came by, in a fancy tabard and everything. With a baton, too." He held out the packet.

Rakóssy took it and turned it over. It was sealed with the Seal of Saint Stephan. He glanced at Denis and put the packet into his doublet.

"Shall I read it?" Denis said.

"No. I know what's in it."

He went up on the walls and watched the people rebuilding the village. He sniffed. The air had a sting of snow in it. There was some light snow already on the rock of the mountains, above the timberline.

"Good enough," he said. In a few weeks, at the most a month, the snow would block passage through the mountains, ending the raiding season. In a little more than a month travel over the plain would be almost impossible except by sleigh.

"It's from the King, isn't it?" Denis said.

"It's the King's seal."

"You might as well read it."

"No."

Denis grinned. "I always wondered what a summons to the Council looked like."

" 'János Rakóssy, son of Alexander son of Stepan, is ordered to Buda to stand trial before his peers on a charge of high treason.' "

"And János Rakóssy does not intend to go."

Rakóssy said, "I can't go until next spring, and by the middle of next spring this whole thing will probably be over and done."

"Is there time for another raid?"

Rakóssy shook his head. "The snow will fall soon. It's no fun to be caught in a snowstorm in the mountains."

"I wanted to go."

Rakóssy looked at him.

"I did," Denis said.

Rakóssy turned back. "Not this year."

"That's too bad."

"Gotten over your crush on Catharine, or is this your way of dying gallantly for unrequited love?"

"Can't you ever take anything the way it's meant?"

"What—a peace treaty? You'll go raiding and I won't push you around?"

Denis looked down toward the village, biting his lip.

Rakóssy pushed himself away from the wall. "Prove it, little brother," he said. "Prove it." He walked away, down the ramparts.

Catherine was sitting with Mari on the kitchen steps, showing her the alphabet. Rakóssy stopped beside them and looked down.

Mari lifted her face, laughing. "My lady says I can go with you to Vrath for Christmas Feast," she said. "Can I?"

"We're not going this year."

Mari's face drooped. Catharine said, "Oh, why not?"

He stamped by them into the kitchen. "Because I don't enjoy being arrested," he said. He shouted at Anna. They listened to him rant around the kitchen. Mari said, "Oh, he's in a mood. He'll be impossible for a while."

"What's the matter?"

"He's fretting over something. The best thing to do is say, 'Yes, Jansci, No, Jansci, May I bring you anything, Jansci?' and go off quietly and forget him for a while. He's got a terrible temper."

"I like the name János better than Jansci."

"Everybody calls him Jansci behind his back. His mother did."

"His mother sounds like an unusual woman."

"I never knew her. They tell some stories about her would make your blood run cold. How she would go for days without saying a word, and take him when he was barely old enough to walk out to gallop around the mountains, and they'd be gone for days. They say when she died he didn't even cry."

"I can't imagine him crying."

"Stop talking about me," Rakóssy said over their heads.

They looked at each other. "Yes, Jansci," they said, in unison, and laughed. He swore and they heard him tramping off through the kitchen. A door slammed.

"He knows some words I'd never even imagined before," Mari said. "Arpád says that he knows every curse that was ever invented."

"He certainly does. In several languages. The young men at the court in Vienna used to follow him around to learn the new ones in German."

"What was it like? What did they wear? Was it beautiful?"

"Yes," Catharine said. "It was beautiful. It was the most beautiful, charming, merry place in the whole world."

* * *

Rakóssy, Catharine and Denis ate supper together in the great hall that night. Denis joined Catharine in bright, witty conversation, and Catharine guided the talk carefully to innocent topics. Rakóssy maintained an absolute silence. Catharine told the servants to take away the dishes, and Rakóssy showed signs of wanting to leave.

Catharine said, "Denis, you remember Miguel de Guzman, don't you? From Vienna?"

"Oh, yes. We had a long discussion about Lauter."

"Luther," Rakóssy said.

"Anyway, the heretic. He says that Luther is promising all the northern German lords that he'll preach submission to the state if they'll support him."

Rakóssy shrugged. "Who needs a new religion for that? I get plenty of submission from my people right now."

"I wasn't implying—"

"Sorry. You've been trying so hard to be . . . helpful lately, I thought perhaps you'd discovered a new way to beat the Turks. Why don't you suggest that we accept Islam? It's the same thing. Submission."

"János, I was only—"

"Being helpful, little brother. Being helpful."

Denis stood up. "Good evening, Catharine." He marched out of the hall. The door slammed behind him.

"Just what are you trying to do to him?" Catharine said.

"I'm not trying to do anything to him."

"What is he to you? The scapegoat for your wrath? You can't do this to him. I'm not going to let you do it."

"Oh?" he said. He sprawled in his chair. "How do you propose to stop me?"

"I don't know," she said calmly. "But I will."

He looked off. She turned toward the door and saw the servants standing there, staring. She signed to them to go. He had not seen them. He was holding a knife in one hand, and his knuckles were white. He turned his eyes back to her. His eyes were black as coal. She stiffened to accept his rage.

"Catharine," he said, "you cannot make me do anything I don't want to do, and you cannot stop me from doing anything, anything at all."

His voice was soft. His eyes were intent and unblinking. She was suddenly afraid to move.

"This is between Denis and me," he said. "I don't want to fight with you, and I don't intend to."

"You're a grown man," she said. "Denis is just a boy."

He stood up, and she winced, lifting her arms before her. He looked down at her. Her heart thundered in her side.

"I don't want you to be afraid of me," he said. "You're acting as if I were going to hit you."

She lowered her hands to her lap. He came around the table and sat on the edge of the table by her chair. She stared up at him. Her back hurt from the tension in her spine. She did not dare to move and ease it.

"I don't want you to be afraid of me," he said. "Believe me. But you are not going to interfere between me and Denis. You have no right to try."

"No right?" she whispered. "No right?"

"Stop being the little champion of the downtrodden, eh?" He bent stiffly and kissed her frozen cheek. He went off, leaving her there alone. Her cheek where he had kissed it burned like fire. She sat, hardly thinking, staring straight ahead. Finally she rose and walked slowly out of the great hall, past the crossed halberds and the badge with its small silver deer.

She went to Denis' room and knocked. Denis opened the door.

"Catharine," he said. "Catharine. You look ill."

"No."

"Are you frightened? Did you fight with János?"

She gave a nervous little laugh. "No. Not at all."

"I'd hate to have you fight over me. Would you like some wine?"

108

"No. I think I'll lie down for a while."

"János is in your room," Denis said. "I'll go down and tell him you want to be alone."

"No, don't. He isn't angry with me, Denis. I'm not in any danger. Thank you."

She smiled at him, and he caught her hand. "Catharine," he said. "If you . . . ever need anything . . ."

She slipped her fingers from his grasp. "Thank you, Denis." She went down the corridor to her room.

Rakóssy's room. The door was open. She saw him at the window, looking out. He turned and saw her, without surprise, and moved away from the window.

"How are your ribs?" she said.

"All right."

"Take off your shirt and let me look at them."

He took off his shirt and started to sit on the bed. He looked at her and the corner of his mouth drew down. He went to the big armchair and sat down in it. She came over and unwound the bandage.

"Breathe," she said.

He breathed and his chest swelled. "Fine," he said.

"Bend over."

He bent.

"Does it hurt?"

"Only a little. The horse wasn't shod. I must have just cracked them."

"I'll bring you some wine."

She warmed wine over the fire and brought it in cups. She stood behind him, looking down at his hair. He said, "Do you suppose that monk's going to get anywhere?"

"I don't know. He has poor Charles in a cleft stick, of course."

"Damn your nephew. Just when I need him, he gets mixed up in some bloody heresy."

She laughed. "Just when you need him. Did anyone ever tell you that you're terribly arrogant?"

"Did anybody ever tell you that the Turks are dangerous?"

"Well, there's not much I can say to that."

"Now that Christianity's in a proper mess, they'll probably attack us. They have to, soon, or they'll lose the whole game."

"You're talking to yourself. Some of my relatives think that this new Sultan will be peaceful."

"There is no such creature as a peaceful Sultan."

"That's dogmatic of you."

"They have to be nasty even to get to the throne. Turks aren't like you nice settled people west of here. They're like Magyars. We're all half barbarian still. Your damned nephew had better get here when the fighting starts, or he's going to lose this nice human moat between the Turks and his territory, and then he'd learn how Turks are."

"Charles is only twenty-five. He's very—"

"Mohammed the Great was twenty-one when he took Constantinople. The trouble with Turks is that they're single-minded. The trouble with Christians is that they're incapable of making up their minds."

"Why are you so single-minded about Malencz, and taking Vrath, if it all depends on whether or not my damned nephew comes to help us?"

"If Charles doesn't come, we'll need all we can—where did you get the idea that I'm going to take Vrath away from Malencz?"

"Denis told me."

"Denis told you?"

"Denis is cleverer than you think, my dear."

He said nothing. He sat staring. She put her hand on his hair. "You're tired, aren't you?" She combed his hair through her fingers, stroking him. His hair was so black there was no trace of brown or even blue in it, curling over her fingers. She watched his face. The cheekbones looked much broader from this angle. She saw him blink. His hands lay on the arms of the chair, relaxed, the fingers curving easily at nothing. He was enjoying the touch of her hands with the selfish pleasure of an animal, forgetting her presence, aware only of her hand giving him pleasure. She took her hand away. He looked up at her.

He stood up and went to the door. He took off his boots with the bootjack there. Coming back toward her, he batted the door shut with his hand. She stood facing him, afraid.

"What did you do that for?" she said.

His eyes snapped and glittered. "Well, why not?"

He turned her around and took the pins out of her hair. He let her hair fall free. She clasped her hands before her. He ran his hands through her hair.

"János," she said, and her voice surprised her.

He stood behind her and put his arms around her. He kissed her throat. "Yes?"

"Please, János. Not tonight." Her voice still had that funny sound to it.

"Oh, Christ, Catharine, I've been celibate for almost a month, waiting for your virgin temper to melt before my ardor. Pity me." He turned her around and kissed her.

"Pity me," she said. "Please."

" 'Belle of Shiraz,' " he said, "you'd better grant me love's demand, or I shall go mad."

She caught the laces of her bodice before he could undo them completely. He kissed her mouth and bent her back until she thought she would fall and flung out her arms, and he picked her up with a sweep that made her dizzy. She felt the roughness of the bedcover against her back and realized that he had lifted her out of her gown. She shoved at him. He let her go and she squirmed into the middle of the bed.

"You are just too good at this," she said. "What kind of life have you had, anyway?"

"Oh, you should have seen what I went through with your sister."

"János!"

"And Mari. It's been hell without you, Catharine." He flopped down beside her and grinned. "Think of all the scheming women who have victimized me, used me." He put his head down on her thigh. "Catharine, if I go mad you shall be unhappy for the rest of your life, and I shall go mad if you don't take pity on me."

He reached for the laces on her busk. She slapped his hand. He flipped over and lay with his head in her lap, smiling up at her.

"You are supposed to write me poetry and to sing under my window and to tell me that I'm beautiful," she said.

"You're beautiful, and I've already told you the only poem I know," he said. "Aside from a filthy rhyme my mother taught me once."

"I am not beautiful."

"Cinched up in that armor, you aren't, no." He put his arm around her waist. "Catharine, if you only knew how I've been abused at the hands of women—"

"Like my sister?"

"Like a lamb to the slaughter. Poor, innocent, pitiful lamb." He rolled upright and kissed her. She liked being kissed, and he made no move to take off her busk.

"You're not going to prevent me," he said, "so you might as well enjoy it." He moved slightly. She put her arms around his neck.

"Please, János. Just let me get used—"

"Just a second." He reared back. She saw the flash of his dagger in his hand and yelped. He tossed the dagger onto the floor and engulfed her. The busk with its slashed laces he flung after the dagger.

"Your body is beautiful," he said. His hands were rough on her skin. He drew her gently down until they were lying side by side. She kept her eyes shut. The light made her eyelids red.

"Put out the candles," she said.

Her petticoats followed the busk. "No."

"Please, János."

He turned her so that a shadow fell across her face and her eyelids darkened. She clung to him. "I'm frightened."

"You're beautiful." He drew the covers over her. She wanted the touch of his hand. "You make Carlotta look like a—"

"How dare you!" She sat up and her eyes flew open. He was naked. He laughed at her and put his hands on her waist and drew her down against him.

"I've never seen a man—"

"Take a long look. I'm the only one you'll ever see."

"You incredible—"

"I mean stripped. Put your head down." He kissed her eyes. She locked her arms around his neck. Don't think. Don't think about it at all.

"This is going to hurt," he said.

"I don't care—oh, please—János. Please." She gulped. Her eyes were shut tight. She clutched his shoulders. "Please, oh, János. János. János."

Rakóssy woke up. Catharine was curled up around his right arm, her fingers wrapped around his wrist. Her hair lay tangled across the pillows. He looked toward the window. It was just dawn. He had a while yet before he had to get up. He felt lazy and empty. He rolled over and nipped her ear.

She leapt awake with a yell and sat up. She blushed. She folded her arms quickly across her breasts and stared at him.

"You weren't so modest last night," he said. "Lie down."

"I was so modest. In the beginning."

"It wasn't the beginning I was thinking of."

"I don't know how—"

"I do." He pulled her down. "You're blushing all the way down to your nipples. Listen to me. There is nothing to be afraid of. You are my wife. It's legal and holy. In fact, we're supposed to do it. How do you think people get born?"

"Have you ever gotten any babies?"

"The Gypsies come through too often." He smoothed her hair down.

"I hurt."

"You don't have to get out of bed all day. Lie still. I won't do anything."

"Don't you want to?"

He snorted. "Women. I will never understand you. If we—"

"Don't you dare use that word."

"What word?"

"The word you used last night."

"Anyhow, you'd hurt too much."

She relaxed. He brushed the hair from her temples. She could see the working of the muscles in his arm and shoulder. She studied the taut framework of his collar-bones. He was very strong. She pulled at the hair on his chest.

"Ouch."

"I'm sorry." She put her hand against his chest. "What do the Gypsies do, steal babies?"

"I don't know. They don't steal ones that are born, but they can keep the girls from having them, or something."

"That's sinful."

"You tore hell out of my back with those nails of yours."

"I'm sorry."

He kissed the tip of her nose. "You're a good lover."

"Good."

She lay still for a moment. He thought she had gone to sleep. She said, "When will you attack Vrath?"

"Malencz is going to attack me in the spring."

"Why don't you attack him?"

"Attack Vrath, with one hundred and eight men?"

"I thought Malencz couldn't fight."

"He couldn't fight his way out of his own nightgown. Anybody can hold Vrath."

"What is it like?"

"It's out on the plain, in a horseshoe bend of the river up there. They call it Vrath's River by the castle. The back wall sits right up against the river. There are three double gates, two with bridges over the river right at the gates, and the other, Main Gate, opens out onto the little plain in front of the castle. The walls are fifteen or sixteen feet thick and the battlements are reinforced with iron braces. The whole thing is practically new. It was built in Sigismund's reign. Hart was almost the first fortress built by Magyars in this part of the country; it's almost three hundred years older than Vrath."

"Is Vrath bigger?"

"About six times bigger."

"Constantinople fell in two months."

"They didn't use their guns well enough, if they used them at all, and they had a hell of a lot of wall to defend. We'll be all right in Vrath." He looked out the window. "I have to go. I'll call Mari."

He got out of bed and dressed himself and went down to the courtyard. The sky was overcast and the wind sliced through him. It was going to snow. He fidgeted while his men finished eating and drove them out into the courtyard to work.

They shot off the heaviest cannon. Denis was there with Arpád and Alexander. The smoke and soot engulfed them all and they choked and coughed until the tears ran down their cheeks.

"Charge too heavy," Rakóssy said. "Where did it hit?"

"About ten feet this side of the village," Denis said. "Shall I go down and clear the villagers out?"

Rakóssy looked over the wall. The villagers were huddled together in the square. Their village was half rebuilt, and in the mess of new houses and debris the little cluster of people looked forlorn and terrified.

"I'll go," Alexander said.

"Tell them I still love them," Rakóssy said. "We won't shoot it off anymore."

Denis was looking out down the slope. He turned and

lay down to crawl half under the cannon. He fussed around for a moment and crept out again, his clothes streaked with grime and black dust.

"I'll be right back," he said.

"Where are you going?"

"I'll be right back."

Rakóssy watched him climb down to the courtyard and go into the castle. Arpád said, "What's got into him?"

"Who knows?" Rakóssy took a swab and cleaned out the cannon.

Denis came back with a little book in red leather binding. He had two pieces of chalk in one hand and two big pieces of paper in the other. He put the book, the paper and the chalk down, lay on his stomach, and pushed under the cannon again.

"What are you doing?" Rakóssy said. "This isn't a toy."

"Don't be cross."

Arpád snorted.

Denis dragged himself out and sat up. "It would be better, wouldn't it, if you could raise the muzzle or lower it as you wished."

Rakóssy looked out at the slope. "Yes. How?"

"If you could fit a screw into the carriage here, you could turn the screw and adjust the height of the muzzle." Denis picked up the little book and flipped it open. "See?"

Rakóssy took the book. Besides the inscrutable characters there were small drawings. One was of a screw, in the drawing, raising and lowering some kind of boom.

"What's this book?"

"It's by a Greek from Syracuse named Archimedes."

Rakóssy sat down. He turned the pages. "Maybe it's got other ideas in it."

"If we rebuild the carriage entirely we can fit screws in to move the muzzle sideways without moving the carriage."

Rakóssy looked over the cannon's breech at Denis, "Prove it."

Denis' face was flushed. "Give me a carpenter, some wood, and I will. I'll try it out on one of the lightest guns first."

Rakóssy tossed him the book. He turned his head. "Sandor."

In the courtyard the carpenter lifted his head.

"Do anything my brother tells you to do." He turned back to Denis. "There's wood in the stable."

Denis nodded. "All right."

He went down to the courtyard. Rakóssy spat.

"Is he crazy?" Arpád said.

"Ask me tomorrow." Rakóssy got up. He went along the wall to watch the assembling of another gun.

All day long he fiddled with the cannon. He put horse troughs from the stable beside each, to hold the round-shot, and rigged up screens to protect the gun crews, if the Turks should use arrows. He fired one of the lighter guns with the screen around it, and the screen, of light wood, caught fire. He had all the screens adjusted accordingly.

Just before dark, Denis came over to him and said, "Look at this." He put down a little model of a cannon. The front of the carriage was wider than on the real guns, and three outsized screws thrust out of it.

"See?" Denis said. He held the model down with one hand and turned the screw on the left side. The muzzle of the toy cannon moved. Denis said, "Turn the screw on the other side to your left. That's it."

The muzzle of the toy moved all the way to one side. They wound the screws back and the muzzle moved across the scale again.

"Will it work with a cannon?"

Denis shrugged. "On the heavy ones—I'm not sure. I've got Sandor carving screws for the lighter ones now."

Rakóssy turned the carriage over and wound the bottom screw. It raised and lowered the muzzle.

"I haven't figured out how to raise it in any position other than dead center," Denis said. "The elevation screw has to be stationary."

"What made you think of this?" Rakóssy said.

Denis almost sneered. "Trying to be helpful."

"Answer my question."

Denis tried to meet his stare. Rakóssy did not blink. At last Denis looked away. "I studied mathematics in school," he said, "and I read Archimedes and some of the Greek geometrists."

A snowflake drifted down between them. Rakóssy looked up at the sky. He turned and called, "Arpád, put everything under cover."

He looked back at Denis. The snow was falling steadily. Denis brushed at his shoulders.

"Hungry?" Rakóssy said.

Denis would not look at him. "I'm starving."

"Come on."

He went down to the courtyard. The wind was bitter, and the snow skittered in curls over the ground. Denis was a few steps behind him. Rakóssy said, "We'll eat in my room. It's warmer there."

"Catharine's room?"

Rakóssy hunched his shoulders against the snow. "In my room and Catharine's room."

Denis stopped. Rakóssy went on a few strides and turned.

"So you got to her," Denis said.

Rakóssy stared at him a moment, spat into the snow, and went on. Denis ran to catch up. Rakóssy whirled in the doorway to face him.

"She is my wife," he said. "Remember?"

"You don't love her."

"Whether I love her or not is no business of yours."

Denis opened his mouth, shut it, and looked down. "I guess it isn't."

"Mother hated Father. I never heard you object to being born."

"She didn't really hate him. She just—"

"She hated him."

Denis looked at his brother's face. "I'm sorry, János."

Rakóssy shoved him gently. "Get married. It's quite an experience, take it from big brother."

The snow fell for three days. The knights sat in their quarters and talked or slept or drank. Mari and Catharine wove cloth in the great hall. Rakóssy, in a bad temper, stormed around the castle for the first two days and on the third disappeared. Nobody asked where he was, being too relieved that he was gone. Denis sat reading Archimedes by the fire in the hall, listening to Catharine and Mari talk.

"Denis," Catharine said, "is there a lute here? Or a harp, or anything? Even one of those Gypsy fiddles? I'm dying for music."

"I've got a lute, but I haven't played for months."

"Does János play?" Catharine said, and Mari giggled.

"God, no."

"Please fetch it, Denis."

"Gentlemen don't play the lute."

"Fetch it. You probably play beautifully."

Denis sighed. "Mari, why don't you get it for me?"

"Charmed, my lord."

Mari ran out. Denis looked after her. Catharine straightened out a tangle of wool. "So we are alone."

"I didn't mean it like that."

"Of course you did."

"You've made a terrific change in János."

"In János? There's been no change in János. In me, perhaps, and in you, but János is as inflexible as steel. Oh, look, here comes Father Zoltan."

Zoltan came in, bowed to Catharine, and said, "What a terrible storm this is. I thought to bother you with my presence for a while."

"It's no bother at all." Catharine indicated a stool. "Bring that nearer the fire."

Zoltan did. "Ah. It's certainly warmer here than down in the basement. My lady, permit me to compliment you. I have never found Hart Castle so congenial."

"Where have you been?" Denis said. "I had the feeling

you were avoiding me."

"Oh, my dear child, hardly that. I was waiting until it was safe to come out again. Your brother was reminded of my presence a bit too precipitously."

Mari came in with the lute. Zoltan smiled. "My lady, you are making yourself quite a court here."

"Yes, and now we're even to have music."

Denis played several Italian songs, passably but not well, and Catharine gave him some instruction. She took the lute and taught him a Spanish love song as old, she said, as the Moors. She played better than Denis, and he knew it and was proud of her.

"My mother used to play by the hour for the King," she said. Her hands moved lightly over the strings. "He had difficulty sleeping at night, and she would play until he did sleep." She sang in Spanish and in French, taught them a round, and they sang it, laughing.

Catharine took the lute up to her bedroom with her that night. She was beginning to worry about Rakóssy, and she sang to comfort herself. The door opened in the midst of a song and she saw that it was he.

"Where have you been?" she said.

"Upstairs. Where did you get this?"

"It's Denis'. Do you play?"

He laughed and sat down, running the heel of his hand over the pearwood. "How is the forlorn lover these days?"

"He's very happy. He thinks you've forgiven him."

"Forgiven him what?"

"For being educated and traveled and witty and worldly."

"That wasn't it. That idea about the screws, it works, it's good. I wouldn't have thought of it."

"You don't have his education," she said.

He glanced at her, amused. "No. He's finally beginning to be useful, in spite of it. He's gotten it into his head to be a Rakóssy."

"He always was a Rakóssy. He was like your father."

"Father was a misfit and a failure. I can leave Denis to command Hart when I go."

She paused a moment. "Do you think that's wise?"

"Well," he said, "he doesn't have my education, but he should do well enough in spite of that."

"I don't know if he will like being left here."

"He'll have to like it."

She frowned. He had been smiling, but his eyes were beginning to sharpen and harden.

"Poor János," she said. "Being stuck in here aggravates you, doesn't it?"

"He'll stay," he said. He put the lute on the table. "If I have to beat him into it."

"János," she said, "come undo my laces."

"I think," he said, "I'll take off my boots first."

The next day, when the snow had stopped, Rakóssy and Denis worked over the cannon. Denis had fit a light gun to his new carriage. It worked almost as well as the model. Denis said, "We could figure out a way to put a lot of barrels on one breech and spray shot all over the place."

"They make that kind. They're called death organs. They're too light and unsure for castle guns."

"Or we could hang a cannon in chains in a kind of A-shaped framework and put that on wheels and take it out onto the field. That way the cannon would be straight no matter how the frame was sitting, up a slope or down."

Denis was looking at a diagram of a catapult. "They're very similar," he said. "Catapults and cannon. Except you can shoot fireballs from a catapult."

"We could heat up the iron balls."

"How would we put them into the breech? And they might fire off the gunpowder too soon."

Denis sketched something on his paper. "I'll see if I can work it out, though. And firing little stones."

"You like this, don't you?"

"Oh, yes. It's like chess. It's an objective problem, you know. It's fun to figure things out."

Rakóssy shrugged. "Well, I'm glad you like it. I've got to go check the feed bins. Want to come?"

"I'm going to work some of these things out."

Rakóssy went down to the courtyard. He was surprised at Denis and Denis' way of thinking, but when he considered it he knew that he shouldn't have been surprised. That irritated him.

There was nothing to do but wait for spring. Rakóssy had the cannon taken down and stored in the stable. Denis drew things on paper and made models. Just before Christmas the Turks made a raid against a winter sheep camp down by the eastern springs. Rakóssy heard of it and took fifty men to the springs, although he knew it would be too late. He left Denis in the castle.

The shepherds had built a snow wall around their camp, and they had fought from behind it, holding the flocks in the middle. Red stains in the old snow marked the edge of the Turks' raiding line. Only one of the shepherds had been killed. The flocks were safe. Rakóssy rode around the camp, studying the tracks in the snow. Arpád talked to the head shepherd. Rakóssy came back and reined in. He was riding a big roan, because the mare was not made for riding in snow.

"How many?" Rakóssy said.

"About forty," the shepherd said. "We killed a lot of them."

The other shepherds were sitting around the fire. They watched Rakóssy covertly.

Arpád said, "How many did they kill?"

"I can't tell. Three or four, maybe. Probably they wounded a lot more. Those longbows aren't much use against Turk armor."

"Late, for a raid," the head shepherd said.

"They're hungry."

Rakóssy nodded to Arpád who brought over a pack horse.

"Harquebuses," Rakóssy said, "and some bolts. Do you know how to use them?"

"No."

Rakóssy dismounted, tossed Arpád his reins, and opened the pack. He took out a harquebus and a bolt. "Come here."

The shepherd came over. Rakóssy said, "You wind it with this crank. Wind it before you put the bolt in. Slide the bolt in here, put the stock to your shoulder like this." He looked around. "Do you want that sheep especially?"

"Not if you're hungry, my lord."

Rakóssy shouldered the harquebus. "Aim through those prongs. And pull the trigger." He shot, and the sheep plunged into the snow without a sound, without a leap.

The shepherd reached for the harquebus, and Rakóssy handed it over.

"For Turks, you understand? If I hear of any of you fighting Magyars or Slavs or Slovenes or Croats—anybody but Turks—I'll make you wish you were never born."

The shepherd grinned.

"Cook me that sheep. It's a long ride back to Hart."

The shepherds moved languidly into action. Rakóssy and his men sat down by the fire. It began to snow, and Rakóssy cursed.

"It's going to be three days going back," he said. "We'll pack some meat with us."

The older shepherd came over and sat on his heels. He directed his men with his hands.

"It used to be that we could count on this water during the winter," he said. "The wind keeps the grass clear, over there."

"And the spring never freezes," Rakóssy said. "I know."

"That's right. What's happened to these Turks, anyway?"

"We burned a lot of their graze last summer. Maybe their herds ran out. Maybe they're starving."

"I hope so," the old shepherd said. He spat. The spittle crackled in the cold air.

Rakóssy blew on his hands and thrust them back into his gloves. "I'm beginning to think that they're going to attack us soon. The whole Turk army."

"How do you know?"

"I just said I was beginning to think it."

"I'll believe you. You always know everything. There's nothing a man can do that ibn Shaitan doesn't know about."

"Don't call me that."

The old shepherd poked the fire with a stick. His hands were bare. The skin of his hands was chapped and red, so rough that looking at them made Rakóssy grit his teeth. "He calls you something else," the shepherd said. "The Lion of Hungary, he calls you."

"How do you know?"

The old man shrugged. "I speak Turk—you have to out here. I listen." He stared at the fire. He lifted his eyes. His face was full of confidence. "You'll beat them."

"I'll try."

The old shepherd spat again. "You will."

If the Emperor should not come . . .

"Kismet," Rakóssy said and shrugged. "I'll do what is possible."

They ate the roasted sheep and slept there that night. Rakóssy thought, Who am I to think that I might lose? The next morning he packed cold meat on the spare horse and led his men back to Hart. The snow fell all the way home. They followed him blindly. They reached the castle in the middle of the night.

"I'm a coward," he told Catharine.

"Ah, my love, cowardice is not one of your vices."

"God damn it," he said. "God damn it."

* * *

Mustafa was in Constantinople before the winter solstice. The Sultan showed him a letter from the King of France, beseeching the Sultan to attack Hungary and rescue the King of France from the wicked clutches of the Emperor. Mustafa, who, like Rakóssy, could not read, admired the fine flourishes of the handwriting and the ornate forms of the seal.

"I will attack Hungary in the spring."

Mustafa bowed. "Your Magnificence is, as ever, direct and purposeful."

"The army has been summoned. I will have seventy-five thousand men, including and centered upon the Janissaries, and three hundred cannon. Do you deem this sufficient?"

Mustafa moved easily around the small room. "Your Magnificence honors me in this. Yet the problem is complex. Such an army would naturally take Hungary in a single month, provided that the lords and kings of the West do not come to the aid of the Magyars. But, even if they do—yes, even then, such an army, commanded by the Magnificence of the Servant of Allah—" Mustafa bowed—"would be enough. But it would be difficult."

"Will they come, these western lords?"

"I cannot say. What I said, Magnificence, would be a lie. I have no certain proof in either direction."

"You are ever wise. What are your suspicions?"

"I suspect nothing, Magnificence." Mustafa looked at his hands. "There is a man in the south who lately married the Emperor's aunt. She is the daughter of a concubine, not of the true wife of the Spanish King. I can say no more of it. I know nothing of her. Nor do I know why he married her."

"Is he a great lord?"

Mustafa shook his head.

"So, then. With you, how goes the campaign?"

Mustafa paused. His eyes swept the elegant tracery of

the ivory screen. "Not well, Magnificence."

"Oh?"

"The past season has nothing in it to equal or recall the successes of past years. I have lost too many men, and my supply lines are too vulnerable to attack, and my . . . opposition too cunning."

"The task is difficult at best. But for one of such ability to find it impossible, that is a thing of amazement."

"Not impossible, Magnificence. I said only that it does not go well. I have gained nothing, and they are wearing us."

"This is this . . . the Count you spoke of?"

"Magnificence. Should I fail to rend this Malencz every time I meet him in battle, should I neglect the laughable task of turning him into a fool and a dupe to make mock of, should I not ride circles around him and rub his proud Magyar nose in the dirt—then I would have no courage to face you. I could not tell you that I had so dishonored my family and my Sultan."

"Who is it, then?"

"Rakóssy."

"This name I have never heard."

"A man of cunning and subtlety, of such a Devil's craft and guile, a lion of a man, a wild dog of a man—in short—" and Mustafa smiled— "a man in every way my equal."

"Mustafa, Mustafa. When you are thus impudent, all cannot be ill. Put it aside for now. I will rescue you from your Magyar lion. When I invade Hungary, I shall do one of two things. The first is the more orthodox. I will ravage the south and east and conquer it, and, on the conquest, move to fight the north. The King and his paladins. The more central task, of course. The second is perhaps the better in this case. I will invade through the south and march directly against the King, pausing only to rest and regroup my army."

"The second is quite the finer plan," Mustafa said. "But if I might make a suggestion."

"Ah?"

"Your Magnificence ought then to take and hold the area due north of Belgrade, in case, by some slim chance and the chastisement of Allah, we need to retreat quickly."

"You anticipate me in every way."

Mustafa bowed. "And may I request one boon of the Magnificence of Allah?"

"It is in your hands. You will command the troops who take and hold this territory. I shall give you sufficient men, although I doubt if I can give you guns. We may, indeed, pause in our march north to destroy any fortresses there."

"I am speechless with delight."

"Am I wrong in assuming that this territory is that held now by your Hungarian lion?"

"Is your Magnificence ever wrong?" Mustafa said.

The winter was short and furious. By the end of January the snow was so thick on the ground that even the sleigh was useless. Rakóssy spent that month composing a letter to Levolt in Kutess. Catharine wrote countless drafts of it. She did not understand the single threat in the letter, and she got tired of it long before he was satisfied. The letter waited for the snow to melt to be sent out.

After January it did not snow again, and one day toward the middle of March, Catharine saw the unmistakable signs of a thaw. She sighed and turned from the window. The winter had been almost unbearable. Now, she thought, I can admit it, because it's over. She almost laughed.

She called Mari and they went down to the great hall and their looms. Catharine folded the cloth she had made and stared at the loom, concentrating on the new pattern she was trying. Mari said suddenly, "A Gypsy came this morning."

"A Gypsy?" Catharine picked up a thread.

"From the north."

"Oh." Catharine wove. The thread flew back and forth. She changed the color and made a small adjustment. Abruptly she realized what Mari had said. She looked up. Mari's eyes were huge.

"But he can't attack us now," Catharine said. "It's too early."

"Arpád says . . ." Mari stopped and chewed her lip. "Arpád says it wouldn't surprise him at all."

Catharine put her hands in her lap. She stared through the mesh of the threads at the long dim hall.

"Arpád says that Jansci thinks the Turks will come this year."

"No," Catharine said. "Not this year. Why?"

"Arpád says that he has never been wrong."

Catharine stood up, spilling the spindle from her lap. The thread looped off into a tangle. She ran to the side door and opened it. In the narrow corridor she paused, wondering where they would be. She went slowly to the library and looked in. It was empty. But the letter to Levolt was gone.

For a moment she tried to govern her fear. I have a right to be afraid, she thought. She ran down the hall to the stairs, climbed them, and ran into her room.

The four of them turned to stare at her. Arpád and Denis stood at once. The Gypsy was Venn, from Columbo's camp. He looked away from her.

"What's wrong?" Rakóssy said.

"You sent the letter to Levolt."

"A month ago."

Denis said, "Catharine, don't be afraid." He glanced at Rakóssy. "Shall I take her downstairs?"

"No." Rakóssy turned back to the Gypsy. "And Levolt did what?"

"Sent a letter. He will not come, he says. You have not been tried and found guilty, and he must have his men to fight the Turks."

"Just a minute." Rakóssy lifted his face toward Catharine's. "Sit down. Malencz has sent to Kutess for men, to meet at Vrath in the first week of April. He knows I have guns and he has asked the King for cannon but the King has none to spare."

Catharine sank down. "Then he may not attack for a while."

Rakóssy said, "I'm going to raid him. I have to get him out of Vrath before the middle of April."

"Why?"

"Because by then the passes in the south will be open, and I don't like being caught with my pants down." He turned again to the Gypsy. "How many men does he have without Levolt?"

"Three hundred at least," Venn said. "Perhaps more. It's said he spent many hours in prayer, wondering if he should attack you or not, when you had not been judged."

"He prays very well. He has more than three hundred."

"Yes."

Rakóssy looked across at Denis, smiling. Abruptly he swung back to Venn. "When did you see Mustafa last?"

Venn jumped a little. "Mustafa?"

"Don't play games. You sold the Turks information about me. You knew the name Mustafa calls me and you had Turkish coins on that fancy vest." Venn looked around at the others. Rakóssy said, "It makes no difference to me. Have you seen him recently?"

"I stopped going to Cliff's Eye last fall. Trig Columbo found out."

"Was he there then?"

"Yes."

"When did he leave?"

"I don't know."

"But he did leave."

"I never said that."

"But you know that he left sometime."

Venn yawned, looked from side to side, and shrugged. "He left after the Turk New Year. I told Trig Columbo. I saw him ride into Belgrade. We could not get a man through the passes then."

"Going south?"

"He went to Belgrade. I swear it on my father's soul. More I don't know."

"It could have been somebody else," Denis said.

"It was Mustafa. I have seen him. And anyway, this man wore the clothes of a ghazi. How many ghazi are there between here and Belgrade?" Venn spat. "Just one. It was Mustafa. He rode that chestnut mare."

"Tell me again that you don't know where he was going," Rakóssy said.

Venn grinned. "You're a tough one."

"How many Gypsies winter south of the mountains? How long were you in Belgrade?"

"Until . . . maybe twenty days ago."

Rakóssy snorted. "You are stupid. You don't lie well enough to look clever. Where was he going?"

"To Constantinople."

Rakóssy blew out through his teeth. "So. Kamal raided the shepherds. It wasn't like Mustafa. I should have known."

"But you did know," Venn said.

"What's the news of the north?"

Venn began to pare his nails. "The Prince of Transylvania has had a fight with the King. He's gone back to his city with his knights and he swears he'll have the King on his knees before he goes back to Buda."

"Good," Denis said.

"They're fools," Rakóssy said.

He stood up. "Venn, go home. Take my thanks to Columbo. You can have the pick of my stables, except for my black mare."

"My king will surely bless your name." Venn rose. He bowed, grinning. "You Devil." He went jauntily out the door. Rakóssy watched him go, frowning.

"Arpád."

Arpád straightened.

"Get one hundred men ready. We're going to hit Malencz."

Arpád went out. Denis said, "Maybe you should send a scout down near Belgrade."

"The Gypsies will tell me if there's any sign of Turks."

"Venn was a traitor to us."

"But Columbo isn't." Rakóssy sat down. "Columbo was in love with Mother. I've known him since I was too little to walk."

"In love with Mother? Did she—"

Rakóssy laughed. He stretched. "Half of Mother's charm was that she never loved anybody. She accepted it as natural that everybody would love her, but she never loved anybody."

"She must have been very unhappy," Catharine said. "A woman needs to love."

"She loved me," Rakóssy said.

"Will we win?" Denis said. "If the Turks come this year."

Rakóssy shrugged. "If we can hold Vrath and Hart, even just Vrath, we will give the Turks some trouble. If the King raises an army good enough to give them one solid whack of a beating, and if Bathóry plays it right—"

"Who is Bathóry?" Catharine said.

"The King's general. If they can hold the north, we will have the Turks in a vise. They'll be trapped. They can't go through Transylvania. They obviously can't go west. If they go south, we can block their way out. We may not finish them off, but we can make a mess of them."

"Shall I go with you?" Denis said.

"Yes. Have you got any mail?"

"No."

"Well, go to the armory and get Georg to give you some."

Denis went out. Catharine said, "He looks very happy."

"Yes."

He stood up and went to his chest. He took out his mail shirt and got into it. Catharine said, "This portrait is of your mother, isn't it?"

"Yes."

"She's very beautiful."

"Columbo says that she was the most beautiful woman he has ever seen who was not a Romna."

"Did she really love you?"

He slung the baldric of his longsword over one shoulder and caught the buckle. "She never loved anybody else but me." He buckled the baldric and went over and kissed Catharine. "Don't be jealous of my mother."

"You never talk about her."

"She's dead." He kissed her eyes and her mouth. "I have to go."

She laid her cheek against his hair. He was kissing her throat. "Then why are you making love to me?" He started to pull away and she tightened her hold on him. "My dearest love," she said.

"Will you miss me?"

Arpád charged through the door. He skidded to a stop and said, "Excuse me."

Rakóssy looked at him over Catharine's head. "Has everybody got bows?"

"Yes." Arpád looked off at the ceiling. Catharine tried to move away from Rakóssy but he held her close.

"Has my little brother got himself armed?"

"Yes. He looks to choke on the baldric."

"All right."

Rakóssy kissed Catharine again and went out the door after Arpád. She went to the window and saw him stride out into the courtyard. He went to the black mare and mounted. He rode over to Denis and they talked for a moment. They swung and the whole band galloped out of Hart.

Catharine turned toward the big portrait. The woman's blue eyes, blazing like jewels, looked over her head.

"I think," Catherine said, "that I would have hated you, madam."

They attacked a large village at the very edge of Malencz's land, herded all the villagers into the fields, and looted the huts. They did not burn them. Denis thought his brother wasted an inordinate amount of time riding up and down the village square. Finally they scattered the village's herds and flocks and started home. They made a camp on a hilltop for the night.

Denis sat in the first round of sentries, watching the north. He felt guilty about harassing the villagers, who after all could not help that Malencz was their lord. He had taken no loot, but he knew that most of the others had—woolen cloth and a few trinkets. He was not entirely sure, either, that he really approved of what his brother was doing. It might be better to let Malencz alone. The more enemies the Turks had to face, the harder they would find the war. If they did ever show up. He had not thought about it all winter.

It was still cold, but the snow on the plain had long since melted. The ground under him was soggy and uncomfortable. He could see his horse, dozing, in the fringe of scrubby trees.

Malencz would not attack them here. It would take the villagers too long to send for him. This whole business was stupid, sham, for the sake of Arpád's and Rakóssy's pride. Denis dug at the mud with his fingers. The cannon were different. With cannon, you paid attention to the engineering of it, but when you fought hand to hand there was blood and people staring at you reproachfully. When this is all over, he thought, I am going to Italy. If there's any Italy left, the way the Emperor and the French are fighting over it.

I'll go to the south, Naples perhaps, or even Palermo. And sit all day under the orange trees and eat cheese and drink goat's milk. I'll be a philosopher, that's what I'll be. And if anybody ever wants me to fight, I'll say, I'm sorry, but I've had my fill of that. I was with Rakóssy at the defense of Vrath.

"Rakóssy?" they would say. "What's your name?"

"Denis Rakóssy. He was my brother."

"Are you the brother who rescued him on the walls?"

"I rescued him once, but he rescued me several times. He's dead, you know."

"How did he die?"

How would his brother die? Not at the height of the battle, of course. Perhaps after the Turks were routed and they were pursuing them, some stray arrow would take his brother neatly off his horse. Denis would hold him while he died and Rakóssy would say something. No, János would never say anything memorable or thrilling. He would say, "The Devil with it," or "Take care of Catharine," or even "I'm scared." Denis thought of what he would say when he died.

"I'll quote from Plutarch," he said. "Or maybe *in perpetua, frater, ave atque vale.*"

"Talking to yourself?"

Rakóssy sat on his heels beside Denis. He was smiling.

"I was just trying to think of what I would say when I die."

"Cheerful thought for a spring night."

"What will you say?"

"I've never thought about it."

"I know you'll never say anything memorable or thrilling."

"Or edifying, either."

"What if we're taken prisoner?"

"In that case, Mustafa will make sure I live long enough to recite the Koran, backwards."

"You mean he'll torture you?"

"I don't intend to find out."

"Will Malencz attack us, do you think? I mean to-night."

"God no. He won't find out about it until tomorrow. Those villagers might. They're tough donkeys, and they've gotten used to fighting for themselves."

Denis yawned. "Let's hope everything goes the way it should. I'm sleepy."

"Well, the Sultan's a tricky fellow, I'm told. Malencz will play right into the trap."

"Good." Denis yawned again.

"Your watch is up. Go to sleep."

"Well, here's to a tough war. Good night." He went off down the side of the hill to sleep. Rakóssy grinned.

Count Louis Malencz, splendid in satin and brocade, listened to the tale of the villagers without change of expression. He dismissed them. He sat a long while, his eyes ranging the books in his study, thinking back over the years before, when in the spring Kamal and Rakóssy had come for the peace talks. There would be no such spring this year. This year the Turks would deal with him alone.

He went to his prie-dieu and knelt. "Oh, God," he said. "Give me strength."

Strength for what? was of course the question. He thought of trying to take Rakóssy by some stratagem. He had planned to have the King's officers place him under arrest at Christmas Feast, but Rakóssy had not come. The King's officers had danced and dined and gone back to Buda with no prisoner.

This attack on his village was a taunt. Surely there was nothing to be gained from an attack on such a miserable little village.

He prayed for a while, arranging his mind.

"Give me the strength to conquer Rakóssy, and I will give a new chapel altar to the cathedral at Buda." That did not sound sufficient. "I will try to take him alive and have him sent to Buda for trial."

Both his sons were still in Buda, at the court. He thought of Peter. He sighed. Peter had been gay, witty, handsome, a true courtier and a gallant gentleman. "You have tried me. Have You found me wanting?"

He thought again of the Masses he had ordered for the repose of the soul of his eldest son. The great ritual comforted him. The mighty swelling of the priests' voices speaking of resurrection and the centuries of tradition and pattern lightened his heart. "If there be heresy, Lord, I have been staunch in Your Service. Why do you afflict me thus?"

Levolt's rebuff had been painful, but Malencz's spies told him that Levolt was not giving aid to Rakóssy. Levolt had always been terrified of Rakóssy; there was an old rumor that Levolt had once dabbled in witchcraft and that Rakóssy had gained some awful power over him.

"I am Your servant. Direct me toward Your enemies."

He was not a young man. Rakóssy was twenty years younger than he. He felt suddenly old and tired and incompetent. They said that Rakóssy had a young wife, the aunt of the Emperor. Was that why the King had suddenly grown silent to his pleas? Someone had told him that a summons had been sent to Hart but that Rakóssy had never answered it.

"Arrogant," Malencz said and clenched his fist. He beat his hands against the top of the prie-dieu. "Arrogant, arrogant."

He wept, and prayed again. There was no one left to help him. Levolt and the King had deserted him. He crossed himself and rose.

"I am Your warrior, Lord. Defend me."

He went out of the room. He sent a servant to assemble his knights in the great hall and went to his chamber to prepare himself. His servants put on his armor. He wore the plate armor his father had commissioned in Milan. He carried the helmet under his arm and strapped the sword around his waist.

The knights were gathered in the hall, rank upon rank, nearly five hundred of them. When he appeared, they cheered him. He waited until they were silent.

"Rakóssy has attacked us," he said. "He sent his men against one of my villages. Are we to let this outrage go unpunished?"

They cheered. He mouthed more phrases. The words tasted foul in his mouth. They cheered whenever he asked a question.

"Tomorrow," he said, "we shall hear Mass in the chapel. After we have asked God and Christ Jesus for aid, we shall march against this traitor Rakóssy." He sobbed and lifted his fist. "I shall lay out his bones to bleach on the hills and beat the flesh from his body with spiked chains."

It seemed to him that the knights cheered this less fervently than before. They were weak-stomached and had not the reason to hate Rakóssy that he had.

Rakóssy took his men back to a place where they could make a good camp and ordered Arpád to keep scouts on the border between his land and Malencz's to find and follow Malencz's army when it appeared. He rode back to Hart to give orders to the remaining ten men in the garrison.

He told them to prepare for a possible Turk attack, to hear all messengers who came to Hart and send him prompt news if the messengers had anything important. He set Catharine over them as temporary commander.

"Will the Gypsies warn us?" she said.

"Yes. There may be a Jew, named ben Jakub, coming from Thessalonika, and he may have some information. He won't strain himself getting here and his news won't be fresh." He looked at Mari standing behind her. "Don't look so frightened."

"What are you going to do?"

"I'm waiting for Malencz. He has to attack soon or I'll go tweak his nose for him. Here it is almost April, and the fool isn't out of his winter underwear yet. I'm only about half a day's ride away. I'll send news. Make sure that the wagons with the other cannon are sound. Tell someone to bring in those oxen, and have the men put the eight marked cannon on the walls."

"I will."

"Be careful."

"I will."

"Don't let anybody inside the gate unless you know him."

"I won't."

He kissed her. "Goodbye."

"János, be careful. Please."

She held him tight. He put his arms around her and kissed her. She shut her eyes. "This is so dangerous."

"Don't be afraid."

"Can I help it?"

"If you're afraid, everybody else here will be. You have to keep them from panicking."

"I will."

She drew back and clasped her hands before her. He put his fingertips to the mole on her cheek.

"Give Denis my love," she said.

He took a few steps away and turned. He smiled. "I will."

He mounted the black mare and rode out the gate. She went to the top of the wall, next to the gate, and watched him jog down the hill. He turned at the foot of it and threw up his hand in salute to her, and she raised her hand. He rode off again, and again he turned and waved. She thought, He acts as if he's never coming back.

"But that isn't so," she said. "It isn't so."

Perhaps the Turks would not come. They might still have a long time ahead of them. How did he know that the Turks were coming? Only that Mustafa had gone south, and that if he himself were Sultan he would attack this year. His intuition. His mind, his eyes, his heart, his mouth, the touch of his hands.

I was born in Jaen, and I was a lady-in-waiting to the Archduchess of Austria. When I was twenty-one years old I was married to the Baron János Rakóssy of Hart Castle in Hungary. Now I am twenty-two, and soon, perhaps, I will have a child, whom he will love and I will love. When I am old, I shall be a dowager. My son will be the Baron Rakóssy. I was born in Jaen . . .

She went slowly down to the courtyard.

"Pál," she said, and Pál came running. "Go get the oxen that draw the wagons with the cannon and put them in the stable. Send Sandor, the Sandor who is the carpenter, down to check those wagons. They've been in the stable all winter and who knows but they are rotten. If you want me, I shall be in the library. All of you must start putting the cannon on the walls. Do you know where they go?"

"Yes, my lady."

She went over to the pump and knelt by it and drank some of the fresh stony water. She ducked under the turnstile and slapped the pony on the rump.

"Poor thing," she said. "You must be terribly bored."

The pony cocked its ears at her. She went up to the library and made a list of all the things she was to do.

A messenger came the next day from Rakóssy. Malencz was on the move and they were going to let him ride into a trap, he said. He needed bread. "We haven't got anything to eat but what we shoot, and the game's gone. Bread and some dried meat. I'll put it on a pack horse."

Catharine stood up. "Come with me," she said.

"They've camped," Imre said. He slid off his horse.

"Where?"

"Near Saint Stephan's Cross, on the top of that knob hill there."

"How many?"

"I counted five hundred seventy, but you know how hard it is."

Arpád whistled. Rakóssy said to him, "Wake everybody up." He turned back to Imre. "Where are their horses?"

"You know that hill?"

"The knobby one with the aspen along the north side?"

"Yes. On the south side there's a kind of a hollow, and the horses are there."

"How well guarded are they?"

"I counted maybe twenty guards."

"Maybe?"

"Twenty."

"Are the horses hobbled?"

Imre shook his head. "They've got a rope fence around them. They're packed in pretty close."

Denis crawled up. "What are we going to do?"

"Run off their horses." Rakóssy stood up and waved in the rest of the men. They gathered in a dense circle around him.

"The knights from Vrath are on the knob-shaped hill by the Stone Cross. Their horses are below the hill on the south side in a rope fence. Twenty sentries. How many here were at the attack on Kamal and Mustafa at Alder Springs?"

Half his men raised their hands.

"Good. We'll do it like that. The ones who were with me then will go with me and the rest with Alexander. My band will take care of the sentries and run off the horses. Alexander's will wait mounted to keep the loose horses bunched up and going in the right direction. We take as many of the sentries alive as possible."

He waited a moment. They all acted as if they understood.

"There are five hundred and seventy knights on the top of that hill."

Somebody gasped.

"Exactly," Rakóssy said. "We have to move fast. Anybody who gets caught or trapped will be left behind. Now are there any questions?"

A skinny young man lifted his hand. Rakóssy nodded. "At Alder Springs we used two men to a sentry. Same here?"

"Yes."

"Do they all have to be taken prisoner? I mean, if we're in trouble can we knock them on the head?"

"And leave them? Yes."

Another arm shot up. "The cover around the south of that hill isn't any too good."

"I know. We'll go in after the moon sets. It could go down just after midnight."

There were no more questions. Rakóssy looked around. "All right. Everybody get some sleep. We'll ride out at midnight."

Denis crept up to him. "I'm going with you," he said.

"All right. You can go in with me. Come over here and I'll explain it."

They left their horses a good mile away from the knobby hill. Rakóssy's men went off in pairs, running easily through the new grass. Rakóssy led Denis along toward the southeastern side of the hill. Denis' mouth was dry. He kept thinking of the knights on the hill and of how they might come charging down on them and cut them to ribbons in the darkness.

It was so dark, now that the moon was down, that he could barely see his brother ahead of him. The ground seemed uneven and pitted under his feet, so that he felt about to trip with every stride. Rakóssy moved like a wraith before him. Suddenly Rakóssy dropped flat on his belly and started to crawl. Denis imitated him. They crawled up to a little ridge and looked over.

The fires of the sentries were banked and dim. Denis

saw the horses, penned and restive, and the blanket-wrapped lumps of the guards. He saw two men walk casually from deep cover across the open meadow before them and back into the deep cover. He glanced at Rakóssy.

"That damned Arpád thinks he can get away with anything," Rakóssy whispered. "Come on, and keep down."

He flopped over the crest of the little ridge and crawled down toward a rock at the edge of the meadow. Denis slithered after him. Suddenly he was not afraid anymore. He hurried, ran into his brother, and was kicked in the chest. Rakóssy pulled up behind the rock.

An owl hooted off to their left. Denis felt the back of his neck break into goose flesh. A gigantic soundless body wheeled out across the meadow. Rakóssy crept out from the cover of the rock, and Denis charged after him on hands and knees.

In the meadow there was a short animal scream. The owl settled to feed. Ahead of him his brother scurried on and dropped flat again behind another rock. Denis looked toward the sentries. He judged they were no more than fifty feet away. He could smell the rank smell of the bunched horses.

Rakóssy was signaling him up. He scrambled up beside him and settled down, trying not to pant. Rakóssy put his mouth against Denis' ear and said, "I'm going to give the others a little while longer."

"What are we going to do then?"

Rakóssy pointed with his elbow at a hummock of grass midway between them and the nearest fire. It did not look large enough to hide a small rabbit.

The owl hooted again. One of the sentries stood, kicked around in the dirt for a rock, and hurled it at the owl, which hooted again immediately from a far-distant place. The sentry swore. Denis could hear him plainly.

"Now," Rakóssy said and scurried out into the open, headed for the tuft of grass. Denis waited, staring at the sentries, his heart banging against his ribs. Rakóssy had reached the hummock and was lying there, waiting. Denis hurled himself after him and flew more than crawled into the feeble cover.

"Keep your head down," Rakóssy said. He put his hands around his mouth, rolled over, and hooted at the sky.

The sentry threw another rock. It bounced against Denis' ankle. From across the meadow a woodcock called. Rakóssy rolled over again and got to his hands and knees. Without a pause he raced in toward the fires. Denis crossed himself and ran after him. The sentries did not see them until they were right above them. Rakóssy had his dagger in his hand. The sentries leapt up to face him. Instantly two of them were struck down from behind. The third opened his mouth to shout. Rakóssy hit him in the stomach with his fist. The sentry fell, clutching Rakóssy. They rolled wildly on the ground, inches from the fire. Denis hopped and danced around them, trying to get in a blow. The sentry's arm arced out of the tangle, holding a great rock. Denis grabbed his wrist. Rakóssy reared up and hit the man in the face.

"He's out. Come on, damn it, come on."

Denis caught the sentry under the arms. Another of Rakóssy's men jumped quietly from the trees and helped him. They carried the sentry to the horse herd, now stamping and surging against the rope fence, while Rakóssy's men tried to catch mounts and get bridles on them.

"Stallions," Rakóssy said quietly. "God damn. Hurry it up."

Denis hauled himself onto a broad comfortable back and felt the long muscles under him tense and leap. Arpád scrambled up on the next horse. "Here," he said and looped a rope over Denis' horse's neck. "Tie it. Hang on to that one."

The sentry was lying across the withers of Denis' mount, face down. Denis made some knots, hardly knowing what he was tying together. It was too late to worry about that anyhow. The horses were moving.

He saw his brother, shouting and waving his arms, on the ground between two trees, and he felt the horse under him bolt, collecting all his weight and flinging it forward. He was in the middle of a sea of horses, all neighing and rearing and riderless and wild. The trees whipped past them. He saw Rakóssy again, briefly, on a horse without bridle and saddle, deep in the center of the charging herd. He thought he could hear shouting from the hilltop.

His and Arpád's horses were roped together, he found. He thought that was a mistake, and he was groping for his dagger when he saw that Arpád was trying to tighten the knots. "Here," Arpád said. "Let me help you." He reached out with one hand and steadied Denis' prisoner. "Grab your reins."

His horse was bridled, but the reins were flying around the horse's knees. Denis took a breath, tightened his hold on the horse's mane, and leaned down over the heaving shoulder. He snatched for one rein, missed, almost fell, and saw the ground driven to a morass by the hoofs of the horses ahead of his, heard the sounds, and saw the legs like scythes slashing back and forth. He snatched again and caught one rein and straightened up. That helped. He used the rein to steady himself and grabbed for the other. Suddenly his horse stumbled. He felt the prisoner sliding limply between his and Arpád's horses, clutched at him, and hung on with his eyes clamped shut. When he looked again, he saw that the horse had stepped on the loose rein and broken it off.

He concentrated on staying on and holding onto the prisoner. He saw his brother again briefly; Rakóssy's horse was fighting with another, fighting at a dead run. The stallions squealed and neighed while they ran, and kicked out and reared and tried to leap on each other. They gashed at each other with their teeth. Denis offered up a short prayer.

"Turks ride mares," Arpád shouted and nodded at him.

Denis laughed. He felt a horse collide with his, and his horse threw its weight back solidly against the other, trying to catch it with its teeth.

"There's Alexander."

Alexander and the others rode whooping out to head off the charge of the loose stallions. Denis thought, They'll never stop them.

"Hang on, they're turning," Rakóssy shouted right beside him. He was systematically beating his horse around the head and shoulders.

Alexander and his men turned the leaders of the wild charge, swung them around in a circle, and headed them into the rear of the herd. The stallions surged together in a ring, slowed to a canter, to a trot, milled around for a while, and suddenly stopped dead. There was a ragged, breathless cheer.

Denis slid down, gasping for air, and realized that he was on foot in the middle of the herd. Rakóssy gave him a hand and Denis climbed up behind him. The men were pushing slowly out of the herd. Rakóssy reached the open and swung down. He almost fell and grabbed for the mane of the horse he had been riding.

"Are you all right?" Denis said.

"I think one of them bit me. Arpád?"

Arpád walked over.

"Did anybody get hurt?"

"None of ours." Arpád wiped his hands on his shirt and counted heads. "I think we lost two of the prisoners."

"Get those stallions neck-roped together and let's get out of here."

They roped the horses into strings of twenty and went back to their camp. Rakóssy counted the horses on the way back; they had taken five hundred and forty-two. He sent three men out to see if they had lost any horses and sat down beside his saddle to tend his leg. He took off his trousers and turned so that the fire shone on his leg.

"You really got it," Denis said.

Rakóssy clenched his teeth and kneaded at the slash on his leg. "God damn horses. Why aren't they sensible, like Turks? A mare wouldn't cut anybody up like this."

His whole leg was bruised and raw. He took a jar of salve from his saddle pouch and smeared it on. It burned and he swore steadily at it and at all stallions.

"What do we do now?" Denis said.

Rakóssy let the cool air in against his leg and sat a moment winking back the tears. "It must be good stuff. It hurts like hell. That depends on Malencz."

He got up and hopped around, getting back into his trousers. Denis said, "What do you think he'll do?"

"Come after us."

"What then?"

"We'll show him that five hundred men on foot aren't worth much against one hundred men mounted. As far as catching up with us is concerned. I'm not going to fight him."

"Oh," Denis said.

"You've gotten bloodthirsty lately."

"You never give me a chance to do anything."

"You'll get your chance."

"When?"

"Soon enough. Go to sleep."

Malencz did come after them, following the great trail of the stallions all that next day, and Rakóssy stayed easily away from him. He took the horses down to good grass and let them graze awhile, watered them up, and circled Malencz's little army once, giving the horseless knights an occasional glimpse of the strings of stolen horses.

That night Malencz camped in the middle of a great meadow. Either he had learned something or someone with him was clever and knew enough not to leave the camp open to a charge, because the knights spent a lot of time gathering brush and making a brush fence around the camp. Rakóssy let his horses rest and graze.

In the morning the knights from Vrath set off grimly for home. They marched in neat columns and sang to keep their spirits up. Rakóssy watched them head off to the northwest and called Arpád.

"They're going to go through the pass by Etzel's Well," he said. "Take seventy of the men and close off the pass from the northwest."

Arpád looked uncertain. "There's more than five hundred of them."

Rakóssy glared at him. "So what?"

Alexander laughed. "God help Malencz." He pulled his horse around. Arpád and most of the men jogged after him. Rakóssy waited until they were almost out of sight. Denis reined up beside him. Rakóssy said, "Little brother, we are going to drive them mad."

He set off after the marching knights, keeping the strings of horses under close control. They caught up with Malencz's men within an hour and Rakóssy ranged his men along a course roughly parallel with theirs. The unmounted knights trudged painfully along in the mud, their packs and saddles and armor on their backs. Rakóssy hooked his knee around his saddle pommel and rode that way, looking very relaxed and comfortable. His men shouted insults down to the men walking below.

At first, Malencz's knights ignored them. They marched close together, and it would be impossible to attack them. The sun rose higher and the ground grew rockier. Toward noon some of the knights suddenly broke formation and charged up the slope toward Rakóssy. He only laughed and, lifting his reins, let the black mare skitter away slightly. The knights subsided.

Rakóssy's men insulted them continually, and Malencz's answered back, swearing and threatening. Once again, just before sundown, they seemed about to charge, and Rakóssy sent the horses in a wild scramble up the slope. The knights drew back, shouting coward at them. Rakóssy laughed.

He made a camp within earshot of Malencz's, kept most of his men in the saddle while the rest made their dinner, and spent the night dozing on horseback while the restless stallions browsed and fought on the slope. The mountless knights made three or four attempts to sneak out of their camp toward the horses, but each time they were seen and Rakóssy and his men scattered, making a great clamor in the night with their moving horses.

The horses would not keep quiet. Rakóssy dared not let them loose to graze. All night long they stamped and neighed and fought. By morning Malencz's knights looked angry enough to try another charge, and Rakóssy tempted them. He charged his own men and all the loose horses straight across their path and up the facing slope, shouting and laughing all the way.

"God," Denis said. "If I were they, I'd be ready to kill you by now."

"Malencz," Rakóssy said.

"What?"

"By the time I get done with them, they'll be ready to kill Malencz."

He followed the tramping column patiently all day long. An hour before sundown they came at last into the little pass onto the plain. The pass was not long, but the sides of the two hills that formed it were rocky and close. When the slow-moving column reached it, they all saw that the far end of the pass was blocked by men with bows.

Rakóssy moved his men and the led stallions down to fill up the other end, catching Malencz and his men between. The stallions were red-eyed and furious. If they were charged down the pass, they would savage anything they could reach. Rakóssy let his black mare trot forward, away from the stallions. They made her nervous and edgy.

Malencz's army rumbled and snarled. Rakóssy moved the mare closer to them, until he was within fifty yards of the nearest knights.

"Do you want your horses back?" he said.

They roared at him. He let his reins slide and waited.

"Listen to me, and I'll give you back your horses."

"Listen?" Malencz shouted. He shoved his way out into the open. "Listen to soft words from a traitor? When the Devil talks of listening to him, a Christian fights!"

Malencz charged, clumsy in his armor. Rakóssy let him get up speed and set the mare straight at him. The mare ran into him and knocked him clean off his feet. Rakóssy vaulted out of the saddle and ran to Malencz. Malencz got to his knees, lifting his sword. Rakóssy dodged the first heavy blow and kicked out. His boot hit Malencz on the shoulder. The sword clattered down. Rakóssy hit Malencz alongside the jaw and felled him. He threw the sword across the little pass, wheeled, and vaulted into his saddle again. Malencz's men had not moved.

"There he is," Rakóssy said. "That's the man who got you into this. He had you camp in a way that made stealing your horses a child's trick. He let you in for a march on foot across the hills. There are five hundred and forty of you. He let you get insulted and harried by eighty men."

They mumbled and talked to one another. Rakóssy looked at the sun. He had less than an hour of daylight.

"What's your proposition?" one knight shouted.

Rakóssy leaned forward. "I need men—good men—Magyars—to fight the Turks. I need Vrath Castle, but I have that. I need knights."

A tall knight stepped forward. "I haven't fought the Turks for three years. Why start now?"

"Shut up, Peter," a smaller man said. "If you don't know who to fight, listen to somebody who does."

"A traitor like that?"

"Treason, to fight the Turks? Man, the King's sitting

up in Buda throwing festivals because he got married and the palatine's giving balls and parties every night. While the Turks are getting ready to knock us off like ripe melons."

"The Turks are overextended. Everybody knows that. They can't go farther than they are now."

Rakóssy said, "They will attack us by next summer at the latest."

"How do you know?"

"I have my ways. The Turk commander in the mountains went to Constantinople this winter. To meet with the Sultan, maybe. To plan the attack, maybe. I don't know. I can guess."

"I believe you," the stocky little man said. "My hand on it. I'm with you."

"You traitor, Béla," Peter said.

"I've been hearing for years you want to fight Turks, you join Rakóssy. You've been sitting on your butt playing gallant knight so long you've forgotten who our enemies are."

"He's a traitor."

"He's smarter than Malencz. That's treason?"

Somebody laughed.

Rakóssy said, "Anybody who doesn't want to join me can take his horse and leave. I don't want cowards."

"Coward?" Peter howled. "I'm no coward, damn you. You can count me for." He took a step forward.

Béla drew a line in the dirt with his heel. "Everybody who's brave and hates Turks and wants to be with us, step over that line."

Arpád came up behind Rakóssy and dismounted. He went over to Malencz. "He's waking up."

"I see him. Tie him up."

The rest of the knights were milling. Gradually, they crossed the line, each to his own taste. Some of them made great shows of it and some pretended that they didn't realize the line was there until it was too late.

Finally there was only one man left on the far side,

Martón Vidor, who had commanded the garrison at Etzel's Well. He stood quietly watching the others cross the line and assemble around Rakóssy.

"Fetch me my horse," he said.

"Somebody bring him his horse," Rakóssy said.

Béla was swaggering back and forth around the line. "Eh, Martón, you've done it again."

"I am still a man of honor," Vidor said stiffly.

The new converts jeered him and laughed at him. Béla made a fig with his left hand. "That for your honor. You don't know what honor is."

Béla wheeled. "Don't mind him," he said to Rakóssy. He grinned; he was missing a tooth. "He still hasn't gotten over what happened at the Well." He put his hand on Rakóssy's arm, and Rakóssy drew away. Béla did not notice, but whirled to shout at Vidor again. Finally Vidor's horse was brought and the man rode off, his back straight as a pine.

They camped there for the night, and the next day they rode toward Vrath. They went slowly. That following night they made a big, noisy camp, and everybody sang songs, and Rakóssy told Denis to go back and take command of Hart.

Denis said, "I am not going. Send Arpád. He knows more about it than I do."

"Arpád doesn't know anything about cannon and he doesn't care. You're going."

"I can't, János. I don't know enough. I haven't had the experience."

"You are going, and you're going to set up a defense that will make the Turks think they're attacking Vienna. You can do it, and you know it, but you're scared out of your mind. You're a coward, but you can do it, and I'm going to make you do it."

The rest of the army was watching them. Denis looked around and turned back to Rakóssy.

"Try," he said and drove his fist into Rakóssy's face.

Rakóssy staggered back, tripped, and sprawled on the ground. He got to his hands and knees, stood up, and walked toward Denis. Denis set himself. Rakóssy charged. Denis blocked one wild swing and caught the next in the belly. He doubled over and Rakóssy clubbed him on the back. Denis fell. He rolled, trying to avoid his brother's boots, and jumped up. For a moment he stood square to Rakóssy, slugging wildly. His face began to hurt. Rakóssy was chopping him down. The pleasure of hitting back was enough to numb the pain. Rakóssy hit him in the chest and Denis fell again.

He got up and backed off, circling. He saw the others around them, packed in a mob. They weren't cheering. They were afraid to cheer for him, and they did not want to cheer for Rakóssy.

Denis lowered his hands. "All right. I'll go."

Rakóssy stepped back. "Get moving. Send Catharine back as soon as you get there." He glared at the others. "Get going. What is this, a festival?"

They scurried off to their jobs. Denis gathered up his belongings. Rakóssy said, "I take it back. You're not a coward."

"Why, thank you, big brother."

"You're just a God-damn fool."

Rakóssy stamped off. Denis heard him cursing.

Rakóssy got his men together, sorted out a garrison for Hart, and sent them back with Denis. He himself went on toward Vrath. Malencz refused to talk. The ground was uneven and marshy and they rode slowly. Rakóssy's face hurt. Denis had given him a black eye.

Everything was going well enough now. He wished it were all over. It seemed to him that luck this good so early in the game was a bad sign.

They reached Vrath in the midafternoon. At first the people on the walls would not admit them, but when they saw that Rakóssy had Malencz, they opened the Main Gate. Rakóssy ordered Malencz taken to a dungeon and locked in.

He rode around to the stable and dismounted. The servants and the retainers of the Count Malencz were gathered in the main courtyard. Vrath was shaped like a squared-off horseshoe and the main courtyard was in the two arms, facing Main Gate, with the stable in the Countess Courtyard and the chapel on the other side. Rakóssy walked slowly around the front of the castle.

He had expected that he would feel triumph when he had Vrath at last. He felt nothing.

He told the servants to go make food for the knights. The rest he dismissed. Before he ate, he found and inspected the quarters for the knights and assigned each man to a bed, distributing them equally among the four common rooms at the corners of the castle. He gave them a lecture while they ate, about keeping their gear in shape and their horses sound. They ate steadily, and his voice was accompanied by a mighty slurping and chewing and gurgling. He told them that Alexander and Arpád were the seconds-in-command but that Béla would be the spokesman for the knights who had been with Malencz. There was a cheer at that and Béla jumped up and bowed.

"I will hang any man who shows cowardice or disobedience," Rakóssy said. "My cannon will be here within a day, and half of us will put them on the walls. One-fourth of you will go to Buda with Malencz's treasure and buy powder and shot. The other one-quarter will start getting food in. Eat well. This is the last time you'll be able to stuff your grimy faces at any meal."

They snarled at him, and he cursed them artistically for a few moments and stamped off. He went to Malencz's old room and sent a servant for food. He could hear the knights shouting and laughing. The knights poured out into the courtyard. Some of Malencz's knights began to sing a song about the advantages of living on the plain. Rakóssy felt the muscles of his back tighten.

"I am the chastiser, I am the defender," the knights sang. "I raise my castle in the grasslands."

By the Countess Gate a little knot of Rakóssy's men from Hart gathered and sang back, "Let the weakheaded build on the plain. I am the attacker, the destroyer. I build my castle in the mountains."

The men from Hart laughed. Rakóssy leaned out the window and shouted for Arpád.

Arpád came running. Rakóssy waited by the window, looking out. The knights had bunched together in two masses and were insulting one another gleefully.

"Stop that," Rakóssy said. "They'll be at one another's throats if they keep that up."

"Well," Arpád said, "after all, we did beat them. There has to be some—"

"We didn't beat them. We tricked them." Rakóssy swung to face him. "And if we tricked them, you didn't beat them. I beat them. Remember that. Get down there and stop that."

"Why don't you?" Arpád said and clapped his great hand over his mouth.

"Why, the Devil take you all," Rakóssy said. "Eight years you've taken my orders and never a word out of you, and now after two days with those rambling idiots you give me back talk. Get down there and stop that before I take you apart rib by rib and eat you for dinner."

Arpád fled. Rakóssy went after him into the corridor and shouted after him, "One more word out of you like that, and you'll wish you were a Turk, you—"

Arpád at the run turned a corner and was gone.

"Pig-eared offal-eating lump," Rakóssy said to himself and went back into his room.

That evening he got all the servants together in the great hall. He divided the men into two groups, those who could fight and those too old or too young. He sent the fighters off to be armed and taught. The others he assigned to the essential tasks of the castle. He would use them in gun crews if he needed more men.

"The women," he said, "can stay if they want. I need women to work in the kitchens. All but you three." He pointed to two women who had babies at their breasts and a third who was pregnant. "You'll have to go. My wife will be here presently and she will supervise the women who stay. Leave me."

They left the hall, all of them but the priest. The priest came forward a few steps.

"Father Halassy," Rakóssy said.

"My lord. If it is acceptable to you, I will go north."

The priest stared at him. He had pale-blue eyes.

"Go with the men going to Buda. With my blessing."

The priest smiled. "I'll decline that honor. Shall I bear a message to the King?"

"No. Why should you?"

"I thought perhaps you felt secure enough now to defy the King directly. If you will excuse me."

"Perhaps you should stay," Rakóssy said. "There may be some need for requiems soon."

The priest turned and walked away. He went quietly out the door and shut it softly behind him.

Rakóssy leaned back in the chair. He had handled that badly. He wondered if he should find a priest. Some of the knights might be pious.

He was tired and he did not want to think about priests and pious knights. The look in the priest's eyes stayed with him and bothered him. He remembered what Columbo had said about blue eyes.

rpád woke him up in the morning. "Is that priest leaving?"

"Don't talk to me about that priest."

"He's saying Mass in the chapel, and half the men are in there."

"He's going to Buda with Alexander."

"Better Alexander than me. Why are you letting him say Mass?"

Rakóssy whirled. "Leave me alone. You hear?"

"Yes, my lord."

A horn blew. "That's Catharine," Rakóssy said.

"My lord?"

Rakóssy turned his head toward him.

"I have to tell you something," Arpád said.

"What is it now?"

"Mari is going to have a baby."

Rakóssy was silent for a time. At last he said. "That's all we need, a pregnant woman. What's the matter, couldn't she get to the Gypsies on time?"

Arpád jerked his head up. His eyes glittered. "She wanted it. And I wanted it. I've told you. That's all." He went out.

Rakóssy stared at the door. He turned slowly and picked up his razor to shave himself. He saw his face, swollen and bruised, in the mirror and put down the razor. He went out into the corridor and down.

Catharine and her train were in the courtyard. Rakóssy helped her dismount. Arpád was standing beside Mari. Rakóssy gave her a measuring look, and Arpád first tried to look angry and finally blushed.

"It is much bigger than Hart," Catharine said, looking up at the walls.

"Yes." Rakóssy turned again toward Arpád. "Take care of the cannon."

Arpád raised his hand, saluting, and went off. Mari watched him go. She stared uncertainly after him, and

Catharine said, "Mari, come with us."

Mari turned, pouting. Catharine smiled and reached out her hand to her. They went after Rakóssy into the castle.

"You might get lost in here," he said. "I'll give you a page until you learn your way around."

"They all joined you?"

"All but one."

She paused to look into a study lined with books. The rug was beautiful, and she went into the room, admiring it. Rakóssy said, "This was Malencz's office. We used to hold the treaty conferences here, he and Kamal ibn Yusuf and I."

"The rug is lovely. I've never seen such colors."

"It's from Baghdad. Malencz and his ancestors were rich."

"But not anymore."

"I'm sending all his treasure to Buda, to buy black powder and cannon shot."

"Take me to our room."

She went out past him. He looked down at her. He took her by the hand. She squeezed his fingers so hard that his signet ring cut his index finger.

When they reached their room, she sent Mari to have her trunk brought up. She admired the rug here, too, and the carving on the great bed and the oil painting on the wall.

Rakóssy sat down. "I'm glad you're here," he said.

"You don't look well. What happened to your face?"

"Nothing."

"You do look ill." She took off her gloves.

"What's the matter?" he said. "You act uninterested."

"I am interested," she said. "But I liked Hart better."

"So do I."

"We'll never go back again," she said. She sat down. "We'll never go back again, will we?"

She looked quickly toward him, and the tears ran down her cheeks.

He got up and came to her, drew her out of the chair, and put his arms around her. She clutched him. She turned her face into his shirt and wept. He rocked her lightly, talking some gibberish, and kissed her hair. She grew tired of standing up and pulled at him. He picked her up and sat down in the chair and held her on his lap. She cried and sobbed and he kissed her. She began to feel much better, and she stopped crying.

"Now, what was that all about?" he said, playing with her hair.

"I don't know." She shut her eyes. "Ever since you left, I've had to be sensible and calm."

"Are you all right now?"

"Yes."

"Get up, then. I've got work to do. Here comes Mari."

"I'm not going to."

"Catharine," he said. He curled her hair around his finger. "Did you know that Mari is going to have a baby?"

"Yes."

"Get up."

"Oh, all right."

She stood and turned to face Mari, who was ordering the porters around with the trunks.

Rakóssy said, "You'll have to go down and tell the cook what to make us for dinner. She has a list of all the food we have. I gave her orders on how much she can use in a day, but she's stupid."

"How many servants do we have?"

"Forty-two. You have charge of them. Thirty-one women, six old men, and five boys."

"Only forty-two?"

"They'll get along." He stopped by the door. "I'll send up a page to show you around." He lingered a moment, watching her, his face guarded and pensive, and went out.

"Well," Catharine said. "I suppose we're here."

"Yes." Mari sent the porters away. "Arpád told Jansci about the baby and he was angry."

"Don't worry."

Mari went to the window. "What's that down there?"

Catharine looked. There was a flat-roofed building just below. "I think it's the stable."

"There's Arpád."

Arpád was putting cannon on the wall by the Countess Gate. The river shone beyond the gate, flooding west. The bridge was of gray-green stone.

"I'm going down to the kitchen," Catharine said. "I'll send for you when I need you."

Mari said, "I suppose it might cause trouble. The baby."

"Don't worry, Mari. I'll take care of you."

She went down to the kitchen. The cook was tiny and very old. Catharine sat at the baking table, drinking milk, while the woman told her what they had in the storerooms. They were curing meat and storing it, and bringing in vegetables and fruit and storing them in the basement, where it was cool. Catharine had never realized how the garrison of a castle was fed, how such quantities of food could be prepared.

All afternoon she listened to the cook and watched the women working in the kitchen. They baked bread for the evening meal until the loaves stood in ranks on the cooling racks. The kitchen was full of the smell of baking.

She went back to her room. It was nearly sundown, and the little page looked weary.

"Are they still working?" she asked.

"They're digging up a trench in front of the castle," the page said, "and making a breastwork."

She looked down at the roof of the stable. A swallow flew up almost to her window, wheeled away, and swept down to the stable and in through the open door. "You may go if you wish."

"If it please you, my lady."

The page bowed very correctly and went off. The little feather in his cap bounced when he walked.

Rakóssy walked along the wall toward Arpád. He gestured with his right hand and said something. Arpád looked as if he were thinking. After a while he nodded and said something, motioning with his hands.

She could see the men digging up the plain, beyond the wall. It was just like chess—first line of defense, second line, and the third the desperation measures when you fought with castle and pawns to protect the King. She wondered if there was a priest here.

Mari's baby. She wondered why Mari could have a baby and she couldn't. She looked down at the carpet. Vrath was full of beautiful things. The table by the window was of some heavy dark wood she did not recognize, and it had been oiled and cared for so well that it glowed almost of itself.

We'll live here from now on, she thought. And I can give balls and feasts. He'll be released from the King's ban and we can live . . . sedately. She took off her shoes and let her feet sink into the carpet. It was so different from Hart, almost like Vienna.

Rakóssy came in. "When are we going to eat?" He sat down and put his head back. "Oh, God. I'm worn out."

She went to stand behind him and massaged his shoulders. "I'll send down for dinner now. You should bathe."

"Do I smell bad?" He sniffed.

She laughed. "Yes."

He stood up, stripping off his doublet and shirt, and poured water into a bowl. Catharine sent Mari to the kitchens.

"How is it going, János?"

"Well enough. We're building a breastwork out beyond the front wall." He rubbed his fingers over his chin. "I don't know what good it will do, but it might slow them down and break up their charges."

"And the cannon?"

He stropped his razor. "If the Turks knock out the front wall, they'll knock out half the cannon. On the bridges I have them stopped. I can hold both bridges from the walls."

He had bruises on his body, too. Catharine watched him shave. Mari and two kitchen girls came in and laid out their dinner. Mari bustled around giving orders. Rakóssy put on a clean shirt and sat down. He looked over at Mari and examined her around the middle.

"My lord," Mari said.

Rakóssy grinned. He ate a little and immediately went to bed. Catharine and Mari went into the study next door.

"Help me out of this gown," Catharine said. "Nobody will come in here except János."

"Everybody's really working," Mari said.

"How is Arpád?"

"Fine. He's made friends with one of Malencz's old knights. Named Béla." She laughed. "He's a real cock rooster, that one."

Catharine turned around, and Mari lifted the gown up over her head and shook it out. "You know how Denis' face was all banged up when he got to Hart?"

"Yes."

"And did you see the bruises on Jansci?"

"How could I miss them?"

Mari grinned. "That's a whacking big black eye he's got."

"It certainly doesn't improve his looks."

"Or his temper, Arpád says. Anyhow, Denis and Jansci had a fight."

"What about?"

"Over Denis going back to Hart."

"Oh, my God."

"Arpád says that Denis saw he couldn't possibly beat Jansci, so he gave in. Everybody was very disappointed."

"Why?"

"Oh, some of them think that Denis could beat Jansci."

"Well, God help us. I hope they never know."

"It might be good for him. Shall I bring you some wine?"

"No, thank you. Why?"

"Nobody's ever beaten him. That's not good for anybody. May I go now?"

"Yes. Where are you?"

"Just down the corridor a turning. On the right side."

"Good night."

"Good night, my lady."

Catharine went into the bedroom and lay down. He was sound asleep. The black eye looked ridiculous. He looked belligerent even in his sleep.

If my mother had known, when she was lying beside the King, that her younger daughter would someday be in a cold, drafty castle in Hungary, married to a baron and waiting for a war, she would have gotten out of bed and never come back. Catharine smiled. There, Mother. That's one I've put over on you.

A week later Alexander and the knights he had taken with him returned from Buda with three wagons loaded with powder and shot. Rakóssy said that there was enough to keep them for a year, and had them take one wagon to Denis. The rest they stored in a dungeon two doors away from Malencz's cell.

Catharine heard that Malencz was still alive and lost her temper. "When a snake's bitten you, you kill it," she said.

"My, my, how ruthless of you. It must be your Hapsburg relations coming out." Rakóssy grinned. "Don't worry about Malencz."

She saw that he was taken food every morning and every night, although she wished that someone would forget about him. She made Arpád set a watch over him. Once she herself went down and looked through the barred window in the door, feeling like a child stealing a look into a haunted room. She saw a man lying on a pallet asleep, a rich blanket over him. His cell was large and dry, and he had water, a razor, soap, clean clothes. But no books, and she knew that he was a bookish man. She gave orders to the warder to give him some books.

"You should kill him," she said to Rakóssy.

"He's harmless," he said. "Don't worry about him."

The men worked like animals. Even Rakóssy took his turn at digging. He and Arpád, Alexander and Béla would sit on the balcony in the front of the castle in the evenings, drinking and talking about the Turks. Sometimes Catharine and Mari were allowed to sit with them.

Béla could not speak Turk, and he did not know very much about them. Arpád was teaching him a little Turk.

"If you're ever caught," Arpád said, "just say, 'La ilaha il-Allah.' " The others laughed.

"What does that mean?" Béla said. "Hello, you swine of Moslems?"

"There is no God but Allah," Arpád said. "It means you're a Moslem. That's their idea of a Credo."

"Better, too," Alexander said. "It's shorter."

Rakóssy shrugged. "There isn't much difference between the Christian Credo and the Moslems', or even the Jews'. They all say the same thing."

"I didn't know the Jews had a Credo," Catharine said.

"Ben Jakub told it to me once."

They waited patiently, but finally Catharine said, "Well, what is it?"

"Hear, O Israel, the Lord is our God, the Lord is one."

"That isn't like ours at all," Mari said.

"Women," Arpád said.

"Christians just go into more detail," Rakóssy said.

"Are you a Christian, János?" Catharine said.

"I was baptized."

"Do you believe in it?"

"Oh, God. What a question. Do I believe that fifteen hundred years ago a man got himself crucified and died and came back to life again? Or do I believe that a religion is a good thing to have and that being a Christian is useful—"

"Useful?" Catharine said. "Dear God, what a terrible—"

Rakóssy put his hands over his ears to shut out the noise. "Don't," he said to the men, "marry an intelligent woman. They are forlorn creatures, misfits, and very nasty when crossed."

"János Rakóssy."

"Do Gypsies have a religion?" Mari said.

"They're Christians," Catharine said. "They were the people who turned Mary and Joseph and the Child from their door on the flight into Egypt."

"Then they can't be Christians," Rakóssy said. "Maybe you're not an intelligent woman after all."

"Why are they called Gypsies if they aren't Egyptians?" Catharine said. "You think you're so clever, all you men do—"

"They don't call themselves Gypsies, they call themselves Romany. That's like you westerners calling us Hungarians, thinking that we are descendants of the Huns. But we call ourselves Magyars, and that's what we are."

"How do you know you aren't Huns?"

"Because we're Magyars," Rakóssy said.

"Maybe your people changed their name. Maybe you're the lost tribes of Israel. Maybe you're even Gypsies."

The four men sat up straight and glared at her. She laughed.

"I knew that would get you all. You're blood-proud, the lot of you."

"And with reason," Arpád said. "Magyars are the best people in the world."

"Your grandmother was a Czech," Rakóssy said.

"Well, she had the sense to bed down with a Magyar, didn't she?"

"Even being part Czech is—"

"You're only half Magyar," Catharine said. "You're half Greek."

"Well, that's better than being Spanish, God knows. I wouldn't be Spanish if—ouch! Quit it. Quit it." He grabbed Catharine by the wrists. "Sit down like a good girl. After all, you're a Magyar by marriage. You can afford to look down on—ouch! Catharine, stop it."

He covered his head with his arms. She smacked him on the crown with her open hand and sat down again.

The other three men were laughing. "Nicely done, my lady," Béla said.

"For a Spaniard," Arpád said and pretended to duck.

"And a Christian," Rakóssy said. "Is it safe to come out?" He lowered his arms. "You're a good little Crusader. You should be a Janissary."

"A Janissary?"

"Infantry," Arpád said. "Turks. They're terrible fighters. Almost as bad as we are in a fight. Pure poison."

"And they're Christians," Rakóssy said. "So you're eligible, Catharine."

"Have you ever fought one?" Béla asked.

Rakóssy shook his head. "God, no. We fight border garrisons, not main-line infantry. We'll see them when the Turks come."

"Spahis are cavalry, aren't they?"

"Yes."

"Mustafa's men aren't Spahis," Arpád said. "There're just horsemen. Mustafa is a ghazi. Whatever happened to that brother of his?"

"He probably sent him to Constantinople faster than he could spit," Alexander said. "That boy was stupid."

"Who is Mustafa's brother?" Catharine said.

"His name was Harun," Rakóssy said. "The dumbest Turk in the world. He came up to join big brother and got himself captured. I got hold of him and ransomed him. That's how I paid back the Fuggers."

"But Mustafa's clever."

"Who is Mustafa?" Béla said.

Arpád reared back. "By God in Heaven, man, where have you been? Who is Mustafa? Mustafa ibn Ismail, the master of Cliff's Eye, the Sultan's commander in the Transylvanian Alps, that's who Mustafa is. And he's clever. My lord, do you remember that time we got cornered up by Turkish Springs?"

"Mustafa," Rakóssy said, "likes to catch people in traps. One time two, three summers ago we went up to burn a supply cache way the hell up on the heights, and he got wind of us and herded us neat as you please into a corner. We didn't even know he was there until we were caught."

"How did you get out?" Béla said.

"That you wouldn't have believed," Arpád said. He leaned forward. "They had us right up on the heights with our backs against a stone cliff. But it started to rain, and thunder and lightning and all, the whole thing. Right up there in the peaks, on the top of the world—it was raining so hard you couldn't see your horse's head if you were in the saddle, and the lightning rolled from one peak to another, the rocks were crashing down around us, and the thunder—"

Alexander said, "So we left. We just beat it out of there like a bunch of drenched rats, and Mustafa couldn't see us or control his men enough even to try to catch us."

"Were you frightened?" Catharine said to Rakóssy.

Rakóssy grinned. "You might say so."

"The lightning," Arpád said. "Big balls of it, jumping from rock to rock like goats. Alexander came running at me—he'd lost his horse—and his mail was all lit up with some kind of blue fire. My horse almost kicked his head off."

"Will Mustafa fight us if the Sultan comes?" Catharine said.

"Probably."

They would talk like that for hours, after they had finished working for the day. Catharine thought that they missed their old kind of war where nobody really ever got hurt. They talked about Mustafa's grand designs and elaborate traps and Rakóssy's lightning strikes. They talked of the stealing of the Sultan's Id-al-Fitr gift to Mustafa, a golden urn, and how they had had to throw it into a lake when the pursuit got too close. They talked of how Mustafa had sent Rakóssy a full suit of Turkish clothes and a copy of the Koran one Christmas, and how Rakóssy had grown a beard and put on the robes and fooled the master of a supply train into thinking that he was Mustafa. Mustafa himself was a Hafiz; he had memorized the Koran.

"Hafiz will give all of Bokhara, all of Samarkand," Catharine said.

"That was another Hafiz," Rakóssy said.

April brought almost constant rain. They had finished the earthworks and planted sharp stakes in it, facing the plain, to stop headlong charges. Rakóssy had a ditch dug beneath the front wall of the castle and ordered brush piled in it as high as a man's waist. The cannon were in place and the larders were bursting with food. Rakóssy found broken and fouled drainage ditches in the back courtyard, on the side against the river, and ordered them cleaned and fixed. He taught all the men in the garrison how to clean, load, charge and fire the cannon.

They gathered up a flock of sheep and goats and put it to graze on the little plain, while several of the men built a pen for them in the back courtyard. The men from Hart and the men from Malencz's old army had a rivalry going. Once or twice it broke into active fighting, and each time Rakóssy roared and swore and beat the offenders. When it rained, it was worse.

Denis sent a letter and told Rakóssy that he should have scraps of metal and stones sewn into canvas sacks for shot. When the cannon exploded the canvas burned away and the scraps flew like a great scythe over the field. Catharine read the letter to Rakóssy. At the bottom she read, "No sign yet. We have seen no messengers. Shall I send my own scouts?"

"Tell him," Rakóssy said, "that the stable at Hart has two feet of little stones under the floor. Tell him not to send his own scouts. Ask him if he's figured out a way to shoot fire."

"Greek fire," Catharine said.

"Nobody knows the secret for that."

The horses grazed on the plain along with the sheep and the goats, saving fodder inside the castle. Cartloads of vegetables from the cellars of the peasants rattled into the courtyard and were sent quietly down to the basement and stored. And yet there was no sign of the Turks.

Rakóssy was having trouble with Arpád, who was the leader of a little bunch of the men from Hart who persistently baited the new recruits. Converts, Arpád called them. Although he and Béla were good friends, Arpád would pick fights with most of the others and beat them, being much bigger and stronger. Rakóssy berated him for it, but Arpád had fallen into a habit of sullen silence.

A messenger came from the north during the middle of April and hailed the porter at the Main Gate. He said that he was from the Diet at Buda.

Rakóssy went to the rampart and called, "What brings you?"

"I bear a message from the Diet of Hungary, signed and sealed by the King."

"Who is it for?"

"Baron János Rakóssy."

"He is not here," Rakóssy said.

The messenger said slowly, "I think he is."

"He is not."

"Give me entrance."

"While he is not here, I can give no man entrance."

"In the name of the King and the Diet of Hungary, I demand it."

"You could come in the name of the Emperor or the

Pope, but unless you come in Rakóssy's name, you cannot go through this gate."

"What should I do with this?" The messenger held up the packet with the summons.

"Take it back with you. Rakóssy cannot read. There is no man here who can." Rakóssy grinned. "Take it back to the Diet and the King."

Another rider was coming. Rakóssy looked toward him and swore. "Open the gate," he said, "but make sure you let in only the Gypsy." He turned back to the messenger. "Go to Buda. And keep your ears open on the way."

"My horse is tired."

"There is a village only a little way west. You probably passed it. Go there."

The Gypsy reined in by the gate. Rakóssy did not recognize him. He went down to the courtyard and called, "What news?"

The Gypsy pretended not to hear him. The gate rose and he rode through. Rakóssy waited for him. The Gypsy dismounted. He looked up at the guns and the men on the walls.

"The Turks," he said and shrugged. "Lots of them, Rakóssy."

Rakóssy called a man to take the Gypsy's horse. "Come up with me." He started across the courtyard. "Arpád, Béla, Alexander, come along." To the Gypsy: "Does my brother know?"

The Gypsy nodded quickly.

Rakóssy knocked on his door. Mari said, "Come in."

They went in. Catharine was sitting by the window, but she stood up when she saw them all.

"Sit down," Rakóssy said to the men with him. He made the Gypsy sit in the big carved chair and sat down himself on the oak chest at the foot of the bed with his legs dangling. "Now. How many?"

The Gypsy looked as if he were counting. He shook his head. "Many."

"Where?"

Catharine sat down again. She looked at none of them. Her face was serene.

"Upriver from the Iron Gate, on the plain."

"How long ago was this?"

"Four days."

"You rode fast. Horsemen or infantry?"

"Most of them were on foot."

"Coming fast?"

"Yes. Very fast."

"Were they all together or spread out?"

"Oh." The Gypsy's eyes were wide. "They were scattered all over the plain. There are drummers and pipes and cymbals. You can hear them miles away. You can hear them marching for miles. There are thousands of them."

"Janissaries. The Jew, ben Jakub. Have you seen him?"

"They killed him."

"What? A Jew?"

"They caught him and killed him. I saw."

"Why?" Arpád said.

"They thought he would tell us," Rakóssy said.

"Venn was with me," the Gypsy said. "You know Venn?"

Rakóssy nodded.

"He said to tell you that Mustafa was with them."

"Guns. Did you see any cannon?"

The Gypsy shrugged. "They had wagons. They had more wagons than I've ever seen, big ones, huge, all covered."

"How many?"

"Three hundred, maybe. Maybe more. In a train."

"You're lying," Béla said.

"He isn't," Rakóssy said. "He wouldn't lie to me."

"I don't lie," the Gypsy said to Béla. "To you, maybe, not to him." He looked at Rakóssy. "I don't lie. Maybe more than three hundred. I think so."

"How many men?"

The Gypsy opened his mouth, shut it again, and shrugged. "I don't know."

"Guess. Think about them."

"I don't know. Thousands. Many thousands. Maybe a million."

"All right," Rakóssy said and shut Béla up with a glance. "Catharine, bring me that Spanish necklace of yours."

Catharine brought the necklace from her trunk. Rakóssy held it out to the Gypsy. "Give this to Trig Columbo."

The Gypsy put the necklace in his shirt. He stood up.

"Trig says," the Gypsy said, "that he doesn't think he will see you again, maybe. If there is anyone you want to send to him to take care of for you, he will do it graciously."

Rakóssy grinned. "Trig Columbo is getting sentimental in his dotage. Tell him for me that if he wants anything kept in a safe place for him while the Turks are here, to send it to me and I will keep it for him."

The Gypsy smiled, showing all his yellowed teeth, and said, "I think we are going to Poland for a while. Goodbye."

He went out. Catherine said, "You should have asked if you could give him my most expensive necklace."

"I should have looked like a damn fool asking you if I could give away anything. You've worn it only once. You don't like it much, do you?"

"It's all right."

"A million Turks?" Arpád said.

Rakóssy stretched. "Try fifty thousand. That sounds like a nice figure."

"When will they be here?"

"That depends on them. It could take them a month. Or they could be here the day after tomorrow. If they come here at all."

"They will," Arpád said.

Rakóssy shut his eyes. "Barricade the two bridge gates.

Use the wagons we brought the cannon in. Make it so that even if they blow the gates to pieces they won't be able to get through. Send me Stepan Hálasz."

Arpád leaned out the door and called for a page, dropping his voice a full octave. When the page came, Arpád sent him for Stepan Hálasz. He turned back toward Rakóssy.

"Is there anything else?"

"Not unless you have any ideas."

"Me?" Arpád touched his chest.

"Yes. Of late you've been acting as if you knew everything, everybody, and all the ways to do things in the world. Don't tell me you're waiting for orders or anything dull like that."

"I—"

"You will get out of here. Now."

Arpád glanced at Mari, turned on his heel, and stamped out. Catharine said, "Mari, go fetch me some water from the kitchen."

Mari went and shut the door quietly behind her.

Catharine smiled. She folded her hands in her lap. "So. So, here we are."

"I'm glad they're coming. I was getting sick of waiting."

He stood up, went to the window, and looked out, looking south. Catharine said, "We have plenty of food."

"We'll have to bring the sheep in."

"I'll have to make sure we've got enough hay and grain."

"We just brought in a crop."

She watched him, keeping her head turned, so that her neck began to ache. "And you've finally gotten back at Arpád."

"Arpád got what was coming to him."

Stepan Hálasz came in. Rakóssy wheeled. "Take two horses and go to the ridge by Hart. Keep a watch until the Turks come, and then come back here and tell me how many there are."

"And if I can't get back?"

"I think you'll be able to."

He thought of sending a letter to Denis. But Denis knew already that the Turks were coming. There was nothing Rakóssy could tell him.

"Denis!" Catharine said suddenly.

He looked at her.

"Denis is in Hart. Will they attack Hart?"

She looked frightened. He said, "I think so."

"You left Denis there—poor little Denis—to fight them all alone." She stood up. "You have to bring him here. He's entirely inexperienced. They'll kill him." She was panting, and she had made fists of her hands in front of her. "It isn't right," she said. "Why should Denis—"

"Why should any of us?" he said. He had it in his throat to say that if Trig Columbo was right, they were all going to die, that probably they would all die. He took her right hand in his and straightened out her cramped fingers.

"Denis will do as well as anybody," he said. "He'll do as well as I would."

"He's too young," she said. She sighed. "I'm sorry. But he doesn't have a charmed life."

"And I do?" he said.

She looked at him, surprised, and suddenly laughed. "Yes, my dear, you certainly do." She kissed his cheek and drew her hand from his and went softly out the door.

Stepan Hálasz came back in the evening of a hot, cloudy day, some eight or ten days after the Gypsy had gone, and said that Hart was besieged by at least five thousand men and twenty guns, that there had been some kind of exchange between a Turk messenger and Denis under a flag of truce, and that immediately afterward the guns had started up. He said that the Turks would be wary of Denis' guns, and he smiled when he said it.

"About half of them charged up that slope, and he held back with the guns until they were almost at the walls. God, I saw it and I was shouting at him to shoot. Then he shot, and he mowed them down. I've never seen so many down, kicking and flopping around."

After that, he said, the Turks settled down to hammer Hart to pieces. He left as soon as he saw that they would not charge again.

Rakóssy ordered a triple watch on the walls and went to bed. In the early morning Béla woke him up. The Turks were at Vrath.

Rakóssy went to the walls and stood between two cannon, looking out at the Turks. They were still arriving. Their trains and columns straggled out across the plain to the horizon. A great cloud of dust hung over the whole plain, rising up into the southern sky. They were unloading their guns and rolling them into line. He heard drums pounding. A detachment of Janissaries jogged toward the river not far from the Chapel Gate. A wagon rumbled after them.

The Magyars were all on the walls of Vrath, watching the Turks roll up. On the wall there was silence. The camp grew on the plain, starting near the river's edge, where Janissaries were erecting a tent of green silk; the camp spread off in a crescent toward the other riverbank. Boys with strings of horses ran through the newborn camp toward the water.

The sun rose higher. The line of the Turkish cannon grew, unbroken from riverbank to riverbank. Rakóssy took off his doublet and leaned against the wall. The air was gritty. He looked up behind him and saw Catharine on the balcony on the Countess Tower. She wore a white gown, and her hair shone. The women were with her.

Alexander, gnawing on a carrot, said, "Big bastards, those guns."

"They are that."

Alexander laughed deep in his chest. "Arpád got his

hat rammed down his throat, I take it."

Rakóssy looked up at Alexander's face. "What was wrong with him?"

Alexander shrugged, still laughing, almost soundlessly. "Are all the guns loaded?"

"Yes."

"With scrap?"

"Yes."

Rakóssy looked south, squinting, trying to see through the cloud of yellow dust. "They'll be getting into position for at least another day."

He went down into the courtyard. They had brought the horses and the flocks in right after Stepan Hálasz got back from Hart, and in the rear courtyard they were slaughtering some of the sheep to cure the meat and store it. Three of the young boys were fishing from the wall. When Rakóssy showed up, they turned to watch him with hungry eyes. He noticed it and went over to them.

"What's the matter?" he said.

"Nothing, my lord."

The boldest boy spoke, but the other two suddenly became very interested in their lines.

"Go watch the Turks," Rakóssy said. "Go on."

"Oh, thank you, my lord, thank you." They ran off down the ramparts, shouting and laughing.

Rakóssy stood looking down at the lines, trailing down over the wall and bellying in the wind, until they dropped into the dark-green river. He called to another page to reel them in, and went on.

He spent the day doing nothing and saying nothing. He did not see Catharine except at dinner. After dinner, when it was dark, he went back to the walls and leaned against one of the cannon and watched the lights on the plain—torches and campfires, clustered all over and for almost a mile away south. He could see people moving in front of the fires. They were still not all collected, and he could hear wagons rumbling around, empty wagons and full. He could tell by the sound they made. In the darkness the great green tent opposite Chapel Gate shook and quivered with the wind.

After a while he went inside and went to bed.

All the next day the Turks made a big pretense of continuing to set up their cannon and move their troops into position, but by midmorning they were ready. In the midafternoon Béla and some of the other Magyars shouted insults and jeers, saying that the Turks should let the Magyars give it a try and it would be done in no time. Rakóssy listened to them, smiling.

"That should tell them it won't work," Arpád said.

"What?"

"They're trying to scare us, aren't they?"

"I don't think they ever thought it would," Rakóssy said.

That evening Rakóssy had dinner with all the knights in the great hall. They all shouted and laughed as loud as possible, so that the Turks would hear. After they had eaten, Catharine and Rakóssy went up to sit on the balcony. It was a beautiful night, without a moon, so that the sky was milky with stars.

"When this is done with," Rakóssy said, "I will buy you ten necklaces, each ten times better than the Spanish necklace."

"Anything would be better than that," she said. "Will we be a Count and Countess?"

"I doubt it."

"Let's go back to Vienna and spend a little time there."

"So you can prove something to your relatives?"

"Of course."

"No. I don't like Vienna."

"Oh, why not?"

"I don't know. I just don't."

"What's that green tent?"

"The Sultan, sweet."

"The Sultan? Oh, my."

He looked at her, and she laughed with a sound like shattering glass.

Early the next morning the Turks raised a truce flag and sent in a messenger. Rakóssy ordered the gun crews to the ready. He thought that the Turks would try a plunge for one or both of the bridge gates as soon as they thought the Magyars were off guard.

The messenger was letting his horse pick its way through the earthworks. It was Mustafa. Rakóssy went out on foot onto the plain, leaving the portcullis raised and the little door in the outer gate open behind him. He walked a little way and stopped.

Mustafa reined in before him. He made his chestnut mare prance and rear and stopped her dead with a great show of horsemanship. He held the white flag on the butt end of a lance. Bending, he stuck the lance into the ground.

"I hope you enjoyed Constantinople," Rakóssy said. He spoke Turk. "It was a cold winter up here. Probably much warmer by the Bosporus."

Mustafa raised an eyebrow. "And you, Rakós'. A most successful winter it was. How can I express to you my surprise and fellow-feeling—my delight and pride—when we heard from your brother that you had captured Vrath?" He paused. "He fought well, your brother. I did not expect it of him. Of course, one charge and . . ."

Rakóssy stared at him. The left corner of his mouth drew down.

"Useless, I see. You amaze me, Rakós'. I am delighted. We knew, of course, that you had gotten cannon with your new bride—The Emperor's kinswoman, I believe? And a plain girl, but one of great intelligence and wit, not what I expected you to marry. Thirty-five cannon. And of course we noticed that there were only eight at Hart, and then your brother said something about

Vrath. What was it? 'If you seek my brother, you will find him waiting for you at Vrath.' He and Kamal should have fun fighting each other, literati that they are. Imagine my master's glee when what seemed to be only a boring war should offer some tidbit of sport."

"I can imagine," Rakóssy said.

"Of course you can. He was overjoyed. And he has sent me now with some distaste to offer you terms. I say distaste, because he does not like to see such sport turned aside. Of course, I have told him that you are a man of some animal cunning, if not wit, breeding and subtlety, and he believes, as I do, that anybody but a complete moron would accept these terms with haste. But he is a generous man."

"You may give your generous master my greetings. Also my condolences on his losses at Hart yesterday morning."

"A feint. They only pretended to die. Allah protects us." Mustafa bowed. "He offers you these terms. Surrender Vrath to him, and you will continue on as his honored guests until he has subdued the rest of Hungary, when he will hold you all for easy ransoms."

"All?"

Mustafa considered this. He looked up at the sky. "My, what a lovely, lovely day. The heavens washed, as it were, with blue, adorned with the marvelous heraldry of the sun, a faint promise of heat, but no matter. Not a cloud there."

"Wonderful."

"There is one man of your troop, Rakós', whom the Sultan—blessed be his name and works—feels should enjoy a more prolonged stay in the bosom of Islam. This man the Sultan will honor with all the glory at his command. He will wash him with rose water and dress him in silks, he will deck his horse with gold and rubies and show him the wonders of the Faith."

"Your master is more than generous."

"More than that, my master would grant this man the

boon of eternal youth," Mustafa said. "Never would this man feel the cold of age or the bitter tooth of time. He would never sense the ebbing of life or the trembling of his ancient limbs or the chill of lost love and the oppression of ungrateful children—"

"You may tell your master that I long to embrace the wonders of Islam and drink the drink of eternal youth from his hands, but I have duties elsewhere. Much as I regret it."

"Rakós'. You have learned grace." Mustafa bent and picked up the lance with the white flag. "This woman must be more than human, if not more than female." He backed the mare three precise steps, stood in his stirrups and looked straight at Catharine.

"Good day, Rakós'," he said smoothly and whirled.

He galloped back toward the Turkish lines. Halfway there, he turned and flung the lance, end over end, to the ground. Rakóssy wheeled toward the Janissaries, gathered by the Countess Gate. Their drums broke out, and they bolted for the bridge. They ran straight for it. Rakóssy shouted, "Alexander."

On the heel of his voice the guns by the Countess Gate went off. The Janissaries pitched down, reeled away, and charged back out of range. The guns above Rakóssy's head roared once. Rakóssy went back through the gate.

The Janissaries apparently had orders to quit the attack as soon as they were threatened. The Sultan would not commit so large a band of his prize troops this early in the game. Rakóssy, on the walls, watched the Turk guns being prepared.

"What did he say?" Alexander said. He watched the men reloading the guns by the Countess Gate.

"Surrender and he'll ransom us after he's beaten the King."

"You too?"

Rakóssy looked at him. "Don't be funny."

Sulphur flared out there behind the Turk guns. Rakóssy knelt down and sighted over the nearest cannon.

"Take it up a turn of the screw."

"Yes, sir."

Alexander bent down to look along the cannon barrel. Rakóssy drew back a little. He sent a boy down to Arpád with orders to try to hit the green tent.

The Turkish cannon began to fire. They seemed soft in the beginning; the guns at either end fired first, and the heavy spring air muffled the sound slightly. The noise grew as the order of firing moved along the crescent, until, when the center guns went off, the roar was like a concussion of the air. The Turk guns fired in a double row, in two long, peeling successions beginning at opposite ends and coming together in the middle and moving on down their separate ways. Rakóssy felt disappointed. It was not even as exciting as a clash between twenty Turks and twenty Magyars.

He saw the shot strike the earthworks before the front wall. A mass of loose dirt flew up and sloughed back down again, spreading over the wooden spikes. The Turks moved their aim up. A ball struck the wall and the stone shuddered.

"Fire when you're ready," Rakóssy said.

It took the Turkish guns so long to fire in their succession that the first gun of each row was loaded and ready by the time the last had gone off. The stone dust and dirt and the smoke of Rakóssy's own cannon made it hard to see. His guns fired whenever they were loaded. The rhythm of the guns inside the walls sounded odd and toneless, almost.

He squinted and looked out. Arpád was trying for the green tent, but it was well out of range. The guns down there paused a moment and opened up again, this time cranked up as high as possible. Still the shot fell far short. Arpád quit.

Because of the order of firing of the Turkish guns, Rakóssy's men could anticipate them. They ducked rhythmically, all along the wall, like a long wave, rising after the gun opposite them had fired. They were not excited either. Rakóssy thought they would have been more excited if they had not known that this would go on for weeks at the least.

The heat was strong. He leaned out to see where the Turkish shot was striking and felt the wall quake under his hands.

"They're raising their aim," he said. "Watch out—and watch that they don't swing their aim around and catch you when you aren't looking."

A Turkish ball flew clear over the wall and crashed into the courtyard, shattering on the paving stones. A woman screamed. Nobody was hurt.

"Dig it out," Béla shouted. "We'll use it for shot."

Suddenly the men all along the wall cheered. Rakóssy jumped up on the merlon of the battlement in front of him and shaded his eyes. One of the Turk guns was lying in a mass of rubble, the muzzle jutting toward the sky.

"We got one," he said. He jumped down. "They'll move their guns back. Keep trained on that wreck, and we'll see if we can get anybody when they go in to drag it off."

"Are they going to go on like this all the time?" Béla said.

"They're just giving us a . . . Duck."

They dropped behind the wall. Another ball, screaming in the air, whirled over their heads and crashed behind them. Rakóssy looked around and saw that one of the young boys had been struck by a piece of flying junk. "Clear that courtyard," he shouted. "Get everybody inside. Go on."

"What was that noise?" Béla said.

Rakóssy shrugged. "They'll concentrate on one part of the wall after a while."

He went down the line a little and had two guns loaded with scrap. A group of mounted Spahis was loitering just beyond one of the Turks. Rakóssy set the aim on the guns himself. He wiped the sweat from his forehead and ducked with the rest of them when the guns opposite them fired. The stone dust sifted down over the men and the guns. The Turks were raising their aim on this side.

"Fire," he said. "This one. Hold the next."

The flame spurted and vanished into the touch hole. Rakóssy counted, automatically, and at three the cannon roared and hurtled back against its braces.

"Fire the next," he said.

The wide scatter of junk from the first gun raked across the front rank of the Spahis. Ten of them collapsed where they stood. Two wounded horses screamed and careened into a gun crew. The second gun went off. Its aim was slightly higher. The Spahis had withdrawn only a little and the shot ripped into them again. This time they whirled and galloped off far into their own lines. The bodies they left behind looked broken.

The Turks were stilling their guns. Rakóssy concentrated on trying to knock out the guns nearest the wall. The whole Turkish army was drawing back, aware now of the range of Rakóssy's guns. They moved quietly and in good order. Their guns all fell silent, and once all their cannon were out of danger, the Turks settled down for what looked like lunch. One of the guns by the Countess Gate had wiped out a gun crew, but before a heavier gun could sight in on the cannon a dozen other Turks had jumped forward to drag it to safety.

"Stop firing, all of you," Rakóssy shouted, and the order echoed down the walls.

The smoke and dust blew slowly off to the east. The ground along the earthworks and way out by the Turkish guns was torn up in chunks and holes, stained black, and in places faintly smoking. Turks with litters jogged out to pick up the dead and wounded. The wind blew off the smoke. There was a strange smell in the air.

"How many men did we lose?" Rakóssy said to Béla, and Béla laughed and shook his head.

"Give everybody a cupful of wine at dinner," Rakóssy said and went down to the courtyard to get himself a drink of water.

* * *

The Turks spent the afternoon building a sort of tower in the middle of their camp. No guns were fired. The Magyars in Vrath cleaned up the mess in the court-yard. The page boy was in a bed in the great hall with a gaping wound in his leg. Rakóssy went in to look at him and thought that he would die. He told one of the women from the kitchen to care for him.

In the evening he went back onto the walls with Ar-pád. The tower was finished. A man in black climbed up to its peak. He lifted his arms. A ram's horn blew some-where.

The Turks shook out prayer rugs and washed them-selves. They knelt, that whole great army, facing south, and in a single thunderous voice began to pray.

Béla had come up to stand by Arpád. He laughed at the Turks.

Rakóssy whirled. "I didn't hear you laughing this morning. Do you think they're children? Get out of here."

Arpád turned to look down at him. Rakóssy said, "Have the women render some of that sheep's fat in the kitchens and store it up here. What's the matter?"

"Nothing," Arpád said. "I will."

"And double the watch."

Arpád turned to look out onto the plain. "One of the women told Mari that she thought you would cast a spell on the Turks."

"That I would . . ." Rakóssy laughed. "Well, tell her to tell them that a Christian sorcerer can't throw spells onto Moslems."

"A Christian?"

"Yes. I am a Christian. They are Moslems." He waved out at the Turks, who had stopped praying and were moving around their camp again. "Come on, let's go. I have something I want to think about."

* * *

Rakóssy leaned on the balcony rail with Catharine, watching the gunners. It was very hot. His shirt was glued to his back. The smoke and dust made his throat gritty, and he coughed.

"There," he said, "that's Mustafa, and I suppose that's the Sultan with him, on the white horse."

"I can't stand the noise," she said.

Half the Turkish guns were pouring heavy stone shot into the Chapel Gate. A lot of the Turks, with some guns, had left that morning, headed down the river. Rakóssy thought they were going to try to ford the river and come up on the other side. Rakóssy's guns fired only if the Turks or their guns happened to come within range, and the Turks were careful about that.

"He's wasting shot," Rakóssy said.

The Chapel Gate's wooden draw gate was splintered and wrecked. The iron portcullis and the wagons stacked against it still blocked the gate, and the Turk shot only added to the barricade. The portcullis was twisted into knots and one broken bar thrust out into the courtyard, spotted with rust.

"I wish I knew how Denis was doing," Catharine said.

"If they take Hart, we'll know it."

"They'll try to fool us. The way Mustafa did."

"The only proof I'll take is Denis."

"You mean if they capture him."

"If they take Hart, they'll tear it apart looking for him. They'll bring him here and pitch his body over the walls."

"Oh, my God," she said. "Don't say that."

"That's the way it will be."

She recoiled and went inside. He leaned on the railing and watched the Turks play their games.

They're going to kill my brother, he thought. Denis with his fair skin and his small light bones.

He thought that the Turks were only testing their

guns. They knew by now that the gates were blocked. He had an idea for protecting the Main Gate, which the Turks were bound to work on next. He stared at his guns and their crews, gathered around and waiting, half naked and sweating, for the Turks to wander within range. A band of Spahis feinted toward one of the bridges, and the gun crews leapt up and stood by their guns. One gun went off. The Spahis skipped away, unhurt, light as sparrows.

Rakóssy went inside. Catharine was sitting with Mari, talking about the colors they would use in a new gown. Mari was big as a barrel already, although the baby was not due until July. They gave him civil looks and words and he went down to the dungeons, where it was cool.

He checked his supply of gunpowder. He had more than he would ever need. The King had not forced prices up on the stock of powder in Buda. The King was stupid.

While he was there he remembered Malencz. He went to his cell and looked in. Malencz was sitting on the bed, reading. He looked up.

His face changed from the quiet, heavy repose Rakóssy remembered to a tight anger. The blood mounted in his cheeks.

"You traitor. You bloody traitor."

Rakóssy shook his head. "You'll have to think of something new."

"Bastard, then. Will you take that? You aren't Alexander Rakóssy's son. You're a stablehand's son." Malencz drew closer to the door. His voice whistled. "Your mother was a whore, bastard. A whore, brought to bed of a Devil's imp."

Rakóssy threw back his head and laughed. Malencz's voice rolled the vowels. "A whore, a whore, bastard."

"She's dead," Rakóssy said, "and she can't hear you. And I don't have to. So tell it to the walls, Malencz. Tell it to your books."

He went down the corridor to the stairs, laughing. He

went up to his room and lay down on the bed, laughing.

Catharine looked up. "What's so amusing, my dear?"

"I think Malencz is going mad."

"János, you can't leave him alive."

"Oh, he's locked up, safe as a church. Safe as a whore in Babylon." He laughed again.

"János, are you well?"

"Perfectly."

"I think you should rest."

"All right."

He put his boots up on the bed and shut his eyes. The women stared at him. He laughed again, sleepily, and rolled over.

Catharine tapped Mari on the shoulder, signed her to come closer, and said into her ear, "Go fetch up something to drink."

Mari got up and went silently away. Catharine stood and put down her sewing and went to the bed. She sat down next to Rakóssy. She put her hand on his back. He turned over and put his arms around her.

"Kiss me," he said.

"If I may." And she did.

Mari came back with a pitcher of cold milk. At the door she heard their soft voices. She smiled. Rakóssy said something, and Catharine laughed. Mari took the pitcher into the next room and went down to find Arpád.

Catharine lifted herself to one elbow and looked down at him. His face, sleeping, was a wicked face. The corners of his mouth were marked by deep short lines. The shadow of his beard was dark and rough. This is why Carlotta loved him, she thought. Because when she lay next to him and he was asleep she could look down at him and see . . . Lucifer naked beside her. Thou son of the morning, morning star, Hesperus, the most beautiful of the sons of God, the chosen angel who presumed too much, the rebel against God. The ultimate traitor, she thought.

"O traitor," she said, "I love you."

"I know." He kissed her wrist. He put his arms around her and drew her down and kissed her mouth.

"Thou morning star," she said. "Who walked in the garden in the heat of the day."

"Accustoming myself to the fires of hell, obviously."

"Condemned forever to walk upon your belly."

"The better to slip through the Turks."

"Won't you ever play?"

"I don't like to play at being guilty, somehow."

"Do you want a boy or a girl?"

"Are you pregnant?"

"No."

"Good."

"Why can Mari get pregnant and not me? I want a baby, János. I want a baby."

"I'm trying."

"Oh, stop it."

He ran the tip of his tongue around the rim of her ear. "Let's have several of both kinds."

"You just want girls so that you can name them after your mother."

"Don't be jealous of my mother."

"Did you love her?"

"Not the way I love you. Go to sleep."

"János."

"Go to sleep, sweetheart. Go to sleep."

Rakóssy went down to the dungeons that night and got two kegs of gunpowder. He followed the dungeon corridor back into the foundations of the castle, curious suddenly. There were torches set in brackets along the walls for a stretch, but after a while they stopped. He took one from the bracket and went on, being careful with the gunpowder. The corridor wound on through the guts of the castle and ended in a blank wall.

There was a ladder standing against the wall. He set down the kegs, put the torch into a socket, and climbed up the ladder. It was rotten in parts and one of the rungs broke under his foot.

He found a trap door in the ceiling above the ladder and opened it. The warm smell of a stable flooded him. He heard the horses stamping and breathing. He put two fingers to his mouth and whistled. The black mare nickered.

He pushed the trap door all the way open and took the kegs out. The black mare nickered again when he passed her. He stopped and scratched her under the chin. "Getting fat, are you?"

He went out through the front door of the stable. He heard the swallows in their nest right over the door. He had thought at first that the cannon would scare them away.

His sentries on the walls were standing around talking. He told one of them to keep a watch on him and went through the Main Gate and walked quietly out to the breastworks. The ground smelled good out here. The stars were out. There was no moon, and the stars were faint and delicate.

He buried the two kegs in the earthworks on the side facing Vrath and tore pieces of white cloth from his shirt to mark them. He sat on the torn, dried earth for a while, looking out at the Turk camp. They had their sentries out, too. He saw men dark against fires talking and strolling. It was almost time for the evening prayer.

When the call to prayer went up, he rose and walked slowly back into Vrath. He found another ladder in the stable loft and lowered it through the trap door. He went upstairs and got into bed beside Catharine and went to sleep.

* * *

The next day the Turks started bombarding the Main Gate. The wooden part of the gate boomed like a drum. Rakóssy ordered some wagons hauled up near the gate in case it had to be blocked quickly.

All that day, and the next, and the next after that, the Turks pounded away at the gate, smashing the wood to a ruin. They knocked out the whole outer part of the gate, so that no two stones remained together. Eventually their shot was reaching through to the inner gate. One of the Magyars walked by the gate and got a wood splinter six inches long in the chest when a Turk ball finally broke through the inner gate.

When the gate was in rubble, the Turks stopped firing. Rakóssy ordered out two hundred men with pikes and held them at the ready, and he had the rendered sheep's fat taken up to the walls. Arpád thought that he meant to boil it and pour it on the Turks, but Rakóssy said that that was an old-fashioned idea and rarely worked.

The Turks waited for a day and a half. On the second day, after the sun had gone down, they started up a heavy gunfire, aimed for the top of the wall all around the Main Gate. The Janissaries lined up, rank on rank. Their armor reflected the red glow of the slow matches and their lances were like blades of grass.

Rakóssy climbed up onto the rampart by the Countess Gate. "Load up with scrap shot," he said. "Swing these guns around and aim for those white patches. Can you see them?"

Alexander squinted, ignoring the pounding of the Turkish guns. "Yes."

"Wait until I give you the signal." He went on down the wall, keeping low, until he reached the Main Gate. There he had the men pour the heavy, stinking sheep's oil over the wall onto the piles of brush in the ditches below. One man was killed doing that, and Rakóssy had his body taken down to the courtyard.

The Janissaries' drums began to rattle. Rakóssy's men

were gathered up in the courtyard, holding the long-bladed pikes. Arpád stood at their head, looking grim.

Rakóssy called down to him to keep the pikemen inside the inner gate. "Never mind. Do what I say for once."

The Turkish shot redoubled. The guns were concentrated on the area around the Main Gate, and they were aimed to strike the top of the wall, so that none of the men could do more than crouch behind the shuddering wall.

"Rakóssy!"

That was Béla.

"Look over there."

Rakóssy looked across the river. A shadowed mass of men and horses was moving up along the far bank, toward the Countess Gate bridge.

"Never mind, they won't be in any position to do us harm."

"Maybe." Béla crawled up beside him; his face was black with soot.

"Not tonight, at least."

There was a monstrous howl from the plain. The Janissaries attacked, screaming. The Magyars could see them only vaguely through the drifting smoke and dust. Rakóssy crept down past the edge of the Turks' fire and shouted to Alexander. He lifted his arm. Alexander was waiting with a slow match. The pipes and drums of the Janissaries wailed almost louder than the guns.

The guns on the wall near the Countess Gate opened up, cutting across the field, but the Janissaries were too far away. They raced on, screaming and beating their drums. They scrambled up over the earthworks, leapt down from the top, and hurtled on.

Rakóssy dropped his arm, and Alexander opened up with the Chapel Gate guns. Rakóssy was holding his breath. The air burned in his lungs. The fusillade from the Chapel Gate guns cut almost across the Janissaries' charge. They could see where the scrap had gone by the lines of thrashing bodies. The two powder kegs ex-

ploded. The Janissaries recoiled from it. The dead
sprawled on the ground around the earthworks in a fan
shape around the kegs.

The Janissaries kept coming. Rakóssy reached for a
torch and hurled it over the wall into the oil-soaked
brush. The voices of the Janissaries were high-pitched
and whining and the guns howled. The fire caught in the
oily brush and flames leapt up, licking at the wall and
shooting down the ditches with a soft crackling.

A wash of Turkish shot struck the top of the wall near
where he was standing. He turned, shouting to the men
around him to get down, feeling the rampart quiver and
buckle under his feet. A gun blew up and a piece of iron
clouted him across the knees. He fell and slid halfway off
the rampart. His head pounded. The noise was driving
him mad. Something heavy struck his shoulders and he
almost lost his grip. He lurched up blindly and caught an
iron brace on the wall. His fingers clamped around it. He
felt the heavy thing slide away from him and heard it fall
into the courtyard. The blood burst forth in a stream
from his nose. He lay, panting, against the warming
stone. He gulped and swallowed his own blood.

The guns stopped suddenly. The silence was like a
benediction.

There was a long Magyar cheer. He wiped the blood
from his face on his sleeve and looked around. Dead men
and a wrecked cannon lay on the broken rampart. Another cannon was in the courtyard on its back.

The drums had stopped too. They must have retreated. He shut his eyes again. Feet ran toward him on
the broken rampart and his men hauled him up, all soft
words and exclamations. One of his legs was cut to the
bone. They carried him to his bedroom. Mari screamed.
Catharine directed them to put him down and help her
undress him and bind him up.

He lay still, listening to Catharine's voice. The men
left and she pulled the covers up over him.

"Are you awake?"

"Yes." He turned his head.

She dabbed at his forehead with a damp cloth. "You were really bashed up, my dear."

He had a headache. "Something hit me on the head."

"Whatever it was was no match for your iron skull."

"Did we lose many men?"

"I don't know. Don't think about it. I'll take care of you. Go to sleep." She kissed his cheek. "Good night."

Pál said, "They've broken in the gate."

Denis stood up. "Let's go take a look."

"What will we do?"

Denis fought down the urge to say, "I don't know," and scream at the top of his lungs. He went down the corridor to the great hall, out that door, and stopped.

The gate was a mass of rubble. One of the big guns on the side of the gate had been knocked out. Two men were clearing away the dead. Denis went slowly across the courtyard, past the motionless turnstile, and looked out.

He could see straight down the slope to the Turkish guns. The infantry—they were not Janissaries; they were just infantry, and he was glad—were standing around talking.

"We have to block it," he said. "What have we got?"

Pál shrugged.

"Get the furniture out of the great hall. It's heavy enough. And the bedding from all the bedrooms. Go on. Get some of the others to help you."

Zoltan came running toward him. "This is insane," he said. His face poured sweat. "What do you think this is?"

"Thermopylae," Denis said. "What brought you out of your hole?"

"Denis," Zoltan said. "Denis, have you gone mad? Fighting—and killing, just like some wild young animal, all the things you hated your brother for, and justly, too. They offered you good terms, honorable terms, and you could end this meaningless, senseless—"

Denis spat. "Go back in your hole."

He went up the ladder and climbed the rampart, sloping from the collapse of the gate, to the last of the heavy guns. They had lost four guns so far. Six men were sitting around the gun, eating bread and cheese.

"They're damned cautious," one of them said. "They could have attacked any time."

"They'll wait until dark."

"How do you suppose they're doing at Vrath?"

Denis took a deep breath. "If Vrath had fallen, we would have heard of it. They would have strung my brother up in seventeen pieces right in front of us."

"As long as they hold out, we're all right," another man said. "We've got someplace to go if this heap gives out."

"If? When." The first man glanced at Denis. "How much food do we have, my lord?"

"Not much," Denis said. "I'm going to start slaughtering horses."

"Horses. You expect us to eat horses?"

"Wait until you start getting really hungry," Denis said. "You'll eat your own mother."

"Why don't we slaughter Anna?"

Denis laughed. "After the horses. And Zoltan."

They laughed softly, rocking on their heels.

"I wonder what terms they offered Vrath," Denis said.

"He probably offered them terms," the second man said. "Christ, he's a tough bastard. I'll bet Béla's sorry he ever threw in with him."

"Ask him," Denis said.

"I will, when I get to hell."

"Hungry?" One of the others offered part of his bread to Denis.

"I just ate," Denis said.

The Turkish guns began to fire again. Denis said, "On

your feet. Let's see if we can get that big gun in the middle."

Rakóssy was in bed for a long time, weak and sick. Catharine thought that he would limp for the rest of his life; she was worried that the wound would get infected.

Arpád and the others stood off a charge against the Chapel Gate bridge and a long, wearying attack on the Main Gate and the bridge together. The Turks seemed to be testing, probing here and there, trying to find weaknesses rather than to take the castle by storm. They bombarded the walls now, forsaking the gates. The noise was continuous. Catharine sat up during the night, watching Rakóssy, and wondered how he could sleep through it.

After more than a week had passed he was suddenly much better and wild to get out of bed. Catharine would not let him. She locked the room when she left. He got out and walked around the room with a staff to lean on, and he made all the men come to him and tell him what was going on.

"We've got a lot of wounded," Béla said. "A lot more than get killed. But they die. We've put them in the great hall."

Rakóssy rubbed his leg. "I was lucky."

Béla grinned. "No. You were Rakóssy."

Catharine said, "Who is tending the wounded?"

"The women from the kitchens," Béla said.

Rakóssy hauled himself around to face her. His face was leaner and his cheekbones looked higher and sharper. "Don't you go down there, you hear me?"

His vehemence surprised her. "I hear you, János."

The Turks hammered away with their heavy guns at the wall between the Main Gate and the Countess Gate, opposite the stable. They pounded at it from the plain and from across the river, never ceasing, but they tried no more charges. They had lost too many men and gained nothing.

Rakóssy left his room for the first time nearly three weeks after he had been wounded. He walked at first with a heavy staff. The Turks must have seen him on the walls; two Turks with bows rode in close to Vrath and shot arrows over the walls with messages tied to them. The messages were identical: "The Sultan congratulates the lord Rakóssy on his recovery."

Rakóssy doubted that the Turks would try to mine under the castle wall because of the nearness of the river. He ordered pans of water set along the base of the wall nonetheless, so that if the Turks did go to digging, the water would show the movements of the ground.

"They must be feeling very disgusted with themselves out there," Catharine said one day.

"Why?"

"Because they've been stood off by less than five hundred men."

"We have more than five hundred. I doubt they're feeling too badly about it. Most sieges are like this."

"Still—"

"Do you think we're low on morale?"

"Oh, no. Everybody's wonderful."

"That's the way it's always been."

Mari had her baby, far too early, and it died. They buried it in the back courtyard, where the sheep had been pastured. Catharine wept bitterly over it, as if it had been her own. Mari and Arpád made it known that they would have another almost immediately.

The long heat broke in the beginning of June, and it rained for four days straight, a heavy smothering rain.

Rakóssy covered his guns with straw and canvas. He did without the staff now, although he limped heavily. While the rain kept up he and his men built wooden roofs to protect the gun crews. The Turks merely sat on the plain waiting.

After the rain stopped, the bombardment began again. The Turks were sending out raiding parties. Rakóssy saw several troops of Spahis leave the camp in the week after the rain. He thought that the Sultan was getting restless.

"Do you feel proud?" Catharine said. "You and he— you are equals. You are matched together."

Rakóssy looked at the green tent. The Sultan was sitting in a chair in front of it, talking with his officers. One of the officers was Mustafa.

"This is nothing more than a game to him," Rakóssy said. "I'm nothing more to him than a fly he could crush with his riding whip."

"No."

Rakóssy shrugged. "The man's been raised in silks and gold. He's waited on by his slaves hand and foot and he's always obeyed without question. He knows nothing of me and I know nothing of him. If I walked over there as a beggar he would give me alms."

"And probably cut off your head."

Rakóssy threw back his head and laughed. "Probably."

"That's enough for me," she said.

"What a bloodthirsty little thing you are."

In the middle of June he counted his men. He had had five hundred and forty at the beginning of the siege, and now he had three hundred and two who were healthy and seventy-three wounded in the great hall. The women from the kitchens tended them under the magnificent hangings and gold inlay of generations of Counts Malencz.

Catharine went down one day to see the wounded. She went through the high door and stopped short. The hall was full of beds and bodies. Two or three women moved among them. She went slowly forward and stopped at the first bed. In it was a man of about Rakóssy's age; there was a long wound in his throat and another in his chest, a hole as if someone had scooped out a handful of his flesh. The wound on his neck was bandaged but his chest was open and bare. She saw the maggots crawling around in the oozing flesh.

"Sania," she said, and the woman came over.

"Look," Catharine said. "Can't you do anything?"

Sania shrugged. "The worms, they eat out the rot."

Catharine turned and ran out of the hall and was sick in the corridor.

She went off to find Rakóssy, her stomach sliding around inside her. He was on the balcony, talking to Béla. She came up and took hold of his arm.

"Yes, my lord," Béla said, and went out the door. Rakóssy looked down at Catharine.

"There's a boy in the great hall," she said, "and the worms are eating him."

"There are seventy-eight men in the great hall," he said, "and the worms are eating all of them. I told you not to go down there."

"Isn't there anything—"

"The women know all there is to be known."

"A doctor?"

"A doctor would prescribe cobwebs and bleeding. A doctor can tend arrow wounds and sword cuts, but what can anybody do when somebody's been blown up? Anyway we don't have one. Don't go down there again."

A horn blew somewhere, and he looked up. He went to the rail and stared out. Catharine turned.

The Turk archers were running forward with their bows. A horseman galloped straight toward the Main Gate, coming from somewhere on the left. He swept down toward the gate, lashing his horse, while the arrows pelted the ground around him and flew past him. Rakóssy shouted, and his gun crews leapt to their cannon. They started up a covering fire.

Béla had come out of the building and was standing almost directly below, looking bewildered. Rakóssy leaned down and shouted, "Rider coming—a Magyar. Go to the gate." And when Béla hesitated: "Get going, damn you."

The horseman was past the shattered earthworks, coming on, closer; Catharine's heart thundered and she held her breath. She could see the light sparkling on his horse's bits and the colors of the hood of his cloak. She cried out to him.

The horse plunged to the ground and the man sailed off. He landed and was still, not twenty feet from the gate. Catharine screamed. Down by the Main Gate, Béla suddenly understood and fought his way through the tangled mess and rubble out to the plain. Rakóssy was straining forward over the railing, shouting to him. Béla ran to the fallen man and heaved him up onto his shoulder. He staggered back through the gate. Rakóssy whirled and ran from the balcony.

Béla got the Magyar through the litter of the gate and laid him down on the paving stones. Immediately he was surrounded by the others. Rakóssy appeared in the courtyard and shouldered and cursed his way through the mob. Catharine watched him, her lungs aching from her pent-up breath.

She saw the way he stood up and dismissed the crowd and she relaxed. He called up four men to carry the man into the great hall and started back into the castle. She could see the relief in the way he held his shoulders. He came back out onto the balcony, and she said, "It wasn't Denis."

"It wasn't anybody I knew. Not from Hart."

"Is he dead?"

"No. He's got an arrow through a lung, though."

She turned and went to the door into the castle.

"Catharine," he said.

She made her step more firm, more confident, and went on, down to the great hall.

The man recovered enough to say that he was from

the King, that the King would raise the ban on Rakóssy if he would provide men and guns to fight the Turks. He told this to Béla, and Béla laughed in his face.

"Yes," the man said. "Yes, very funny, isn't it?"

Rakóssy was summoned, and he came to the man's bedside. "The Emperor," he said. "Has the King asked his help?"

"They won't help us. None of them. The heretic has told them it's God's will, the coming of the Turks." The man swallowed. A pink froth clung to the corner of his mouth. "Will I die?"

Rakóssy stared away, not listening.

"Will I die?" the man said.

"I'll take care of you," Catharine said.

Rakóssy went out into the corridor. He walked to the stairs and up to the door of the balcony. He could see through to the sunlight and the plain beyond the wall, and the light outside made the darkness just within the door more distinct.

The Emperor . . . chooses not to come. He thought, There's no use for it. All the things I did, and they called me a traitor. He's betrayed us all. That stupid boy. That Burgundian-Spanish-German and the Devil knows what else lout waving his sword at peasants. What was the use? I should go out now and give it up to him and let him kill me and at least the rest of them could live through it. Oh, God, you stinking—

He plunged out into the sunlight. He leaned his fore-arms on the rail and looked east toward the green silk tent, shaking in the wind. The Sultan in his chair was watching Vrath.

He stared at the Sultan, thinking about the Emperor fighting his wars in Italy and France and scratching where the heretic monk itched. The Emperor, who could not be bothered about a little war on the edge of Europe. The Magyars had always fought to keep out of the Empire, to keep from being hauled by the heels to the Hapsburgs in their golden chairs. It was hard to think of how the Emperor had decided it that way.

He thought of the Emperor and the Archduke and all their advisers sitting in Vienna and the Emperor saying, perhaps, "It would be difficult now. Let him have Hungary. We can give him Hungary for now. Let him gnaw on Hungary. Let him trample Hungary. Let him—"

Suddenly Rakóssy had the irresistible feeling that the Sultan was looking straight back at him, that across hundreds of yards of the fighting ground they were looking into each other's eyes.

No, he thought. You aren't looking at the Emperor's ally and kinsman, Turk. You're looking at a Magyar, damn you. A free Magyar. Let you choke on Hungary.

The feeling passed. He saw the Sultan rise and shake out his sleeves. Mustafa turned and mounted the chestnut mare. Rakóssy watched Mustafa ride across the field. It had been fun fighting Mustafa with his schemes and tricks and jokes. That was over now. He wondered what Mustafa was thinking.

Catharine tended the King's messenger, washed his wound, and fed him. She nursed him through a fever that lasted two days, staying by him all the time. When the fever broke, she thought he would get well. She slept in her own bed that night. In the morning, when she went to the great hall, they told her that he had died.

"It isn't fair," Catharine said.

"No," Rakóssy said.

"I hate it. I hate it."

"I know," he said. He went up on the ramparts.

They ate that evening in silence, the two of them. He pushed back his dish and said, "Still brooding over your lost lamb?"

"Must you be quite so snide?"

"With the number of people who have been killed or hurt so far, I don't see why you're so upset over one of them."

"Has compassion gone out of style? You may have a heart of stone, but I don't. And I have the right to be unhappy if I want to." She stood up, trembling. "Haven't I? I'm stuck out here in the middle of a war, away from everything I've ever loved, and I can't even save a hurt man. What's wrong with me? What's wrong with all of us?"

He came toward her, and she backed away.

"Don't come near me. I'm unhappy and I have the right to be. I'm going to cry and scream and—"

He slapped her. She swayed and put her hand to her cheek.

"How dare you."

"If you're going to cry and scream," he said, "go someplace where nobody can hear you. Every time you put on one of these exhibitions, you're helping the Turks. Shut up and go to bed and sleep. You'll feel better in the morning."

"I suppose I have to be strong. And smile all the time. Why me? If you'd married Carlotta—"

"I didn't marry Carlotta. I married you. Shut up or I'll hit you again."

"Go ahead. Hit me. Hit me. Because I'm—"

He slapped her, much harder, and she fell. He picked her up and undressed her and put her to bed. She stared at him.

"Good night," he said and went out.

He went down to the great hall and looked at the wounded. They were carrying out two corpses, wrapped in their knights' cloaks. They would bury them in the back courtyard, where the sheep had been penned before they slaughtered all the sheep. Rakóssy went back after them and watched.

Béla read a part of the burial service from a book left behind by the priest. The moon had set already, and no stars were out. The sky was like charred wood. It would rain again tomorrow. Rakóssy twitched his shoulders under his shirt.

The Turks would break through the wall by the stable within a few days. He would have to remember to move the guns off. They could put them on the stable roof, which was flat. The two corpses were put into the graves and covered over. There were many graves here now, all marked with slabs of wood, all crowded together.

"My lord," Béla said.

Rakóssy looked up at the wall. A rope with a heavy stick tied to the end flew over the wall from the other side. The rope slithered back until the stick was wedged against the battlement.

"Who's there?" Rakóssy called.

"Somebody's climbing," Béla said.

"Not even a Turk's that stupid. Who's there?"

"Gently, gently, brother." A blond head appeared over the top of the wall. "Nobody but me."

Denis crawled over the wall and let himself down. He shook his rope loose and coiled it. Rakóssy stood motionless. Denis was soaking wet and wore only a ragged pair of trousers. He came over to Rakóssy, stopped before him, and said, "What, no greeting for the Prodigal?"

"Prodigal, hell." Rakóssy lifted one hand awkwardly, and Denis with a laugh embraced him. Rakóssy wrapped his arm around Denis' neck and hugged him.

"Jesus," he said. "Jesus." He pushed Denis back. "Let me look at you. Are you alive? You look more like a ghost."

"Very like. I'm starved."

"Come to the kitchen. I'll feed you with my own hands." He put his hand on Denis' arm. "By God, you're real."

Denis pushed his soaked hair out of his eyes. "Yes." He smiled.

They went into the kitchen, and Rakóssy called out a

woman to feed Denis. He sent Béla and the others to find Arpád and Alexander and sat himself down opposite Denis at the table. Denis ate steadily. Rakóssy put his chin on his hands and watched.

Finally Denis sat back, sighing. "Well," he said. "I suppose you want to know about the fate of the ancestral home."

"You sound like Mustafa. Yes. What happened?"

"We lost Hart five—no, six days ago. They came in over the front wall, through the gate, and over the back, all at once. I didn't know if I was supposed to stay and die or not. So I didn't."

He wiped his mouth. "I finally found out that it was Kamal who was commanding there. They beat at us until we had only two guns left. Then they just came up the hill like the Great Flood and we were finished. I only had forty-three men left. Even Leonidas had three hundred. So I ran like a dog."

"How did you get here?"

"I ran." He grinned again. "I had a raw rabbit and some old vegetables. Turnips. Pulled them out of an old field. There isn't anything left to eat between here and Hart. You can see where the Turks marched like a burn."

Rakóssy said, "Do you want more to eat?"

"No. I'm stuffed. Before I left Hart I blew it up. I blasted my way out through the back of the stable with some of the powder and the rest just went off by itself, I guess. They had gotten into the kitchen, where I was keeping my wounded, and they were killing them. I don't think there were many left. I got a lot of Turks."

Arpád came in. "By God," he said. "By God."

Rakóssy said, "They took Hart—or what was left. Where's Alexander?"

"Right here. Hah!" Alexander pounced on Denis and wrestled him around the kitchen, finally plumping him back down again. "Now that you're here the Turks will all run and hide."

Denis said, "You may kill me with all this sudden affection, the bunch of you."

"We missed you," Rakóssy said. "I didn't have anybody to shout at. Did I, Arpád?"

"Oh, he did well enough." Arpád nodded several times.

Mari came in behind him. Her body had shrunk down around her bones, but she smiled as well. "Denis. You look perfectly healthy to me."

"And you look as beautiful as ever."

Arpád snorted. "Listen, boy—"

"Shut up," Rakóssy said. "Mari, go up and get Catharine, will you?"

"How is she?" Denis said.

"She's not feeling well," Mari said.

"Denis will do her good," Rakóssy said.

Mari left. Denis said, "What's wrong?"

"She's nervy. God knows she does enough. You can see the Crusader sticking out of her like . . ." Rakóssy shrugged. "But she does get unhappy."

"She's a good woman."

"I should have sent her away," Rakóssy said. "When the whole thing started."

Denis studied him for a while. It seemed to Rakóssy that Denis' face had changed, somehow, deep in the bones; he looked the same, no older, no more worn, and yet he looked different.

"That wouldn't have helped," Denis said.

"No," Rakóssy said.

Catharine came through the door, smiling, holding out both hands. "Denis. My dear Denis."

"Catharine, I came all the way back here to see you." He got up and kissed her forehead. "But what will we do with your husband?"

"Well," Mari said. "Isn't he the fresh thing."

Rakóssy looked up at Catharine, and she smiled at him. She put her hand on his hair and stood with her hip against his shoulder. "Let's have some wine," she said.

"Let's celebrate."

"There," Rakóssy said, "is an intelligent woman."

Arpád went down into the basement and came back with two jugs.

"Did you talk to Kamal at all?" Rakóssy said to Denis.

"Yes. He tried to convince me that they'd taken Vrath and that you'd been made into stew for the Sultan. He may have been killed in the explosion."

Arpád filled cups. "Shall we send some to the Turks?" he said, holding up the jug.

"Let them drink horse urine," Denis said. Catharine laughed and put her hands over her ears.

"Kamal leads a charmed life," Rakóssy said. "He's so stupid he should have died long ago. What happened to Zoltan?"

Denis paused a moment, fingering his cup. "He put a knife through his heart," he said.

"Well, well," Rakóssy said and smiled into his cup.

"Why do you dislike Zoltan so much?" Denis said.

"I don't anymore."

"Did it have something to do with Mother?"

"Why, I loved Zoltan like a father."

Denis filled up his cup again. "He wasn't much good to me. How are you doing here? I swam down and didn't see a thing."

"Oh, hell," Rakóssy said. "We're setting them back on their butts. They've got over fifty thousand men out there and they can't take an inch without our permission in writing."

"What's going on up north?"

Catharine said, "That's the touchy subject."

"The Emperor," Rakóssy said, "the Holy Roman Emperor his Universal Greatness Charles, fifth of that name, first lord of Europe and God's own warrior on earth—"

"I get the idea," Denis said. "Is he not coming at all, or just delaying?"

"He's not coming."

"Do you think the King can—"

"For Christ's sake," Rakóssy said. "The King is twenty years old. He turns pale whenever he sees a piece of armor."

Arpád said, "Do we tell the others, or not?"

"They probably know already."

"We didn't."

"Tell them." Rakóssy shoved his cup away. "We're finished no matter how you look at it. They might as well know."

"János," Catharine said soothingly.

"It's the God-damn truth. If I were—"

"Don't shout," Denis said.

"If I were inclined to be a martyr I'd surrender and let as many as possible get out with their skins whole, at least."

They were silent. He lifted his head and looked at them, one by one, surprised. Catharine went across the room and sat down.

"You aren't inclined to be a martyr," she said. She looked at Denis, smiled slightly, and turned back toward Rakóssy. "As for surrendering, you're acting like a child. I'm surprised that you should even think of something like that."

"We aren't finished," Mari said. "We can't be finished. We're beating them here."

Arpád was pulling his mustaches. He glanced over at Alexander, and they both looked down at the floor.

"All right," Rakóssy said. "Forget I ever said anything. Denis, you're tired. Come with me and I'll show you where to sleep."

He got up, pulled his doublet straight, and said, "Arpád, we have to move the cannon off the wall they're bombarding. Do it tonight. Come on, Denis."

Denis followed him. When Rakóssy passed by Catharine's chair, he paused a moment and looked down and said in German, "Wrong fairy tale, sweet." He touched her cheek briefly and went on.

On the way up the stairs Denis said, "What's wrong?"

"Nothing."

Denis shrugged. Rakóssy put him in the rooms just past his, said good night, and went back to his room. He took off his boots and lay down on the bed, on his back, with his arms behind his head.

Catharine came in almost immediately with Mari. Mari helped her undress and left quietly. Catharine moved around the room, putting things minutely in order.

"If you think I help the Turks with my tantrums," she said, "you just almost lost us the game, my dear."

"Well, well," he said.

"That's what you said about Zoltan. You're in a terrible mood." She moved a chair slightly and sat down, drawing the light cloth of the dressing gown over her legs. "What exactly is the matter?"

"I hate to lose."

She laughed. He moved slightly, hitching himself around on the bed.

"If we had been born in another time," she said, "perhaps we would have been happier, but we weren't. We were born now, and we have to take what we were given, and we might as well make the best of it."

"You and your bloody homilies."

"János, please tell me what's bothering you."

He hauled himself up on one elbow. "Do you really want to know? I'll tell you. I sweated and schemed and got myself called traitor to get here, and where am I? What have I done? I've gotten you and my brother and five hundred men into a death trap."

He flopped back down flat on the bed. "That's what's bothering me."

She sat still a moment. After a while she said, "You may look at it that way, or you may want to think that you've done the best you could possibly do."

"Oh, well," he said. "What difference does it make?"

"There's a question of honor involved."

"Honor? What's honor got to do with it?"

She burst out laughing. "János, you're so funny sometimes." She went over to the bed and sat down next to him and put her long hand on his forehead. "You don't have a fever. Perhaps I should dose you with a purgative."

"That would be wonderful. I can see me now, running back and forth between the ramparts and the nearest drainage ditch. Just as the Turks attack I say, 'Oops, excuse me a moment, men, I have this irresistible urge to—'"

"Kiss your wife," she said and bent down and kissed him.

"Exactly," he said. He put his arms around her. "Do you want me honorable, I shall fight thirty thousand Turks from the balcony to defend your virtue. I'll challenge the Sultan himself. I'll—"

"Shut up," she said. "My dear."

The following morning the section of wall opposite the stable collapsed at last under the Turkish guns. Rakóssy put Denis to command the rest of the cannon and set about organizing a defense against the charge that must come. He sent Alexander with fifty men to get pikes and shields and put another fifty men with crossbows on the stable roof. Arpád and several other men brought cauldrons of oil from the kitchen to fling on the brush in the ditch before the destroyed wall. The Turks were still firing, trying to knock the rubble flat, and the shot streamed through and smashed into the stable. The horses began to neigh and kick inside the stable, but Rakóssy had no time to move them, and the shot was doing no great damage.

The Turks had attacked that section because, once the guns were knocked out, there was no way to prevent the Spahis across the river from charging over the bridge. Rakóssy had moved some of the guns up onto the stable roof. He put Arpád up there to command them and the crossbowmen, and he himself went up on the wall beside the breach. He saw Catharine on the balcony with Mari and waved.

Béla came up beside him. "Will we hold them this time?"

"We're going to hold them until their beards turn gray. Go down there with Alexander." Rakóssy took a torch from the pile near the edge of the rampart and lit it. The ditch with its dry brush was half choked now with the fallen rock of the wall.

"Stepan," he shouted, and the nearest man ran over.

"Fetch me two kegs of powder and a sack of scrap shot. Two half-empty kegs. Hurry."

Stepan ran off. The Turks suddenly stopped firing. The drums beat, and the flutes and pipes picked up the rhythm in their reedy voices. Stepan came back, panting, and Rakóssy said, "Watch them while I do this."

He could hear the sound of feet, thousands of feet padding over the earth, softer than the drums. Down by the Main Gate Denis' voice lifted in command, young and fresh and firm.

They were coming from the plain and from across the river. The guns on the stable roof roared out. Rakóssy looked up from putting the scrap into the powder kegs and saw that the bridge rail had blocked most of the shot. The cannon would not be fired again; by the time they would be reloaded the Spahis would be across. The crossbowmen lifted their bows. The Spahis were galloping across, packed together on the narrow bridge. A horse reared and fell, almost blocking the bridge, and two of the Spahis leapt quickly down and flung the horse into the river, forcing it up before it died and driving it over the rail.

Rakóssy tore two strips of cloth from his shirt, soaked them in oil, and threaded them through the bungholes in the kegs. He hooked the inside ends of the cloth fuses over the sharp edges of the scrap and pounded the covers on tight.

Denis' guns began to roll, a light patter like rain.

The Turks from the bridge plunged into the gap in the wall, howling, their lances thrusting forward, trying to get in and hold the breach by momentum alone. Rakóssy lit another torch from his and tossed it down into the ditch. The brush flared up, half strangled by the dust and the debris on top of it. It did little good, and Rakóssy swore.

The Janissaries from the plain rushed in behind the Spahis, and the Spahis withdrew back through the ranks of infantry, their horses wheeling and neighing at the fire. The Janissaries forced themselves into the gap. Alexander and Béla and their men closed with them.

Rakóssy lit the fuse on the first keg and stood up. He threw the keg into the Janissaries, well behind their front lines. The keg hurtled out and down, spilling gunpowder through the hole, and vanished into the mass of tight-packed infantry. They shoved away from it, confused, and for a moment nothing happened. Rakóssy held his breath. The keg exploded. The scraps slashed out, whining in the air. The Janissaries howled in rage and pain. The scraps flayed down the men nearest. A man almost below Rakóssy went to his knees, his hand pressed to his side.

"*La ilaha il-Allah!*"

"Just made them more angry," Rakóssy said.

The fighting in the breach grew more intense. Alexander's men stood shoulder to shoulder, solid as rock, taller than the Turks and stock-still in the rubble. The Turks' great numbers hampered them here, and the long pikes and halberds kept them from using their scimitars.

Rakóssy picked up the other keg, cut off the fuse almost even with the wood, lit it, and threw. The keg turned end over end. Gunpowder crackled and flashed around the fuse. The keg exploded over the Janissaries' heads. Rakóssy heard men screaming. He swore to hear his own voice. He turned back to the fighting in the breach.

"Magyar, Magyar." He shinnied down the edge of the

rubble from the rampart. He leapt onto a Janissary's back and struck him down. "Die, Christian." His own men roared his name.

Rakóssy stood with his back pressed to the uneven stone, and the Janissaries charged him, turning almost their whole weight from the other Magyars, flinging themselves against him. Their eyes shone over the cheekpieces on their sleek helmets. A sword smashed against the stone beside his head. He struck back and the blood flew over his hands. He could not hold them off; they were smothering him.

Abruptly they rushed off, charging away, answering the different note in the drums. Their voices, hoarsely raised, grew fainter. The cool air rushed in around him.

"Alexander."

It was Arpád, shouting from the stable roof.

"Alexander!"

Alexander, swaying, standing to his hips in rubble and dead men, drenched in blood, looked up, raised one hand in salute, and fell forward. Rakóssy started toward him, but Arpád was there immediately. He lifted Alexander gently and carried him into the courtyard. He put him down and bent over him.

Rakóssy went slowly toward him. He stood not far from Arpád and watched. He was still panting. The guns on the other side of the castle stilled. The silence sprang up all around him.

He looked up and saw Denis on the walls, half naked, his chest and face black with grime. Denis waved.

"Arpád," Rakóssy said.

"He's dead."

Rakóssy got his breath. He put his sword back in the sheath. "Better this way, you know."

Arpád looked up. Rakóssy almost reached out to touch him.

"I know," Arpád said. "I know."

Rakóssy went over and knelt beside Alexander. His big, ugly face looked no different. He felt an immense sadness that Alexander should have died.

"Don't worry," Arpád said. "He got the best of it."

Rakóssy nodded and got up. His leg hurt. He put his hand against his thigh to hold his leg together and went inside.

"You see," Mustafa said.

"I see. I will send a messenger to tell him that the southern fortress has been taken. It would be better if we had the brother."

"Kamal searched the ruins from the pit to the height." Mustafa poured chilled milk into a cup and put it on the little table beside the chair. "There was no sign of him. Either the brother was blown to pieces or he escaped."

"He is of no use to us either way. I cannot be held up here any longer. The King of Hungary has an army and he advances on us now. Twenty thousand men."

"I think you will find better sport here."

"Indeed. On the other hand, when the Chinese invented gunpowder they took the sport out of war. When I have attended to this King and his . . . plaything army, I shall march back and we will give proper attention to this Rakóssy. You are aware of my wishes in this matter, should Allah grant you a victory in my absence."

"Yes."

"I am moved by this defense. There is great craft here, and courage and a stubbornness I admire. Deal honorably with them. I have given orders to prepare all but ten thousand men for a march. I can give you no guns. I know that in your hands ten thousand are as a hundred thousand, and I offer you my blessing. Take your truce flag and tell him that the southern castle is in our hands."

Mustafa bowed. He went out into the blazing sunlight and called to Kamal.

"Fetch me a flag of truce," he said. "And my mare."

Kamal bowed and called a slave. Mustafa stood arranging the cloth of his turban. He mounted the mare and took the lance with the white flag.

The ground between the Turk camp and Vrath was broken and scarred and stank. Mustafa guided the chestnut mare carefully around the uneven places. He saw the portcullis on the Main Gate rise and Rakóssy came through, limping slightly. Mustafa reined in, put the mare through some fancy trickwork, and stopped her.

"Greetings, Rakós'. We meet again, and it is yet another magnificent day."

Rakóssy picked his way through the shattered earthworks. "So it is."

Mustafa studied Rakóssy in detail. He sat back in his saddle and shook his head. "There is no justice in Heaven. You look well. One would think that Allah would smite you down, if only for dismissing the lovely days of war. Completely recovered, I see. A trifle dirty." Mustafa sniffed. He folded the immaculate messaline of his sleeve.

"Hell's made of filth," Rakóssy said.

"Why, you spoke the words before I had them on my lips. And your wife? Well, I trust?"

"Very well."

"And Arpád, my dear friend?"

"Very well."

"And your brother?"

"In remarkable good health."

"Hmmm." Mustafa stroked his beard. His eyes traveled the walls of Vrath and fastened on one blond head. "So I see. Amazing, the resilience of the Rakóssys. Compliment him for me. It may amuse you to know that my master leaves tomorrow to seek out and destroy your King and his army, which numbers somewhat less than twenty thousand men."

"I'm amused as hell."

"Leaving me and my men as arbiters of your doom. Including some veterans of Cliff's Eye. Rakós', do you know the Koran?"

"Vaguely."

"Then picture me as Israfel." Mustafa lifted his reins. His eyes swooped to Rakóssy's. "And I read what is written on your forehead, Rakós'."

He turned and galloped off. He heard Rakóssy's shouting laughter.

"A touch too dramatic," Mustafa said to Kamal, reining in. "Just a touch."

The Turks attacked once more, a halfhearted feint for the Main Gate and a brief plunge to the breach, beaten off almost before it was begun. Only one of Rakóssy's men was hurt: Denis, who was knocked against a cannon and broke his arm. He fell from the rampart and landed in the middle of a bunch of men and was safely borne up, "like Christ," he said, "if he had leapt when he was tempted." He was carried in state to his room and tended there. Outside, the men cheered the departure of the Sultan. The ten thousand left behind seemed as few as the men in the castle.

Rakóssy had one hundred sixty-one men whole and slightly more wounded. The wounded were dying more than they were recovering. The little burial ground was full of dead Magyars.

Denis sat in bed reading. Rakóssy moved restlessly around the room.

"What is that?" he asked.

"Ovid. Love poetry."

"In Latin?"

"Yes. I wish we had Father's library here. I'm homesick for Petrarch, and Malencz seems to have leaned heavily on moldy Hellenic poets."

"Anything about how to win a war in that book?"

"That depends on the kind of war." Denis put down the book. "You look tired, János. And thin."

"I'm fine."

"Do you think that the King might be able to beat them?"

"The King's coming to meet them and he has about one third the men the Turks have."

"Maybe Mustafa was lying."

"Oh, no. He took far too much glee in telling me."

Catharine came in with a tray of food. She drew up a little table and put the tray down. "Denis," she said, "can you eat by yourself?"

"Thank you, yes."

She arranged the food for the three of them. Rakóssy took a bite of the meat and a chunk of bread and said, "You eat it. I'm not hungry."

"Don't be a fool," Denis said. "You have to fight."

"I'm not hungry. Eat it. Or save it, if you want."

"Well," Catharine said, "sit and talk to us while we eat."

He sat and listened to them discuss Ovid. When Denis was finished, Catharine pulled the covers up over him and stood up. She called Mari to take the tray and the dishes down to the kitchen and went with Rakóssy to their room.

"János," she said, "maybe now that the Sultan is gone we can figure out some way of beating them."

"I'd rather we didn't talk about that. Don't worry about it. There's no reason to."

"It's hard not to worry about dying."

"I worry a lot more about being dead."

"Look how thin I've gotten. It's frightening the way this dress hangs on me. I'll have to take in everything I own."

She went to the chest and took out another gown and held it up to her. "This will be hard," she said.

"I should have sent you back to Austria," he said. "When this whole thing started."

"I don't think I could have persuaded Charles to do anything else."

In the little awkward pause she looked at him and saw that she had misunderstood him. She put the dress down. "You would have sent me away?"

"I don't like what I've gotten you into."

"Will you stop that? You'll go mad that way. Stop it." Her hands shook and she pressed them against her thighs. "You're just feeling sorry for yourself."

His eyes widened slightly, and he appeared to consider that. "All right," he said. "Maybe between now and the time the Sultan comes back, I'll think of something."

"Do they know about me? The Turks."

"Yes."

"Good. They can make up a song about us and sing it around their fires."

"I think," he said, laughing, "that you should have been born about five hundred years ago. When those things were still possible."

"They are possible now. Heroes, and heroines—"

"And poetry and romances and Crusades and wild charges and things like that." He patted her head.

"I'll make it possible."

"You do that. I'm going down and see about the meat supply."

"Let me do that. I don't think there's much left. We'll have to start eating the horses." She went over to the door and called Mari, and the two of them went off, talking steadily and laughing.

Rakóssy went into Malencz's old study and got a cup of the best wine. The books ranked neatly around the room reminded him of his father. The room was musty. He opened up two of the windows and stood before one of them, breathing the warm air.

It was just evening, and the air was soft and fine. He could hear the last words of the call to prayer, out in the Turkish camp, and the voices of the men in the courtyard below him. It was almost like before. When his mother had been alive she and he had often gone out in the summer evenings and drifted around the hills, walk-

ing sometimes with their horses hobbled and grazing behind them. He wondered if it were true that souls could
look down from Heaven and up from Hell to see what
was happening on the earth, and, if it were, what she
thought of him now.

He thought he was much different from the little boy
he had been when she was alive. He wished there was
someone he could talk to about her, but the only men
alive now who had known her at all were Trig Columbo
and Malencz. She had called him Lajos instead of Louis,
which had infuriated him.

"That is an affectation, Jansci," she had said. "As if you
were named Jean or Giovanni instead of János."

He wondered if she would have liked Catharine. She
had never liked women much. My wife believes in
heroes, Mother. Why in hell am I thinking about my
mother?

"I must leave you, Jansci, my son Jansci."

And the Gypsies and the deep forest where the sun
doesn't shine where you told me stories and swore that
they were true.

He turned away from the window and poured himself
another cup of wine. Naturally, Mother, I am going to
think of some great bold stroke that will save us all the
moment before the Sultan's big ugly fist lands on top of
us. All the horses will grow wings and we shall fly like
Mohammed over the heads of the Mohammedans. I'm
sure Catharine will wave to them.

He drank off the wine and put the cup back beside the
keg. There was no use thinking about it. No sense in
worrying about it. The Devil take it. He drew the shut-
ters closed and locked them. János Hunyadi died one
hundred years ago.

He went out of the study and down to the courtyard
and helped some of the men repair the damage the Turks
had done to the stable.

* * *

Sometimes Malencz heard thunder over the castle, although the walls were so thick that if he were asleep the storms would not wake him up. It was hard to visualize what was happening; it was getting harder and harder to understand and remember, to describe things to himself. He had not spoken aloud in so long that he came at words gingerly when they entered his head, stalking them like ferrets, unsure.

The words in the books he had were in Latin or in Greek, and it was odd that they should be; sometimes he was struck with amazement at it. They were much different than the words inside his head, the words he said to himself when he thought of something—two things related but not the same. The relationship he found increasingly difficult to recall. Certainly, some of the words on the pages meant much the same thing as the words in his head, so the difference wasn't there.

He thought it had something to do with which was real, the word on the paper, which he could see, or the word in his mind. Once he thought that he understood, and jumped up in triumph, but the book slammed shut and he couldn't find the proper word again, and the idea vanished. Later on he could sometimes feel it tickling the edges of his mind but he could never catch it.

That was puzzling and sad. He lingered often over particular words, savoring them, pronouncing them soundlessly in the original and in Magyar, but the meaning always eluded him.

He did not like the occasional sounds that penetrated here. They reminded him of something else, some other, terrible thing. He knew that the world was divided into circles, and that the words moved in their own circles, and that there was another circle like a fence around something else. He quested after it now and then but always felt the subtlest small voice telling him, Stop, no more, don't look, not yet.

Not yet. That was it. That was why he was here, he had been confined to be purified, to be purged of base matter (once he had seen silver smelted and seen the scum of dross on the liquid in the crucible), to be made worthy of something. In the end, he would be told, he would be fashioned like the molten silver into something rich and proper, for uses unknown to other men. Not yet.

In that other circle, the one he wasn't allowed to see, there was something to be dreaded and avoided, but when the time came it would be revealed, all of it. That other circle held something dark and ferocious, alternately a pacing creature chained up and a sort of storm held in a box (perhaps like the storms he heard, now and then? His mind probed timidly at it, hopefully: was this part of the revelation, was it now?), something perhaps he would have to serve, or to destroy. He longed for it to be massive and awesome and forbidding, something mighty and great, and in one corner of his mind feared that it would be a little weak thing like a sick rat.

The sentry outside this room occasionally looked in, and when he did Malencz composed his face and hunted up the proper words to say—soothing, tempting words. But the sentry never spoke. Whatever he did, Malencz must never betray that he had been given this trust. It was something so completely secret that he realized it must be fantastically dangerous, and he must hide it, always hide it, behind the proper words (if he must ever speak) and behind a mild and yielding manner, bearing the secret trust inside, guarded and tended until the day came when it would burst out in splendor, gathering him up and transforming him, glorious as the sun, to bear it forth with trumpets into the world.

Mustafa did not attack them. He sat in his camp out there on the plain, and they sat in Vrath, and it looked almost as if the two had nothing to do with each other. Rakóssy saw flocks of sheep driven into Mustafa's camp and slaughtered, and on days when the wind blew right they could smell the roasting mutton. Mustafa knew what he was doing.

Two of Malencz's old knights deserted over the wall in the back of the castle, obviously thinking that if Denis could come in that way, they could go out. The sentry found the ropes hanging over the edge of the wall the following morning and sent for Rakóssy. He and Arpád and the sentry stood on the rampart looking down at the river, dark and full of sand, and the ropes hanging down to the water's surface.

"Who were they?" Rakóssy said.

"We'll find out when the Turks throw their heads over," Arpád said.

"He won't. Get Béla up— No. Come on."

Rakóssy went off along the rampart. Arpád said, "He won't?"

"No. He'd like it if they all got the idea that they could desert. They weren't from Hart, were they?"

"God no." Arpád looked over at the river. "Do you think he caught them?"

Rakóssy stopped and pointed down the river toward the bridge. A little band of Turks was fishing over the railing.

"They probably hauled them out there," he said. "The current's too strong for them to swim against it." He went on, walking fast.

Béla was sitting in the courtyard, in the shade of the balcony, dicing with two more of Malencz's old knights. Rakóssy climbed down the ladder and walked across the courtyard. Arpád saw that his limp was suddenly more pronounced.

The three knights looked up. Their faces sharpened and became wary. Arpád thought, They knew.

Rakóssy stopped in front of Béla. "Who were they?" he said.

Béla stood up slowly. He looked around. The courtyard was suddenly full of Béla's friends. They made a thick circle around Rakóssy, Arpád, and Béla.

"Who were they?" Rakóssy said. His voice was almost soft.

"Peter Bársony and Milo the Czech."

The men around them murmured, angry that he had told. Béla glared quickly at them.

"Did you know they were going?" Rakóssy said. He had not looked at the crowd of men, only at Béla, since he had come down off the wall.

Béla did not answer, saw that that was a mistake, took a breath, let it out, put his thumbs in his belt, threw out his chest, and said, "I did."

Rakóssy backhanded him. Béla fell against the castle wall. He flung his arms out to brace himself.

Rakóssy watched him a moment, standing easily with his hands open at his sides, and turned his head and looked slowly all around. The men were poised, ready to attack him, their faces wild.

"God damn you," Béla said.

Rakóssy brought his eyes slowly back to Béla's. "I should hang you high as Heaven," he said. "Don't tempt me."

"Give us the word, Béla," somebody said.

Rakóssy did not bother to look around. He watched Béla. The left corner of his mouth drew down.

"Give them the word, Béla," he said.

Béla said nothing.

Rakóssy turned slowly, putting his back to Béla. He looked at Arpád and said, "We have to slaughter a few more horses. Take three of these men and do it."

He walked straight at the thickest part of the circle of men. They trembled, longing to attack him. He went straight at them and they parted to let him through. He hardly seemed to notice that they were there.

Denis was on the rampart beside a pair of cannon. Rakóssy went over to him. Denis said, "Catharine was on the balcony."

Rakóssy looked, but the balcony was empty. Denis said, "If they had put a hand on you, I would have shot them to pieces."

"Mustafa would have loved that," Rakóssy said.

Horse meat was not bad, once they got over the idea that they had ridden it. The summer was cool, and it did not rain. Rakóssy got bored, and once led thirty men out to try to steal some of the sheep Mustafa held so invitingly near, but the Turks swooped down on them and they barely got back into Vrath.

They never found out what had happened to Peter Bársony and Milo the Czech. No other men deserted. Arpád said, laughing, that they would rather fight the Turks than Rakóssy.

"Béla's a coward," Arpád said.

"Oh? I thought he was your long-lost love, the way you were carrying on before."

"That was before."

Denis was still wearing a sling, but he was as busy as any of them. Catharine often pleaded with him to rest more; she was afraid that his arm would heal crooked.

"I'm fine, Catharine," Denis said. "There's nothing wrong with me. My arm's almost healed up. See?"

"Don't you dare take it out of that sling."

Rakóssy said, "She's right. Do you want to be ugly?"

Catharine sat back, sighing. "The two of you are impossible. János, we have to save more food than we are."

"If they eat less than they're getting now," he said, "they'll drop in their tracks from hunger. We have enough meat for another month, counting all the horses, and there are plenty of vegetables."

"If we didn't have to feed Malencz—"

"He's still alive?" Denis said.

"Down in one of the dungeons," Rakóssy said. "What he eats will make no difference."

"It makes me uneasy," Catharine said. "I dreamt of him last night. I dreamt that he got out at night and prowled around with a sword in his hand, looking for you."

"He's locked up and harmless."

Denis hardly heard them. Malencz was alive. He was locked up below, probably entirely forgotten by all but a few, forgotten in his own castle. He saw Malencz clearly in his mind, and his heart jumped with pity.

He went down to the dungeons and found Malencz the next day. He had the warder unlock the door and he stepped into the big, dim room. Malencz rose at once and moved softly across the room to the corner.

"Sir Denis," he said. He rushed forward and embraced Denis. "Is it really you?"

"Easy, sir," Denis said. He smiled. "I just heard that you were alive."

"God knows why he doesn't kill me."

That, Denis thought, is an interesting question. "Do you need anything?"

"More food. I get one meal a day, and it isn't enough to feed a half-dead cat."

"We're all starving, slowly but surely."

Malencz's eyes were sunken. Denis thought that he might be a little mad. Malencz smiled. "Denis. I'm glad you're here. He's turning me into a wild animal."

"Oh, Louis. Sit down, let's talk."

Malencz told him about the time Rakóssy had come down to see him. "He's a devil. He's not human. I could almost see the horns on his head."

"He certainly fights like one."

"Tell me how it's going."

"Well, the main part of the army's gone, and all the guns, thank God. They don't attack us and we don't attack them. They're waiting until we starve or give up. They've broken through one wall, but it's too narrow a gap to make their numbers count, and I think they've given up trying to take us by storm."

"She's a fine old castle."

"Marvelous."

"Hart. Weren't you at Hart?"

"Yes. I held it until the beginning of June, I guess. What is it now—July? Almost August." He shrugged. "I finally had to blow it up."

"Can you bring me some books? Someone had these brought down—I don't know who."

"Probably my brother's wife."

"Can you bring me some Pliny and Procopius?"

"And some of your rotten Hellenic poets. Of course. And pen and paper, too, if you want."

"Good. Fine. Bring something you like, and we'll talk about it. How did you hurt your arm?"

"I knocked it against a cannon. It's almost healed now."

"That's too bad. But . . . the ill wind. You don't have to fight."

"I . . ." No use. "Yes, I suppose so. I've read Procopius. We can talk about that, if it's all right with you. And Ovid, I'll bring."

"Thank you." Malencz caught his good hand and wrung it. "You won't tell your brother?"

"Not if I can help it."

"Good. Good. You're looking well. Very well. Thin but well. I'd like some water to wash in, too."

"I'll bring it."

"Tonight?"

"As soon as I can."

"Good. Good."

They talked for a while, and Denis left. He went thankfully up to the open air and gulped it down. Malencz, he thought, never understood, never had a chance against my brother. Denis was sorry for him. He paced across the courtyard and took his turn on the watch, wondering if he should tell Rakóssy. Malencz was not well, and if anything happened he wanted his brother to know where he was.

He went up to his brother's room after his watch was over and sat quietly until Rakóssy woke up.

"What time is it?"

"Nearly dark."

"You should have woken me up."

"János, I've been to see Malencz."

Rakóssy got up and shaved. "Oh?"

"I'd like your permission to take him some books and talk to him."

"Oh."

Denis waited. He saw the long scar on Rakóssy's leg and said, "How did that happen?"

"A cannon exploded right next to me." He washed his shoulders and put on a shirt. He sat down on the bed to pull on his boots.

"Take a sword with you," he said. "Be careful. Don't go near him."

"Oh. Yes. I will."

Denis stood up. Rakóssy was buckling on his sword-belt.

"Thank you, János."

The corner of Rakóssy's mouth drew down. "I trust you, Denis."

Malencz groped over the problem of Denis. He was pleased with himself, he had spoken normally and without revealing anything, although the sight of Denis had turned everything suddenly around until it all fit. He was amazed that he hadn't thought of it sooner, and recalled that he had needed much deep thinking and concentration before he had understood. He knew everything now, everything, and he could remember all the things that had happened. It was amazing that so many things had happened that he had been almost totally unaware of, but they had, and he remembered everything.

Denis might be the helper that had been promised. Probably he was unwitting of it now, he was too young and too innocent to know, and it was for Malencz to take him in charge. The time would present itself. In the meantime he had to think, to consider, to scheme everything out and take careful note of everything that happened. But he was pleased that it was Denis who would help him.

Kamal said, "They keep half their men in the breach. Wondrous careful, our little Magyar friend."

Mustafa, half a roast fowl in his hand, looked up and frowned. "Careful? We should go out there and sit at his feet, like disciples." He turned the fowl to the plumpest part and bit into it. Gripping the fowl with his teeth, he reached both hands to water and cup, poured, and set down the jug. He took the bird in one hand and chewed thoughtfully.

"Rakóssy must be dying of boredom in there."

"When you take him," Kamal said. He sat down. Tenderly, he surveyed the camp, spread out in the morning sunshine. "When you take him, Mustafa, will you grant me a boon?"

"O Kamal," Mustafa said. He set down the fowl, belched comfortably, and called for water to wash his fingers in. "O Kamal, whom I love as my own fool of a brother, is there a star in Heaven I would not give you if I possessed it? The seas I would give you, to fish pearls from them."

Kamal smiled. He inclined his head slightly. "You do me great honor, and yourself more honor than I can—in my poor person—give you in return."

"Honor." Mustafa lifted his head. His eyes searched vaguely in the sky. "Honor. Ah, we live for honor, Kamal. There is no greater thing a man can possess than honor in the eyes of Allah. Honor, Kamal, the finest word in our tongue. Which is why, my beloved brother, I cannot grant you the boon you desire."

Kamal's face fell. For a moment, Mustafa saw, Kamal was dangerously close to impropriety in speech and vulgarity in thoughts. Mustafa lowered his eyes to the rings on his left hand. He said, "Honor, Kamal, is beyond

barter and beyond revenge. And honor is not the possession of any one race—however much Allah may in His
Mercy have ordained us its chief priests. The Magyar
tongue has a word for honor in it too."

Kamal bowed. "I defer to your judgment, my lord."

"Kamal, Kamal." Mustafa spread his hands. "I do you
honor in this. You are . . . a rash child, my brother. A
man of principle, and yet a man of some unsteady pride,
of a certain—" Mustafa gestured vaguely—"not to say
base, not to say in any way ignoble—of a certain—shall
we call it narrowness of mind? Ah, Kamal, do not look
so. I chastise you for your own good, and in my love for
you I chastise myself."

Kamal said nothing.

"Rakóssy is the child of the Devil, but forget not that
the Devil was gently born, even as we—and what are we
but devils whose redemption is not entirely impossible?
But I will not dwell on theology. Rakóssy is a man of
honor."

Kamal sputtered.

"I know that you still itch from the trick he played on
you. But I will not grant you a boon that will cast dishonor on you and on me. You want to avenge yourself
on him when he is helpless, and that I will not permit. Do
you understand me?"

Kamal understood him.

"I have instructions from the Sultan," Mustafa said,
"to take Rakóssy alive."

Kamal nodded. He had known that.

"I am under orders to hold him until the Sultan summons him into the Presence. The Sultan was impressed
by the defense of Vrath. He will offer Rakóssy a place in
his army, if Rakóssy will renounce Christ and submit to
the true Faith."

Kamal did not trust himself to speak.

"Rakóssy," Mustafa said, "will refuse. He hates priests
and he is, after all, a child of Satan, but he is at heart a
Christian, as, doubtless, all wicked men are. He will re-

fuse, and he will be mercifully destroyed."

Mustafa smiled fleetingly. "I myself do not believe that we will be able to take him alive. I do not intend to lose fifty men to take one man who will die anyway." He picked up the fowl again. "Go. Go watch his walls."

Kamal left, swirling his robes around him.

"Rakós'," Mustafa said, "you are still a great soldier."

Denis saw Malencz every three or four days. They did not talk about the war or Rakóssy. They translated Procopius into Magyar and read Ovid and Catullus. Malencz seemed better for it, and Denis felt easier about going down there. He did not particularly like it, but he felt guilty if he did not, and the glow in the man's eyes was rewarding.

One day Denis went to the burial service for the last of the men from the great hall. They had all died or gotten well, and the last two were buried almost on top of another grave. Arpád recited parts of the burial service.

He said, "These men died here for the honor of Magyars. They lie in Magyar dirt. This land will never be Turkish. If they take it, the Turks will be thrown off by the earth they stand on. The rivers and the fields will not teem for them, the mountains will have no game for them, and the birds of the air will not nest here. Nobody will ever own this land but us."

Denis listened to that voice and forgot that it was Arpád's. The voice was steady and deep. He shut his eyes.

"We will die here. Everybody dies. The name of Vrath Castle and the names of the men who die here, you and I, will not be written down in books. We have been forgotten, except for God. Our lives will be written, for good or for wickedness, on the heart of God. If we fight for God and the honor of our race, it is for good. If we fight for nothing, only to fight, then we die for nothing, and it is for wickedness."

Denis opened his eyes. Arpád crossed himself. "God help us."

"Amen."

"The Turks. They will remember us. We'll make them remember us. The Turks. The Turks."

Arpád turned and went off. Denis was stricken to his heart. His brother was not there, and he went to find him and could not. He wanted desperately to find him. It was like a bad dream, when he looked for his mother or his father and could not find them.

He did find Mari, when it was almost evening, and flirted halfheartedly with her. She was thin. The bones of her shoulder jabbed through her dress. She said, "I had a baby, you know."

"No, I didn't. I'm sorry."

"No," she said. "We will have more, Arpád and I."

"Mari . . ."

Her eyes stared at him.

"We will have more."

He took an armful of books down to Malencz, determined to escape the bad dream. He called to the warder in the dungeons to tell him that he was there. He whistled a little, watching the warder open the cell door, and said, "Good evening, Louis."

Malencz looked terrible, as if he had not slept. Denis said, "Are you well?"

"I'm feeling . . . strange." Malencz went to the cot. "Sit down. What have you brought?"

"Tibullus and Sallust. More ink, paper." Denis sat down and made himself comfortable. He took pens from his sling.

"I had a dream last night," Malencz said. He put his hands to his temples. "Or maybe it wasn't a dream. Maybe I actually saw it."

"What was it?"

"I can't remember it all. Your brother means to kill me."

"Louis, he's forgotten all about you."

"He forgets nothing. I remember in the dream he was watching me, waiting for me to sleep so that he could stab me. He was watching and laughing."

Malencz's voice was perfectly normal. His face was hidden by his long hands. Suddenly he lowered his hands and turned the full baleful glare of his eyes on Denis, like a blow.

"He means to kill me," he said. "He has to kill me. Because I know."

"What do you know?"

"When the Turks take Vrath they will find me and question me. I know. He raised a devil to enter into the Sultan and killed him. I saw it, out in the hall. He was digging in the dirt and whispering."

"There is no dirt in the hall."

"That was how he killed my son. My son, Peter. He summoned up a devil. I saw that, too. I saw him drawing circles in the dirt and speaking strange words. The Gypsies taught him that, you know. He changed himself into a wild boar and ravaged the countryside and killed my son. When the boar attacked Peter it shouted in a human voice."

"Louis—"

"At night he never sleeps. Devils don't sleep, you know. They prowl around. He walks back and forth and snarls and hisses in the hall. Everybody knows that. He never takes off his boots because he has hoofs for feet. Once I had a vision that I saw him dead and I saw a little blue devil come out of his mouth. Everybody knows that. He threw a spell over all my men. He bewitched them all."

"He doesn't have hoofs, he has feet. I've seen them."

"He's bewitched you, too." Malencz looked suddenly afraid. "Are you bewitched?"

"No, Louis."

"I saw his face all lit up with sulphurous fire and I saw his footprints burning," Malencz said. "I saw, and I know. He has to kill me. He knows everything. He sits in his room and he sees everything. The devils come and tell him what happens. I saw Lucifer himself come out of the circle he drew in the dirt."

"When did you see this?" Denis said. He leaned forward. "Louis, please, you must get hold of yourself."

"I saw it. I saw it all. I saw him outside, and he was digging in the dirt and drawing his circles and summoning up the devils. Jew-talk, he used, and Greek that he learned from his witch-whore mother, and Gypsy, and he spoke all the prayers backward and he throws spells on men, so that they can only see if he lets them and they must do as he wills. He won the Emperor's daughter with a love potion."

"Louis."

Malencz rose. "He's bewitched you, too. I see the mark on your forehead." He stretched out his hand and touched Denis' forehead.

He is mad, Denis thought. I mustn't disturb him. I must get away and tell János.

"Shall I bring down some Ovid?" he said.

Malencz's hot, shiny eyes looked confused and dulled. "Ovid? Oh, yes. We have to translate more of it. That helps, you know."

"I'll get some," Denis said. He went carefully toward the door. Malencz stood by the bed, hunched slightly.

"Take some of these back, will you?" Malencz said in a perfectly normal tone.

Denis knelt to gather up a stack of books in his arms. Instantly Malencz's furious weight was on his back. Denis straightened, reaching behind him with his good hand to drag Malencz off, and Manencz raised one arm and stabbed Denis in the chest with Denis' own dagger. Denis gasped and tried to shout and the knife stabbed again and again into his chest.

"You Devil's instrument," Malencz whispered. He let Denis go. Denis slid quietly to the floor and lay still. There was blood all over the room. Malencz looked at the knife in his hand and forced his fingers open. He went to the door and said, "Warder. Warder, Sir Denis is ill."

The warder came running. He threw open the door. "Dear God," he said. "You've . . ."

Malencz caught him by the throat. The warder snatched at his hands, striking at him. Malencz threw him to one side and jumped on him with both feet when he fell. He grabbed the warder's sword and stabbed him through the chest.

"So much for you," he said. "You traitor."

He had to hurry. Even now Rakóssy might be calling up his legions of imps to go find out what the turmoil was. He had seen them flying around the castle. The others were bewitched so that they couldn't see the imps. Rakóssy had left his black powder here someplace. Vrath was his, lawfully his, and he could do with her as he wished. He must hide from the imps some way.

He had thought Denis was all right. All this time he had waited, testing Denis, and he had thought that Denis was still all right, but he wasn't, after all; he had been worming his way into Malencz's confidence, trying to trick him, and like a fool he had told all he knew. They were all around him; no decent man was safe. He thought perhaps he should save the Emperor's sister or daughter or whatever she was, but then he thought that she was probably bewitched too.

He found the cell where the powder was stored and took two kegs. He couldn't carry more than that. He didn't know if that was enough. It had to be a big explosion. He thought probably Rakóssy had raised a wall around the castle. The Turks would have taken it otherwise.

He went up to the kitchen and through that little door into the courtyard. The sentries were watching the Turkish camp, and he stayed away from the side where the wall was breached, lit brilliantly with torches and packed with men. He made his way to the high corner on the chapel side, hiding in the shadows.

* * *

"Denis has been looking for you," Catharine said. "He's frantic."

"Where is he?"

"He took some books down to Malencz," Mari said. She sighed. "I'm tired. May I go to bed, my lady?"

"Of course. János, have you had anything to eat?"

"No. I'm going to find Denis."

He went to Denis' room, and it was empty. He was with Malencz. Rakóssy swore. He went down to the kitchen and found Catharine there, fixing him something to eat. He went down to the basement.

He saw the warder lying dead, half in and half out of Malencz's cell. He stared at the body. He turned.

"Catharine."

"Yes?" She came to the kitchen door at the head of the stairs.

"Call Arpád."

"What's wrong?"

"Call Arpád." He went slowly down the corridor and into the dungeon.

Arpád and Catharine came after him, it seemed almost at once. He looked up.

"Take her upstairs," he said. "Arpád, Malencz has escaped. I want him. Alive."

Catharine said, "It's Denis, isn't it?" She went by Arpád and walked toward the dungeon. Rakóssy thrust out his arm to hold her back. She looked at him. He drew his arm away from her. She went by him. She looked into the dungeon and shut her eyes.

Arpád ran up the stairs.

Rakóssy put his arm around Catharine to keep her from falling. "Now will you go?"

She went back down the corridor.

Rakóssy stepped into the dungeon. The books were scattered all over the floor, and the ink had spilled. He knelt and lifted Denis in his arms. He carried him up to the kitchen and put him on the table there. The pale hair seemed to have faded. Sometimes when they opened the graves of the long dead they found blond strands of hair still golden in the fresh light, but touching them destroyed them and the hair turned to dust. He felt that Denis had been long dead, that he had known long before that Denis was dead.

He lifted one of Denis' hands, the long fingers cool in his own hand. There was an ink spot on the index finger. The light bones of Denis' face seemed malleable as clay. He looked like a wax saint, neither dead nor alive.

"Better this way."

He had not meant it the other time he had said it. Better this way. Oh, yes, better. I never meant to hurt you. Or if I meant to, I had my reasons.

But he wasn't alive. I'm saying this to myself. Bereft.

There was an explosion, somewhere, outside. He lifted his head. The explosion rippled the floor under his feet. His legs shook. He went quickly to the door into the courtyard. The hot air struck him in the face.

Malencz. Malencz.

He ran to the front of the courtyard. The whole front wall was down in rubble. Only the frame of the Main Gate stood. Malencz. Denis had told him about blowing up Hart. That was why. The cannon were in the debris, scrap and garbage, iron shards worth nothing. The sentries . . .

Arpád was shouting at him. He turned. Arpád said, "Shall I get everybody out?"

"Yes." Rakóssy moved so that he could see the Turkish camp through the breach. "Will you look at that?" He looked up at the full moon. "Malencz, God damn your soul."

He went back inside and found Mari and Catharine with the other women in the great hall. He drew Catharine aside.

"They've broken through," she said.

"It was Malencz. He must have poured a couple of

kegs of powder into a hole in the wall. The whole wall's down."

"It's ended, isn't it?"

"Yes. They'll attack us. When they come in here, tell them who you are. They'll ransom you."

"I don't want it," she said. She pressed her hands against her skirt.

"I don't want it either."

He looked at the other women. "Please," he said. "Stay here, tell them who you are. Please."

"János, don't."

"Catharine . . ."

Arpád came into the hall. "They're coming."

"You take the guns on the stable roof, I'll take the ones by the Chapel Gate. We'll catch them in a crossfire." He turned back to Catharine. "You do as I tell you."

She kissed him. He thought, Maybe, somehow, and pulled away from her, almost rough. "One kiss before dying," he said. "Christ, I sound like one of your fairy tales."

He walked out of the hall. He thought she spoke behind him.

The men were gathered up by the guns. He went up with them. Their faces shone and their eyes were full of fears.

"All right," he said. "Let's ram it down their throats."

She had better go. Get away. She could be carrying his child.

That's dynastic of you.

Out on the plain torches bloomed, first a few, spreading, leaping from hand to hand, like the lightning on the mountain that time. The plain was full of torches like a field of asters. The torches moved, coming closer, an army of fire. "Ready," he said.

"Ready, my lord."

Not your lord much longer, friend.

"In nomine Patris, et Filii, et Spiritu Sanctu."

The men around him were crossing themselves. His

hand was like lead at his side. He closed his fingers over the hilt of his sword. *Te absolvo.*

"Light your matches."

They heard, dimly, the sound of many hoofs on the beaten plain. The slow matches dipped over the torches and the smell of sulphur reached his nostrils, bitter and itching. He rubbed his nose.

"Shall we cry *'Deus le vult,'* my lord?" Béla said.

"Shut up."

The Turks were there, in the great breach, charging. Rakóssy said, "Fire."

There was a moment of nothing but the hissing matches and the odd rolling charge of the Turks. The cannon roared. The Turks in the gap stopped short against the wall of shot closing from either side. Rakóssy saw Arpád on the roof of the stable, one arm raised, immense. There was no time to reload. The Turks were swarming toward them. He saw their faces in the shining torches. Their eyes were brighter than their shields. A lance flew past him and a Magyar shrieked and tumbled from the wall.

In this last fairy tale. He drew his sword, pulling back to the wall. The courtyard was flooded with Turks. They had ladders, they were scaling the wall. He and the men with him ran to turn the ladders over. The lances pelted the stone around him. Rakóssy snatched at Béla. Béla flung his hand aside, clasped the lance in both hands, and drew it out of his belly. The black blood sprang after it. Béla raised the lance and leapt, shouting, into the Turks below.

Rakóssy kicked a ladder away. He ran down the wall toward the breach, climbed down the edge of the broken wall, and raced toward the Turks, silent, his sword held low. The Turks whirled to meet him.

He hardly knew what he did. He held the sword in both hands and stood spread-legged, cleaving around him, seeing nothing, feeling only the contact of the sword with the Turks. A horse reared over him and he dodged it and killed it when it came down. He used it as a shield. The Turks charged him. Their swords swept the air around him like feathers.

The Turks drew back, making a wall around him. He looked up at the wall. There were no more Magyars there. His men were dead. He charged the Turks and they faded away before him. He rushed into the angle of the wall and stood with his back to the stone.

Arpád's voice sailed over the heads of the Turks. He looked over them and saw Arpád, gigantic, jump from the stable roof into the midst of Turks. He saw Arpád's head, swaying, the eyes darting back and forth, above the Turks. Arpád went down. He was washed over by the mob of the Turks.

There was a sudden stillness. He looked at the wall of Turks around him. Beyond them he saw Mustafa, sitting on the chestnut mare, watching him. On all their faces was the same waiting. They meant to have him alive.

He feinted, rushed them, drew back, and worked his way down the wall. They would not meet him. Arpád they would kill but not him. He heard his own breath sobbing through his teeth. He charged them and they parted to let him through and followed him like herders' dogs. Over the heads of the Turks Mustafa regarded him with cold eyes.

"János."

He whirled toward her. She stepped from the shelter of the wall. She had a sword in her hands, and she lifted it. She ran on light feet toward the Turks. They backed away; they would kill no woman. He screamed her name. She turned her head toward him, the eyes unseeing, and attacked.

The Turks shouted. A lance ran through her breast. He saw her white gown, her white body, lying on the courtyard stone. The Turks rolled and howled around her. Over their rushing heads Mustafa said, "I think it best that we kill him."

Rakóssy turned and ran for the kitchen door. He made

it two jumps ahead of the Turks and slammed it shut. Mari was there, sitting by Denis' body.

"Are they all dead but us?" Mari said.

He nodded.

She began to cry. "I'm not going to die. Nothing they can do to me would be worse than dying." She put her head down.

"Pray for me," he said. "Or something."

He went down the steps into the dungeon corridor and ran along it. He passed the place where the torches stopped and ran through pitch-darkness. His leg began to ache. He ran limping. Malencz. Malencz.

He ran into the wall at the end of the corridor. For a moment he stood pressed against it, gasping. His leg almost refused to bear him. He reached out and felt the ladder's rung. He groped to it and climbed up.

The sound of horses reached him. He pushed the trap door open. He smelled moldy hay and manure. The horses were stamping and neighing. He climbed up into the stable.

The last of the hay was piled against the back wall. He lit the tinder in his tinderbox and flung it into the hay. He went along the lines of horses, cutting them loose. There were almost one hundred of them left after the slaughtering. Their manes tossed like branches in the wind, and the dim flickering firelight shone on their skins. They screamed at the smell of the fire and kicked out at him.

The black mare thrust her head under his arm. "Good girl," he said. "Good girl." He pulled her rope loose and mounted her. He rode her into the midst of the pack of loose horses. He could see the hay burning; the flames ran like mice through it.

The horses plunged against the stable door. Their hoofs rang on the floor and the walls. The door opened, and Turks, Turkish faces, slick with sweat, showed in the doorway. The horses galloped over them. The black mare ran in the middle of the pack.

The horses burst into the courtyard, running with their heads high, screaming, mad to be loose. The Turks scattered before them. Rakóssy bent over the black mare's neck. He reached back to touch the hilt of his sword, in its scabbard. The mare raced toward the open plain. She slowed to pick her way through the litter of rock and nameless men. He clutched her, his face pressed against her foaming neck. She jumped the last of the fallen rock and bolted.

He dozed through the night. The dawn broke suddenly over him, and he straightened. The mare was grazing, the rope trailing down from her halter.

He turned her west, to the village there, and met a man at the edge of a field.

"Count Malencz? He left before dawn." The man spat. "Got beaten, didn't you? Not so great now, are you?"

"I want some rope."

"Ask for it."

Rakóssy looked down at him. The man spat again. "Turk or Magyar, you're all the same. What difference does it make? In my hut. Ask the woman."

"Just remember," Rakóssy said, "that a Magyar didn't kill you."

He rode off to the hut and the woman came out. He said, "Get me some rope."

"Rope."

She went inside and came out again with a coil of grass rope. He dismounted and took it and made a bridle for the mare. The woman sat in the door and watched him.

"The King's dead," she said.

"When?"

She shrugged. "We just heard."

"Malencz. Which way did he go?"

"West." She paused. "He's mad, that one. He's mad."

He rode off. The sun rose higher. He rode west, across the plain, watching for Malencz ahead of him. There was a spring up ahead. He thought that Malencz would be there, but he rode slowly toward it, letting the mare take her own pace.

He reached the spring and rode around it. Malencz was there, sitting under a tree, and he didn't look surprised when Rakóssy rode in.

"Is there no killing you, Rakóssy?"

"None."

Malencz got up and drew his sword. Rakóssy slid off the mare. Malencz said, "I knew you would come after me."

"There's blood between you and me, traitor."

Malencz raised his sword and attacked him in a short rush. Rakóssy parried his thrust, struck back, and narrowly missed.

"Playing with cannon has lost you your skill, traitor."

"Come on, then," Rakóssy said.

They fought quickly together and drew apart again, circling. Malencz lunged, Rakóssy parried him and struck in over his sword, and Malencz's quick return slit his arm above the elbow.

Rakóssy backed off. Malencz was hesitant. He attacked, almost tentatively, and withdrew a little. Rakóssy started after him. Malencz was working him slowly around so that the sun would be in his eyes, but Rakóssy stopped moving and forced Malencz back a step, toward the spring.

Suddenly Malencz leapt in with a wild rush, flailing with his sword. Rakóssy backed off a few steps, parried a hard thrust, drew Malencz's sword out of line, and struck in over the blade, straight to the heart. Malencz slid from the sword into the grass. He lay still. Rakóssy saw that he was dead.

He wiped his sword on Malencz's shirt and mounted the mare. She drank at the spring. Her mane was snarled, and he straightened it while she drank. When she was satisfied he turned her west.

It began to rain around noon. He cantered the mare up to a little wooden bridge that crossed Vrath's River and led her under it. He sat down, waiting for the rain to stop. Bubbles rose from the stream where the rain struck it, and the rain rattled on the bridge overhead like hoofs. The swallows flew in and out under the bridge, flying low over the water, singing. They swooped wildly, their wings stretched on the wind, dipping and circling.

Rakóssy watched the bubbles burst on the surface of the stream. The swallows ignored him and the mare. The sun was out but it had not stopped raining. The sun cast the shadow of the bridge over the water; the sunlight picked out the pebbles in the stream bed.

The rain stopped. He led the mare out and vaulted onto her back. He started east again, toward Hart.

A while later he saw a band of Spahis riding over the plain. He stopped and waited for them. They wheeled toward him and trotted forward, curious. He drew his sword. When they were so close that he could see their faces and know that they were not Mustafa's men, he charged them.

They were surprised. They spread apart, slowing their horses. He raced the mare into their midst. The leader flung up his arm and hurled his lance. It passed over Rakóssy's head. He swerved the mare to attack the leader. She charged in, gathering herself, and put her shoulder to the Turk's horse and threw it.

The other Turks closed in and surrounded him. The mare went down with a lance through her chest. Rakóssy leapt off and rolled. He came to his feet among the Turks. He struck up at them. They leaned down to kill him. He ducked between two horses and gutted one and leapt to kill the rider. One of the Turks tripped him up, and when he fell they sprawled over him. He lost his sword. He drew his dagger and stabbed at the bodies twisting over him. He was thrust hard back to the ground. A boot stepped firmly on his wrist. He looked up and saw the sword above him and watched it descend and died.

"They were not my men," Mustafa said. "They could hardly have known him. Or are Turks to think every man who fights so well to be Rakóssy?"

"But they brought him to you."

"Yes. I buried him. They were all dead who knew

him. Only I was left, and I buried him."

"I have heard that he was a sinful man."

"He was not buried in any holiness. I buried him where his old castle stood. He will rest better there than anywhere else. I doubt he will bother us from there."

"You did well. I only wish that I had seen his face. Now there are more important things to talk about. Are you thirsty? There is milk and sherbet there, on the table."

Cecelia Holland

Cecelia Holland was born in Nevada on New Year's Eve, 1943. Raised in Metuchen, New Jersey, she now lives in Woodbridge, Connecticut. She is the author of an earlier novel, *The Firedrake*, dealing with the Norman invasion of England.